# Cast of Cha

MW00454051

**John J. Malone.** A short, plumpish, un. _ _ _ _ _ _ _ whiskey and keeping blondes from going to the electric chair.

**Jake Justus.** A redheaded press agent, manager, ex-reporter and sometime amateur detective. He's currently between jobs and feels very fortunate to have married

**Helene Brand Justus.** Blonde, beautiful and rich, she can out drink and out drive most men. In between drinks, she got Jake to the altar.

**George Brand.** Helene's father. He's a bit of a character and is usually accompanied by **Partridge**, his valet or—some say—his keeper.

**Daniel Von Flanagan.** He added the "Von" so people wouldn't think he was just another Irish cop. He'd rather grow pecans that catch crooks.

**Mona McClare.** A bored widow, she wrote a bestseller, hunted tigers, flew the Atlantic solo, went on a polar expedition, and has been engaged to every eligible bachelor on three continents. She bets Jake her nightclub, The Casino, that she can pull off the perfect murder.

**Lulamay Yandry.** A Tennessee widow, the water is deep where it appears to be shallow. So is the corn liquor she dishes out.

**Willis Sanders.** A broker, his first wife died under mysterious circumstances. Now married to **Fluerette**, he's father to the jealous **Daphne**.

**Wells Ogletree.** Helene refers to him as "Heart-of-Stone Ogletree." He's father to

**Ellen Ogletree.** She was once kidnapped and ransomed for $50,000. She recently broke off her engagement and is now seeing

**Leonard Marhmont.** An Englishman known to have no money of his own..

**Max Hook.** A mob boss, he once owned The Casino.

**Little Georgie la Cerra.** He works for Hook, as does **Blunk**.

**Gus.** He runs out trio's current favorite watering hole.

**Joshua Gumbril.** The murdered man. What possible motive could Mona have for killing him?

**Garrity** and **Lally.** Chicago cops.

## The John J. Malone books
*8 Faces at 3* (1939)
*The Corpse Steps Out* (1940)
*The Wrong Murder* (1940)
*The Right Murder* (1941)
*Trial by Fury* (1941)
*The Bid Midget Murders* (1942)
*Having Wonderful Crime* (1943)
*The Lucky Stiff* (1945)
*The Fourth Postman* (1948)
*Knocked for a Loop* (1957)
*My Kingdom for a Hearse* (1957)
*But the Doctor Died* (1967)
(It is highly unlikely that this was actually
written by Rice)
*The Pickled Poodles* (1960)
(an authorized continuation of the Malone series
by Larry Harris, aka Laurence M. Janifer)

Short story collections
*The Name is Malone* (1958)
*People Vs. Withers and Malone* (1963)
(with Stuart Palmer, who maintained Rice
participated in the plotting of
the stories)
*Once Upon a Train*
(with Stuart Palmer, edited by
Harold Straubing)
*Murder, Mystery & Malone* (2002)
edited by Jeffrey Marks

The standalone novel
*Home Sweet Homicide* (1944)
has been reprinted by
The Rue Morgue Press

# The Wrong Murder

## Murder

A John J. Malone mystery by

## Craig Rice

Rue Morgue Press
Lyons, Colorado

ISBN: 978-1-60187-074-2




Rue Morgue Press
87 Lone Tree Lane
Lyons CO 80540




PRINTED IN THE UNITED STATES

# About Craig Rice

"Murder is not mirthful and there is nothing comic about a corpse," Craig Rice wrote in a 1946 essay, "Murder Makes Merry," for Howard Haycraft's *The Art of the Mystery Story*. Yet Rice herself was able to make murder mirthful, perhaps because she made it abundantly clear that it was all in good fun. "She never forgot," said critic J. Randolph Cox, "that the primary purpose of the detective story was entertainment."

And entertain readers she did. She got serious once in a while, in the novels written as by Michael Venning or in the stand-alone, *Telefair*, but for the most part she went for the laugh, especially in a dozen or so novels featuring Chicago criminal lawyer John J. Malone and his sidekicks, Jake and Helene Justus. Starting in 1939 with *8 Faces at 3* and ending with *My Kingdom for a Hearse* in 1957, published two weeks after her death at the age of 49, Rice's inebriated trio of sleuths prowled the streets and bars of Chicago, vowing that no blonde—or redhead or brunette—would ever be convicted of murder. Mostly, they hung out in Joe the Angel's City Hall Bar where they playfully tweaked the nose of homicide cop Daniel von Flanagan (he added the "von" so as not to be deemed just another Irish cop). Such antics eventually earned her the unheard of sum (for a mystery writer) of $46,000 a year by 1945 and in 1946 *Time* put her on its cover, the only mystery writer ever to be so honored.

While her nonseries book, *Home Sweet Homicide* (1944), in which the three children of a mystery writing single mom attempt to solve a murder and at the same time find their mother a man, won her much praise and a place in the Haycraft-Queen Cornerstone list, it is the Malone books that she is best known for. For more information on Rice see Tom & Enid Schantz' introduction to *The Corpse Steps Out*.

# *Chapter One*

Later, they were able to trace the little man in the rusty black overcoat as far south as Van Buren Street. At an indeterminate point somewhere south of the corner of State and Van Buren, the trail was lost. Not that it mattered greatly, after the man was dead.

His first appearance on State Street that could be proved beyond the shadow of a doubt was at the north-west corner of Van Buren, just below the steps leading to the elevated. He had paused there briefly to buy a newspaper. The newsstand boy remembered him clearly, especially the manner in which he had fished the depths of a worn leather change purse for the odd penny.

When they found the little man later in the day, the newspaper was still tucked under his arm unread, just as the boy had folded it.

No one would have expected him to be noticed anywhere, especially not on State Street in the last week before Christmas. He was a trifle under the average height, stoop-shouldered, and exceedingly thin. His skin, drawn tight over the bones of his sharp-featured face, had an unhealthy pallor; his eyes were so light a blue as to be almost colorless, protuberant and peering as the eyes of a fish. A few wisps of untidy gray hair showed under his dusty black derby. The newsstand boy remembered he had spoken in a thin, wheezy voice punctuated by an asthmatic cough.

On the whole, he was an ordinary, inconspicuous little man. So it was amazing later (though not to Dan Von Flanagan of the Homicide Squad) how many people remembered seeing him on his progress up State Street, after a photograph of his remains had appeared on the front page of the *Times*. It seemed almost as though everyone who had been on State Street that afternoon in the peak of the Christmas-shopping rush had seen and noticed the little man in the rusty black overcoat.

Nevertheless, it was from just such volunteered information that it was possible, later, to find out where the little man had gone and what he had done between Van Buren Street and the corner where his stroll had ended abruptly. It appeared that he had not been in a hurry. The newsstand boy was positive that it had been exactly five minutes to two when the man stopped to buy a paper. He remembered it because his next customer had been a girl in a red hat who had

7

asked him the time, and his watch (a present from his grandfather) was never wrong.

There was no possible doubt that it was just fifteen minutes past two by the big clock over State and Madison Streets when the little man reached that corner. A hundred witnesses were ready to swear to it.

The distance between those two points was only four longish blocks, so his progress had been slow. Just north of Van Buren Street he had paused before the Rialto Burlesque Theater to examine the colored posters that adorned its façade. For a moment it had seemed that he was going into the theater, then he had apparently changed his mind and continued on his way north. Still farther in the same block he had paused again before a window filled with inexpensive garments that could be purchased on convenient credit terms. At the corner of Jackson Boulevard he had barely escaped being run down by an automobile driven by a Mr. Louis Whitman of Oak Park. It was a close shave, but the little man made it to safety just in time.

The State Street sidewalks were jammed from wall to gutter with holiday shoppers. Lampposts were transformed with Christmas wreaths, Christmas decorations of every kind glittered in the windows, chimes and amplified recordings of a dozen different Christmas carols came from loud-speakers, each trying to outdo the other in volume. Salvation Army lassies and Volunteers-of-America Santa Clauses rang their little bells furiously on every corner. At State and Jackson the gigantic Rothschild Christmas tree dominated the entire street as far north as the Lake Street Elevated. Even the raw wind and the occasional flurries of cold gray rain failed to dampen the enthusiasm of the holiday throng. The whole street was one enormous, noisy, crowded carnival.

It appeared, however, that the man in the rusty black overcoat had no Christmas shopping to do. At least there was no evidence of his having done any.

He did pause at the drugstore on the corner of State and Adams Streets long enough to ask the soda-fountain clerk for a little baking soda and a glass of carbonated water. The clerk, when questioned later, thought that it had been just about two o'clock, perhaps a few minutes past.

The little man emerged from the drugstore and stood for a moment in front of the doorway, jostled by the passing crowds, as though deciding which direction he should take. Then at last he appeared to make up his mind and plunged into the sea of holiday shoppers crossing Adams Street.

Just beyond Adams Street, by the corner window of the Fair store, there was an almost impenetrable pedestrian traffic jam. Evidently the man hesitated an instant at the edge of the corner, watching the shoppers who were trying to fight their way up to the toy display in the window, and then decided to skirt the crowd by going out to the very last inch of sidewalk, instead of trying to push his way through.

That may have been his second narrow escape of the afternoon.

He went slowly past the Fair store, past the little shops just south of Monroe Street, and past the big variety store on the corner, paying no attention to the extravagant displays in the windows. At the southwest corner of Monroe Street he paused again, waiting for a traffic light to change. While he stood there a Volunteers-of-America Santa Claus waved at him hopefully, and received a blank, disinterested stare.

Beyond Monroe Street he went more slowly, staying now on the inside edge of the sidewalk, pausing once or twice to stare reflectively at the displays of women's shoes in the windows. The two Kresge stores he ignored completely, but as he reached the southwest corner of State and Madison Streets he made a prolonged stop before the Liggett's drugstore, examining a window display of fountain pens. He stood there so long, indeed, it may have been he felt a sense of apprehension, a feeling of foreboding, about crossing the street. It would not have been such a surprising thing, after all. It may even have been that he glanced nervously across the street once or twice as he stood there by the drugstore window, though surely he could not have known of any danger. Perhaps he felt a certain chilling of the blood, an impulse to turn back. That remains forever speculative.

The corner of State and Madison Streets, long acclaimed as the busiest corner in the world, was more crowded now than at any other time of the year. Directly below the great clock on the Boston Store, the mass of people was almost im-movable, as shoppers tried to push up to the window filled with animated toys, as other shoppers attempted to fight their way into the revolving doors of the building, and as still others, trying to go any one of four different directions, shoved and struggled to make their way through the jam. The air was filled with voices, with the racket of streetcars, automobiles, and taxicabs, with two differ-ent Christmas carols shouted from loudspeakers on opposite sides of the street, and with the continual, insistent jingling of the little bells.

It was into this mass of people that the little man plunged when he decided to cross Madison Street. This time he did not go around the edge of the crowd.

Later, of course, there were those who claimed to have heard the sound of the shot, even over the roar and clamor of the crowded street. At the time, however, no notice was taken of it.

One large section of the crowd was moving northward, and the little man in the rusty black overcoat was caught in the middle of it, carried on for ten or fifteen feet by the impact of the moving bodies around him. Then, as the crowd began to thin, a little beyond the entrance to the Boston Store, he seemed sud-denly to lose his balance.

No one noticed him when he fell. There was no outcry of any kind until a large woman with her arms full of bundles (a Mrs. J. Martin of Evanston) saw that a man had collapsed at her feet. She screamed, and dropped the bundles. Another woman, seeing only Mrs. Martin, screamed likewise.

By some thoughtfulness of providence, the body was not trampled beyond all recognition in the melee that followed, before a policeman managed to shove his way through the milling, hysterical mob of people to the center of the disturbance. It was believed at first that the man had merely fainted in the midst of the holiday crowd, not an unusual occurrence. Then the policeman, one Edward Gahagan, discovered that he was dead.

But it was not until help came, and the crowd was pushed back a few feet more, that it was possible to examine the body of the little man more carefully, and discover the bullethole in his back.


## Chapter Two

No one knew it at the time, and only a very few ever did know or even suspect it, but if a party had not been given the day before the unfortunate occurrence at State and Madison Streets, the little man in the rusty black overcoat might never have been murdered at all.

Certainly the tall, lean, red-haired man sitting on the concrete-and-iron stairway of the famous hotel where the party was being held knew nothing of the sort. He wouldn't have cared much if he had. At the time he was too busy trying to balance a glass in each hand while he stared at the girl he considered the most beautiful blonde in the world.

He was Jake Justus, ex-reporter, and, by his own admission, the second greatest press agent alive. (He never told who the first one was.) He wouldn't have cared about the fate of the little man because, frankly, he was a little bored with murder.

As manager of Dick Dayton's dance band, he had become involved in the murder of Miss Alexandria Inglehart of Maple Park, and had done his bit toward exonerating Dick Dayton's bride, accused of the crime.* As manager of Nelle Brown, the radio star, he had been drawn into an insane tangle of murders and disappearing corpses. Jake felt, not surprisingly, that he had had more than his share of homicides.

There was, to be honest about it, a singular lack of appreciation in his attitude. For the first murder had introduced him to Helene Brand, the exquisite blonde debutante of Maple Park. The second murder had brought her back to him at a time when he felt he had lost her forever.

Today he had married Helene Brand, and he wouldn't have cared if fifty little men in rusty black overcoats were murdered on every street corner in the Loop.

There were three of them on the stairway. On one side of Jake sat Helene, her pale-gold hair beautifully in place, dressed in something composed of light-green wool and enormous quantities of brownish fur. On the other side was a tall, stout, and extremely impressive man with a round, pinkish face, heavy gray hair, and a neatly trimmed mustache and imperial. He was George Brand, father of the bride, who had flown from Hawaii to give his daughter in marriage, and was about to take a plane for Florida.

On the step just below them was a bottle of gin, a shakerful of Martinis, and a few extra glasses, thoughtfully brought along in case of breakage. The Martinis, Helene's father had explained, were there to be used as a chaser for the gin.

The solemnity of the occasion was almost overwhelming. For a long time all three of them had been completely speechless. Once, indeed, Helene's father had exclaimed "My children!" with a sonorous sigh, and laid a hand on Jake's shoulder. For a moment Jake had felt his new father-in-law was about to break into a song, a speech, or tears. In fact he wasn't at all sure but what at any minute all three of them would burst into tears.

He took a tentative sip at his drink, with a vague feeling that if anyone rashly lighted a match in his immediate vicinity, he would probably come down in some obscure place, such as Michigan City, if, indeed he came down at all. With half a dozen of his father-in-law's drinks under his belt, anyone attempting to convey him anywhere would probably be arrested for shipping munitions without a permit.

It was hard to realize that he was actually married to Helene. He tried to remember the exact words the justice of the peace had used an hour or so before. *"Air P.A. signs deb in big tie-up."* No, that would hardly have been in the marriage service. That would be in *Variety*.

Soft, discreet steps on the staircase behind them made Jake turn his head. There stood Partridge, a small, thin, grayish man, with perpetually anxious eyes. Jake had long since given up trying to decide if he were George Brand's valet or his legal guardian. He always seemed to be just on the verge of some disapproving comment which was never actually spoken. He seemed especially on the verge of some such comment now, though all he managed was one little, reproachful, and infinitely sad cough.

George Brand rose lumberingly to his feet. "Partridge is right. We ought to return to our guests." He frowned and pulled at his beard. "There must have been something terribly important I wanted to say to you, or I'd never have brought you out here where we could be alone. Oh well, perhaps it will come to me."

He stalked majestically up the stairs. Jake and Helene gathered the empty glasses and followed him.

In the big living room of the apartment the crowd had thinned a little, but the room was still full of people. Most of them were strangers to Jake, but at the far end of the room he saw one familiar face. He headed for it like a shipwrecked sailor setting out for an island.

The face, red and a little perspiring, belonged to a short, stocky man with rumpled dark hair, a badly wrinkled suit, and a necktie that was slowly crawling under one ear. He was the center, as usual, of an admiring group. John J. Malone, Chicago's famous criminal lawyer, always drew a crowd, in his private life as well as in the courtroom.

Jake sat down beside him and managed to take part in the conversation without hearing a word of it. He was not an altogether happy man, indeed for one who had just married Helene Brand, he was singularly unhappy.

In a few hours he and Helene would leave for Bermuda and a two-weeks honeymoon. Then they would return to Chicago, and he would look for a job.

Nelle Brown had left for Hollywood a few days before and Jake was without a star to manage. A hell of a time to get married, he told himself, even if he had married an heiress. Rather, because he had married an heiress. Helene's money was her own business. He was just another guy out of a job.

The rent on the expensive apartment had been paid for a month in advance. There was enough left over for a honeymoon in Bermuda and a few weeks' living. Oh well, he consoled himself, he'd find a new client. He always had.

He looked around the room and wondered how many people in it had ever looked for a job. He took another drink, and began wondering who they all were. He'd met them an hour or two ago, now he began trying to match names and faces.

The middle-aged, rather haggard man who faintly resembled Helene's father, save that he lacked a beard, was Willis Sanders, a broker. The small, delicate, almost too perfect woman who sat twirling a cocktail glass in tiny, nervous fingers was Willis Sanders' wife.

The girl beside Mrs. Sanders—who was she? Jake tried hard to remember. Whoever she was, she looked unhappy, sullen, almost brooding. She was a big girl, a tall girl, yet perfectly proportioned. Her hair was dark brown and glossy, falling in great waves to her shoulders. Her eyes were large and dark and liquid, with the longest lashes Jake had ever seen. There was a kind of violence about her beauty, Jake thought, almost a tempestuous quality. She looked the way heroines of Italian operas were supposed to look and never did.

He remembered suddenly that she was Willis Sanders' daughter by his first wife.

He went on looking round the room. There were two rather ordinary young women in what were probably Paris frocks, a slightly bald man with a dark mustache, and a small, noisily vivacious woman with bobbed gray hair and an almost smothering Southern accent whom nobody knew and who had been invited because she happened to live across the hall.

There was one woman in the room he would never have any trouble remembering, however. Mona McClane!

Sitting there in the overcrowded room, she seemed a little too disappointingly like other people. Her hair was short, jet black, and very sleek, with a heavy bang that fell over her forehead nearly to her eyebrows. Her pale face was thin, pointed, foxlike; her enormous, shadowy eyes were almost green.

When had Mona McClane's name first appeared in print? Jake couldn't remember. At her birth, he guessed. The birth of a child to the McClane clan had undoubtedly been news. At the age of six her picture had appeared when her blue-blooded terriers took first prize at the dog show. It had been printed again, and often, when the ballroom of the enormous and incredibly ugly McClane mansion on Lake Shore Drive had been completely remodeled for her debut. Its next lavish appearance had been when she had made a thoroughly satisfactory and noteworthy marriage.

At that point Jake's memory of newspaper pictures and stories began to crystallize. Mona McClane had vanished from all but the society pages for a few years while she lived the life of a model young matron, produced one daughter, and managed, expertly, a number of society bazaars. Then a few years later the socially satisfactory and noteworthy husband of Mona McClane had shot himself accidentally while on a hunting trip (some were so unkind as to hint it had not been entirely accidental), the story had exploded in a front-page splash, and from that day on Mona McClane's life had been lived in printer's ink.

She had been publicly engaged to an Indian rajah and broken off the match two days before the marriage was to take place. She had married a titled Hungarian and been a Princess with an unpronounceable name for a year and a half. She had married an impoverished Indiana farmer, retired to live the simple life, and divorced him in four months. After that divorce she had resumed the name of McClane.

She had written a best seller, become a licensed airplane pilot, hunted tigers in India and elephants in Africa, run for Congress unsuccessfully, gone on a polar expedition, made a transatlantic solo flight, been sued twice for alienation of affections, met the Grand Lama of Tibet, had a screen test, and been reported engaged to every eligible man on three continents.

It was faintly disappointing to Jake, meeting her for the first time, that she looked like other human beings. He'd half expected her to glow like a neon sign.

He was struggling with mental arithmetic, trying to guess at her age, when a minor explosion seemed to take place at his elbow. He looked up and saw Helene. A wide green hat framed her face, furs were slung over her arm. George Brand and Partridge were with her, both ready for traveling.

It had just been discovered, Helene explained, that George Brand's plane left in exactly seventeen minutes, and it was easily a thirty-minute drive to the airport. Obviously, no one but herself could possibly get them there on time.

Later Jake claimed to have had a premonition about it, but nobody believed him. He did go so far as to point out that while Helene could undoubtedly get to the airport with time to spare, her driving was of a nature fit for neither man nor beast. But there was no time for discussion. Helene gathered up her furs, promised to be back within the hour, and was gone.

Jake sighed, accepted a drink, and settled back in his chair. He wondered how he was going to live for an hour away from Helene. He wondered how he had lived so much of his life away from Helene.

It was then that Mona McClane leaned forward in her chair, her pointed chin poised on her little fist, her green eyes sparkling, and said, "I wonder what it feels like to murder someone. One of these days I'm going to find out!"


## Chapter Three

Afterward Jake could remember how, at that casual remark from Mona McClane, his mind had seemed to snap into focus, like a camera that had been improperly adjusted before. The whole day, from its moment of waking, had been hazy and unreal, somehow dreamlike; he had been only half conscious of sights and sounds and words.

Mona McClane's voice cut into his thoughts sharply, clearing his mind of its fog. For the first time he became completely aware of the room around him and of the people in it. He noticed, and was to remember forever, how the snow was falling softly, almost lazily, in a thinnish veil past the wide window just behind Mona McClane. He noticed how the ash from Malone's cigar broke off suddenly and fell in a little cascade, settling in grayish drifts in the folds of the lawyer's dark-blue suit.

Jake knew that the woman meant it. Everyone else in the room laughed politely and appreciatively and leaned a little closer to catch what that clever Mona McClane might say next. But Jake knew it hadn't been one of those soap bubbles of polite conversation tossed in the air to be blown back and forth until it finally collapsed. He knew, and he didn't care.

He emptied his cocktail glass and set it down on the table beside him. "Well," he said, "why don't you murder somebody? Who's stopping you?"

"I intend to," Mona McClane said. There wasn't a flicker of expression on her pointed face.

"Anyone in particular?" Jake asked.

Mona McClane shrugged her narrow shoulders. "The identity of the victim isn't important, is it? When you're hunting elephants, you don't ask the name of the elephant before you shoot, do you?"

Everyone laughed except the tall, flamboyant Daphne Sanders.

"A new kind of big-game hunt?" Willis Sanders suggested.

Mona McClane lifted her shoulders again, lightly, carelessly. "Not exactly. It's a little hard to explain."

"Then why bother?" said the thin, reedy voice of Fleurette Sanders. "We can all imagine your wanting to murder someone, Mona darling."

The woman sitting near Mona McClane giggled. Jake thought she was a little vague about what was going on, but she was certainly enjoying it. She was an ordinary-looking, dowdy little woman in a badly fitting flowered print dress, with graying hair that straggled down the back of her neck. A Mrs. Ogletree, he remembered. Helene had warned him that she was a walking gossip column.

John J. Malone aimed an installment of cigar ash at the tray and missed by a good three inches. "There's a difference," he said, "between just wanting to murder, and wanting to murder someone."

Mona McClane smiled at him. Her eyes seemed fixed on a misty point on some far horizon. "I've never taken a human life. I can't possibly imagine what it's like." There was a musical little laugh. "I know what almost everything else is like."

"Don't brag," said Willis Sanders in playful reproof.

She paid no attention to him. "To know that someone who has been alive is dead—dead by one's own hand—what is it like? How does it feel? What's the sensation of knowing you've killed, intentionally, another human being?"

"It must feel uncomfortably like being dragged off to jail for a long stay," said a tall, angular, pallid man who had just joined the group. Jake recognized him as Wells Ogletree. Heart-of-stone Ogletree, Helene had called him.

"Not necessarily," Malone said softly. "That's what lawyers are for."

Mona McClane looked at him and beyond him. "I don't know that I'd need a lawyer," she said, musing. "No, I think I could get away with it."

"Oh, stop!" a voice burst out unexpectedly. It came from the girl just at Jake's elbow. "Stop it," she said again. "It isn't a thing to joke about."

Jake turned to look at her. She was a small girl, almost blonde, not exceptional in any way, with a thin, petulant face and a pinched little mouth. He fished his memory for her name and found it. Ellen Ogletree. He wondered why her face and her name seemed so familiar to him, as though he'd known them a long time.

"Who's joking?" Mona McClane asked in what seemed to be surprise. "I'm in earnest. You might say, deadly earnest."

A nervous little laugh ran around the group. The man who was holding Ellen Ogletree's hand possessively giggled foolishly. He was a pale young man, with hair and skin that seemed to be the same indiscriminate color, a rabbity chin, and no eyebrows whatsoever. Jay something-or-other, Jake remembered. Ellen Ogletree's fiancé, and stinking rich. He'd have to be that rich to be anybody's fiancé, Jake thought.

Mona McClane said, half dreamily, "Get away with it? Of course I could get away with it."

Jake forgot he was on his best behavior and said "Nuts!" in a loud and skeptical voice.

She turned to him and lifted one eyebrow. "Care to bet on it, Mr. Justus?"

"Come now, Mona," said Willis Sanders uneasily. "This is going just a bit too far."

Willis Sanders might have whispered into the wind for all the attention anyone paid to him.

"Hell yes," Jake said crossly. "I'd bet on anything. Name your terms and pick your victim." He shook John J. Malone's restraining hand off his arm as he might have shaken off a fly.

No one said anything. There was just the faintest suggestion of a smile on Daphne Sanders' lovely, sullen mouth. The gray-haired Southern woman seemed shocked speechless.

Mona McClane's voice was very clear and very cool. "I'll commit a murder and you pin it on me. I'll bet you can't do it. I'll bet you—" she paused only an instant, "the Casino."

Jake felt something like a minor electric shock. The Casino was the night spot where out-of-town visitors always wanted to go first. It was the place that had stayed open for fifteen years, through good times and bad, rolling up reputation and prosperity. He'd had Dick Dayton's band there for a season, Nelle Brown had sung there. Twice he'd tried to get the job of press-agenting it. Anyone who owned the Casino would never need to worry about getting a job to support his heiress bride.

He tried to keep the surprise out of his voice. "The Casino belongs to you?"

Again Mona McClane lifted one eyebrow, the left one. "The McClane estate includes stranger things than that. Well, is it a bet?"

"Suppose you win?" Jake asked.

She laughed. "If I win a bet like that—the satisfaction of winning ought to be enough."

Jake lit a cigarette. "Lady," he said happily, "it's a bet."

Then everyone laughed.

John J. Malone selected a cigar, looked at it, lit it, and stared up at the ceiling. "I'd suggest there ought to be certain stipulations," he said slowly. "Obscure poisons ought to be ruled out, for instance, and as for completely destroying the remains—"

"Oh, please!" Ellen Ogletree exclaimed. No one noticed her.

"I promise," Mona McClane said, "my murder will be committed in broad daylight on the public streets, with the most ordinary weapon I can find. I'll even promise you plenty of witnesses."

There was only the barest pause before Fleurette Sanders said lightly, with a tinkling little laugh, "You ought also to agree that the victim won't be missed. It would be rather a shame to pick on the head of a large family, or a young man about to be married. By all means, Mona, pick someone who won't be mourned."

"That's easy," Mona McClane said. Her voice was incredibly sweet. "I can think of any number of people who wouldn't be mourned in the least."

Daphne Sanders smiled, ever so slightly. Jake wondered how a woman who looked as smart as Fleurette Sanders would lead with her chin like that.

"The motive, too," Malone said suddenly. "That ought to be another stipulation. If you're going to go out and just indiscriminately murder some perfect stranger, you're putting Jake under an unreasonable handicap." He cleared his throat and began, in his best courtroom manner, "Motive and method are the roads to follow in tracking down a murderer. Opportunity, a silly thing that has to do with alibis, can be ruled out by any intelligent person who has read the memoirs of Houdini. But if there is no motive, one of those roads is blocked. Therefore—"

"Don't worry," Mona McClane said evenly. "There will be motive. That I can promise. Also, that my murder will be a matter of personal motive—though there are some people that perfect strangers ought to shoot down in the streets, like rabid dogs."

This time no one laughed.

Fleurette Sanders stirred uneasily. "I think the whole conversation has been a trifle silly," her voice faded. No one seemed to notice that she had said a word.

"Someone no one will mourn for, and someone I have a motive for murdering," Mona McClane repeated clearly. "Shot down in broad daylight on the public streets. I'll be looking for you with a pair of handcuffs in your pocket, Mr. Justus, and I hope you make a fortune out of the Casino if you win. A bet's a bet."

"Sure," Jake said casually, "but for the love of God stay away from people you don't like for the next two weeks. I'm going on my honeymoon."

A little ripple of laughter ran around the room. People began talking here and there of other things, in little groups. Mona McClane pulled her furs about her shoulders with a quick, graceful gesture, picked up her cigarette case, said, "Give my love to the bride," and was gone.

The very briefest of awkward pauses passed before Willis Sanders cleared his throat and said, "Of course Mona is a remarkable woman, but I don't consider her joking in the best of taste."

No one else had any comment to make.

The party began to disintegrate slowly. Darkness had fallen outside and people began drifting away, the Sanders family, Wells Ogletree, Ellen Ogletree and her rabbity fiancé, the bald-headed man and his fattish wife. Jake managed by some miracle to say what was necessary to the departing guests, but he barely noticed them. He was engaged in wishing Helene would come back, that he had either one more drink or one less—one more drink or one less, he thought, either one seemed almost impossible to arrange at the moment.

The room displayed just the faintest inclination to spin.

It had been a lovely party, he told himself. A very lovely party. He only wished he had known the people who had given it a little better. Still, he had managed to make a date with that beautiful girl in the pale-green suit, the one with the gorgeous long legs. She'd be back any minute now, too. He'd never had a date with a girl like that before. In fact he'd never seen a girl like that before. There couldn't be any other girl, anywhere, with beautiful, long, slim legs like that. She'd gone to take someone to a plane, but she was coming back. Someone. Her father. Father-in-law. Airplane. Honeymoon. *Helene.*

He came in out of the fog long enough to realize he had just married the only girl he'd ever loved.

That was when the telephone call came for him, and Helene's silvery voice came over the wire.

"Hello darling," she said cheerfully. "Get Malone. I'm in jail."

He wrestled with that for a moment. "What jail?"

A muffled voice away from the telephone said, "Where the hell am I?" then there was a pause and then Helene said, "First District station. I hope you have some money. You and Malone come and get me."

"What are you in for?"

"Reckless driving," she said, "and speeding and driving while intoxicated and leaving my driver's license in my other purse and going through a stop sign and driving without a taillight. Don't worry," she added confidently, "Malone can get me out."

He made a futile gesture at the telephone. "Your father's plane?"

"He'll never make it," Helene said crisply. "He's in jail, too."

It took a little over thirty seconds to cope with that. "But," Jake said stupidly, "you were driving the car. What's he in jail for?"

"Resisting-an-officer-in-the-attempt-to-do-his-duty," Helene quoted. She added, "For knocking down a cop and kicking another one in the stomach. Tell Malone he'd better bring quite a lot of money with him."

"Partridge?" Jake asked feebly. He had a feeling that not only was he at the end of his rope, but that the rope was getting badly frayed.

"Partridge is in the hospital."

Jake's flesh froze tight to his bones. "There was an accident. Sweetheart, are you all right? Why didn't you tell me? How badly were you hurt? Darling, tell me you're all right. Angel—"

"Don't be a dope," she said. "There wasn't any accident."

"Partridge," Jake said helplessly. "Partridge. Hospital."

"He fainted," Helene told him. "Now will you get Malone, and please hurry?" She hung up.

## Chapter Four

Jake Justus and John J. Malone were in a taxi and halfway to the Michigan

Avenue bridge before Jake recovered enough breath to speak.

"Well, it was a swell party, anyway."

Malone snorted. "I threw a better one the time I smuggled twelve jurors out of their sleeping quarters and engaged a suite in my hotel—"

"I remember," Jake said, quickly and unhappily. "I had to carry in the liquor and see that all the girls got home safely afterward. And then it turned out you would have gotten an acquittal anyway."

Malone said, "I never believe in taking chances with a client's interests at stake. That's ethics."

Jake made a rude, horselike noise.

"Malone, did you think you recognized that Ogletree girl?"

"Sure," the lawyer said, "so did you. Don't you remember?"

Jake said, "Damn it, today I'm having enough trouble remembering who I am."

"The Ogletree kidnaping," Malone reminded him. "It was about two years ago. Ellen Ogletree was snatched. Her old man kicked in fifty grand to get her back unharmed. Personally I don't think she'd be worth ten per cent of that, harmed or unharmed. No one ever got the kidnapers."

"It comes back to me now, but vaguely."

"You ought to read the newspapers once in a while," the lawyer said. He tossed a half-finished cigar out the window. "Damn near every face there was familiar to me, one way or another. Willis Sanders' first wife was killed in rather mysterious circumstances a few years ago. Some people said it was no accident, especially as he'd been keeping company with Fleurette—her name used to be Flossie—for quite a while. Daphne Sanders ran away from home when her old man married again and was on every front page in the country for three weeks. Of course everybody who can read knows Mona McClane."

"Malone, have we enough money with us?"

"At the First District station," Malone said confidently, "I don't need money."

He was almost right, but not quite. The problem of rescuing George Brand from the clutches of the law was merely a matter of transporting his huge, and by that time supine, bulk to a taxicab. That was something of a problem in itself, but the cab driver and three husky policemen managed it nicely. Partridge, his nerves, but not his aplomb, badly shaken, was dispatched to look after his employer, and the taxi departed in the direction of George Brand's club.

Helene, however, was a different matter.

"She stays right here," the desk sergeant announced firmly. "It was purely a matter of luck we laid hands on her in the first place."

Malone agreed with that, but protested against the indignity of keeping a friend of his in jail. "Especially," he added, "for a little matter of a traffic violation."

The sergeant snorted very impolitely. "Traffic violation!" he said, and added,

"She stays right here till we hear from Kansas City. Imagine," he said incredulously, "a guy like Mr. Brand getting tangled up with a dame like that."

Malone was too puzzled to do more than swear questioningly.

"We'd never have recognized her," the sergeant volunteered cheerfully, "if Von Flanagan hadn't happened to drop in. He knew her right away."

A chilling suspicion began to grow in Malone's mind. The lovely blonde heiress and Daniel Von Flanagan of the Homicide Squad had become the best of friends, in spite of a few bad hours Helene had given him in the past. But Von Flanagan was known to have a heavy-handed variety of humor.

Malone's worst suspicions were quickly confirmed. Helene, according to Von Flanagan, was wanted by Kansas City on a serious charge. Not under the name of Helene Brand, or Helene Justus, of course. No one, not even Malone, could do a thing about it.

"Imagine the nerve of her!" said the sergeant, "claiming to be George Brand's daughter. Daughter—!"

In vain Malone argued, explained, demanded, found and offered identification. Nothing could be done until Von Flanagan would admit his "mistake," or word would come from Kansas City.

And no one seemed to have any idea where Von Flanagan was.

"How soon will you hear from Kansas City?" Malone asked at last in desperation.

The sergeant yawned. "Sometime tomorrow." He added, "If they hurry."

The little lawyer grabbed Jake's arm just before a healthy swing landed on the desk sergeant's jaw.

"She's my wife," Jake howled. "You can't keep her in jail."

The sergeant answered him with an icy stare. "I remember you when you was with the *Examiner*, Jake Justus. I remember when you and your boss sprung a dame from the can, claiming she was your wife, and kept her hid out some place for five days, running her story in the paper all that time, while everybody was giving us the laugh because we wanted her for questioning in the McGurk killing. Once maybe I fall for a gag, but twice I don't fall for the same gag."

Malone's tactful and hasty removal of the red-haired press agent from the police station certainly saved the latter from landing in jail along with his bride. It may also have saved the desk sergeant from becoming the center of interest at an inquest.

Jake was still struggling when they reached the sidewalk, and repeating, "She's my wife. They can't do this to me."

"Shut up," Malone said tersely, "and get in that cab."

He shoved Jake into a waiting taxi and told the driver to go north.

Three blocks later Jake was able to speak again. "What the hell goes on?"

"Von Flanagan's idea of a practical joke," the lawyer told him.

Jake talked loudly and in an objectionably personal manner about Von Flanagan for three more blocks. "Malone, get her out of there. She—" he gulped. "I—" he gulped again. "The reservations. Bermuda. Two and a half hours."

"Stop gargling and tell me what you mean," Malone said crossly, lighting a cigarette and handing it to the distraught man.

Jake took two long drags on the cigarette, tossed it out the window, and said, "Helene and I have reservations on a plane leaving two and a half hours from now. We're going to Bermuda for our honeymoon. In two and a half hours, mind you."

"I doubt it like hell," the lawyer said. "You'd better get those reservations changed. On second thought," he added, "give them to me. I'll get them changed for a later plane, get your bride out of jail, and deliver her to you."

"Where the hell is Von Flanagan?"

"He's probably hiding under a bed somewhere. Not a bad idea, either. Give me those damn reservations."

Jake handed them over silently.

"And stop worrying," Malone added.

"You go to blazes. Listen, Malone. Helene and I were just married today. Today, understand? When people have just been married—"

"I know," Malone said, "my mother told me, too. I said to stop worrying. I'll get your bride out of jail for you."

"Where are you taking me now?"

"Back to your apartment. Just curl up with a copy of *The Police Gazette* and keep cool."

Jake became almost unnecessarily profane. As he paused for breath Malone said gloomily, "All I wish is that you hadn't made that damned-fool bet."

"What bet?"

"The one you made with Mona McClane."

"Mona McClane?"

Malone roared, "You made a bet this afternoon with Mona McClane. Remember?"

"Oh," Jake said, "Oh, that bet. I'd forgotten it."

"Mark my words," Malone said, "she hasn't forgotten."

"Nuts."

"She wasn't just making talk," the lawyer told him. "She meant every word of it. She's probably out murdering somebody right now."

"I hope to God it's Von Flanagan, if she is," Jake said soulfully. Suddenly he groaned. "If Helene finds out about that damned bet, she'll want to stay here in Chicago just to learn whether or not Mona McClane really did mean it."

"All right, don't tell her."

"If I don't tell her, somebody else will, and she'll be sore as a goat."

"Then do tell her and resign yourself to staying in Chicago."

"But I'm going on my honeymoon, and—"

Malone bellowed, "Damn it, if you want advice, write to Dorothy Dix." He added in a softer tone, but with a tinge of bitterness, "If I'd known you were going to be this much trouble, I'd have married Helene myself to save you from her."

Jake said nothing. For the rest of the way he sat staring moodily out the cab window, watching the snow that still fell in great feathery flakes to be ground to a grayish mud by the wheels of passing cars. Early winter twilight had settled over the city; Michigan Avenue windows were a blaze of colored lights in the violet haze. They passed the Water Tower, half veiled in the snow, a reddish glare against its white curtain, passed Oak Street Beach, now a desolate area of sand, snow, and heaps of ice, and turned west on Schiller Street. A few blocks more and the cab skidded precariously to a stop before the hotel that had housed a wedding party an hour or two before.

"A hell of a wedding night," Jake growled.

The little lawyer looked at him with affectionate sympathy. "After all the trouble you had trying to get married to Helene, you ought to consider yourself lucky, even if your bridal suite is the First District police station."

Jake grunted and climbed out of the cab. "What's the rap for breaking into jail?"

"Well," Malone said thoughtfully, "it would be the first time in your life you weren't bothered by house dicks." He added, as Jake started across the sidewalk, "Stay home and don't worry. I'll get your bride out of the jug and deliver her to you almost as good as new. Meanwhile, curl up with a copy of—"

Jake wheeled around. "And if you don't bring her back?"

"Then I'll bring you Von Flanagan."

He slammed the cab door and was gone before Jake could answer.

## *Chapter Five*

The distance from the bedroom door to the corner behind the blue chair to the window and back to the door again could be covered in approximately seventy-five fair-sized steps.

Jake knew because he'd counted them after the first half-hour.

After the second half-hour he began a new circuit: from the door to the window, then to the corner behind the chair and back to the door again. It was the same distance, but a new route.

When the third half-hour had gone by he sat down on the davenport and looked around the room. This was going to be his home, he reminded himself; he was going to live here, with Helene. He closed his eyes and pictured Helene in house pajamas, making coffee in the kitchenette. He decided he didn't want coffee, and pictured Helene in house pajamas, blue ones. The hell with the house pajamas. He pictured Helene.

He opened his eyes again. It was a pleasant room, badly marred now by the remains of the party. A little house cleaning wouldn't do any harm. Jake rose, straightened a picture, carried three cocktail glasses into the kitchenette, emptied an ash tray, and sat down again.

Perhaps Helene and Malone were on their way right at this exact moment.

He rose and began walking again, this time going all the way round the room in a complete oblong. It was a little farther that way.

In a few weeks he'd be back here. He began thinking about the future. Maybe there wouldn't be any good jobs for press agents when they came back from Bermuda. A fine time to be getting married, when he was out of a job. Still, if he hadn't been out of a job, they couldn't have gone on a honeymoon. Press agents didn't take vacations. Maybe he should have gone to Hollywood with Nelle Brown. But that hadn't appealed at the time.

Oh well, something would turn up. Something always had. Suddenly he grinned. Now if Mona McClane only carried out her threat and he could win that bet he'd made with her! For a moment he imagined himself owning the Casino.

Oh well, he might as well imagine himself owning the Michigan Avenue bridge.

He discovered that by standing at one side of the window and craning his neck a little he could see the cars and taxis turning onto Schiller Street. Maybe one of them was bringing Helene.

He decided that when twenty-five cars and taxis had gone around that corner, he'd stop watching from the window. Maybe he'd better make it twenty-five taxis. No, he'd count cars too.

After the seventeenth car had passed, there was an almost unendurably long wait. He'd almost given up, when nearly a dozen cars and taxis came by in a bunch, too many for him to count.

This time he'd watch until exactly ten cars and ten taxicabs had gone by.

He added several paragraphs to the long list of things he'd planned to say over the telephone to Von Flanagan when Helene was safely out of jail. Thinking about them distracted his attention from the scene below, and he lost count entirely.

There was no sense in going on like this, he told himself sternly. He'd sit down calmly, smoke a cigarette, and think about something else.

He was out of matches.

Searching the apartment he found over a dozen packages of assorted brands of cigarettes, and a battered folder holding exactly two matches.

Well, that would last until Helene arrived. Surely it couldn't be very long now. This time tomorrow they'd be in Bermuda. He looked at his watch. Nine o'clock.

That reminded him he'd had no dinner.

The hell with dinner.

Perhaps if he left the door ajar he could hear the elevator as it stopped at the floor. He tried it, and found that he could. He could also hear the elevator every time it approached the floor from either direction. During the next half-hour he was halfway down the hall every time he heard a sound.

He was returning from one of those luckless excursions when a door across the hall suddenly opened and a voice called out.

"Oh, Mr. Justus."

He wheeled around. The voice, dripping with honey and Southern accent, came from the gray-haired woman who had been at the party. Jake blinked at her for a moment before he remembered her. Then he smiled. He had reached the stage of loneliness where he would have smiled at anyone, save Daniel Von Flanagan.

She beamed at him. "I kept hearin' you go up and down the hall, and I got downright worried about you, Mr. Justus. I do hope there's nothing wrong."

"I'm—waiting for someone," Jake said lamely. It was a slightly difficult situation to explain.

"But yo' charming bride—where is she?"

"She's not here. It's—she who I'm waiting for." It occurred to him that his explanation only added to the confusion somehow.

The woman's tact rose to the occasion. "Oh." She managed to make three syllables of it. "Won't you come in and have a drink while yo're waiting? I do just hate to think of you in there all alone."

Jake hesitated only an instant. Five more minutes of solitude were going to make him a gibbering maniac. Besides, he needed a drink.

She cocked her head on one side in a pleasantly birdlike manner and added, "Now please don't feel embarrassed because you can't remember my name. Nobody gets names right at parties. My name is Lulamay Yandry, I'm a widow and I come from Tennessee, and I'm sure we're properly introduced. So come right in."

He didn't need any more urging. He followed his hostess into a room shaped like the one he had just left, cozily littered with sewing, knitting bags, and innumerable small, unframed photographs of extremely uninteresting-looking people.

"Kinfolk," Mrs. Yandry explained casually, waving an arm. She motioned Jake to an easy chair and vanished into the kitchenette, returning with a large decanter full of a translucent, watery fluid, and two glasses. "I bet yo're sitting there wondering what I'm doin' up here so far away from home. That's the first question anyone asks me, what am I doing up here so far away from home. It's a long story, Mr. Justus, and I'm not goin' to bore you with it even if you urge me."

Jake hadn't the slightest intention of urging her. He hadn't wondered for even a split second what Lulamay Yandry was doing so far away from home. However, he managed an expression of polite interest while she continued to chatter, filled the glasses and handed him one. "I'm so glad to find some folks who are really neighborly. Northern folks don't seem neighborly, like the folks at home." She smiled at him amiably. "Here's how, as you say up No'th."

Jake's first impression was that all hell had broken loose in his throat. He tried a second taste and wondered if he could, by any chance, be drinking some newly developed high explosive. His third taste convinced him that the liquor, whatever it was, was not half bad.

"Just a bit strong when you don't expect it, isn't it?" Lulamay twittered. "It's a shot of real corn liquor from Tennessee."

"It must have been the shot heard round the world," Jake hazarded. He had a feeling that the rest of the nation ought to secede from Tennessee, and at once.

Lulamay Yandry looked almost, but not quite, like the ideal of a dear old grandmother. She was a small woman, somewhere beyond middle age, with a faded, pretty face, and immense blue eyes. Her dress, Jake guessed, was expensive, it fitted perfectly, and was fashioned in a new and rather extreme style. Over it she wore a shapeless sweater coat that had seen its best days long ago. Her stockings were sheer and shimmering, her tiny feet were thrust into frayed heelless carpet slippers.

She refilled the glasses, sat down, picked up a knitting bag, and began to knit. For a while Jake forgot his troubles as he watched her managing four knitting needles, a cigarette, and a glass of real corn liquor from Tennessee, all with only two hands, and without losing a syllable from the flow of monologue that went on and on. There was something wonderfully soothing and comforting about Tennessee corn liquor, Jake found. He was able to listen to Lulamay Yandry without having the faintest idea of what she was saying.

During the first two drinks he looked at his watch every fifteen minutes. After that he didn't bother. At the fourth drink he gave up all hope of dining with Helene and telephoned to the Pit for barbecued ribs, which Lulamay declared were her favorite food. A perfect combination with corn liquor, too. Jake licked his fingers and wished Lulamay kept a couple of hound dogs. He was in just the mood for throwing bones to hound dogs.

After the fifth drink Lulamay became hopelessly involved in her knitting and laid it aside. By that time they had turned the radio on, turned it off again, and were swapping stories.

The sixth drink made Jake remember Von Flanagan, and he decided to go out, find him, and beat the everlasting living daylights out of him. After a lengthy debate about it with Lulamay, who didn't know what on earth he was talking about, he gave it up.

He forgot Von Flanagan with the seventh drink. He was adrift on roseate clouds above a wonderful, wonderful world. If only Helene were there. Helene would like Lulamay Yandry. Who wanted to go to Bermuda anyway? Besides, the plane had probably left by now. Lulamay Yandry was a marvelous old girl.

She reminded him of the grandmother that he'd never seen. He repressed an impulse to weep.

Helene. Who wanted to spend his wedding night on an airliner, anyway? All he wanted was to be alone with Helene. He'd wanted to be alone with Helene for a long time now. Not on an airliner, either.

He noticed that his hostess had stopped chattering. She was, in fact, as silent as the grave. Well, never let it be said that he, Jake Justus, was one to wake up a dear old lady. Not he. In fact, he could do with forty winks himself.

Besides, a little sleep would make the time pass quicker until Helene was there.

He looked at the decanter, noted regretfully that it was empty. Oh well, it was clear across the room. Too far to walk, anyway.

Just a little catnap, that was all he wanted. Just a little, tiny, teensy-weensy catnap.

He hummed a line of "Rockaby, Baby" to himself, pulled his long legs up on the sofa, took one deep breath, and slept like the dead.

## *Chapter Six*

Jake Justus heard bells ringing somewhere. There were fire-alarm bells, church bells, chimes, telephone bells, doorbells, a large assortment of buzzers, and two small carillons.

They were all, he discovered, inside his head.

He opened his eyes for a divided second, shut them hastily, and tried to remember what he had been dreaming. Something about betting on a horse race. He'd bet on a horse, and when it came by the grandstand he'd been surprised to see that it was being ridden by Mona McClane instead of a jockey. There had been something else in the dream, too, something confused and horrible. Then the bells had wakened him.

He opened his eyes again, gingerly. It was broad daylight. He sat bolt upright, suddenly wide-awake.

Lulamay Yandry still slept peacefully in her chair, her gray hair straggling over her face, her mouth open. After a terrible moment of pulling himself together, Jake rose slowly and cautiously to his feet, tiptoed to the door, and went out without disturbing her.

He was probably in enough trouble right now without letting a gray-haired Southern belle know that he had compromised her.

The bells were still ringing, fainter now, but definitely there.

What on earth was he going to tell Helene!

He opened the door to his own apartment quietly and timidly, and stood listening for a moment. Not a sound. He crept in and closed the door carefully.

The room was empty.

He thought it over for a while. Of course. She was asleep. Probably it was early morning, just barely daylight. He looked at his watch and found it had stopped. Oh well, it couldn't be much past dawn.

He tiptoed to the bedroom door, encouraging himself with the thought that he could put over a very convincing story. He'd explain that he had been there for hours, and hadn't wanted to disturb her. She'd probably be appreciative, even grateful, for his thoughtfulness. He congratulated himself admiringly, and opened the bedroom door an inch at a time, praying that its hinges wouldn't make a sound.

*No Helene.*

No Helene anywhere. No sign of Helene.

The bells began to ring more loudly, and something strange was happening to his knees. He had a curious conviction that he had died during the night. If that was true, perhaps he ought to lie down. He wondered vaguely if he'd better call the coroner. Maybe it would be illegal for him to move until the police had come to examine his remains.

What time could it be? He looked hopefully toward the window. The snow had stopped falling, but the sky was gray, heavily blanketed with clouds. The sun might be anywhere.

With what he recognized as an extremely heroic effort he picked up the telephone and asked for the correct time, adding, "And no matter what time it is, it's going to be a very, very unpleasant surprise."

The time was eleven thirty-two.

Half the day gone and nothing done. Almost twelve hours since plane time. What had Malone done about the reservations? Almost twenty-four hours since he had been married.

*Where was Helene?*

Helene was still in jail. Helene was out of jail, but she and Malone had been in an accident and were in the hospital. Mona McClane had murdered her. Something terrible had happened.

It was then that he saw the note, scrawled with lipstick on a piece of hotel stationery and propped up against the mirror of the dressing table:

> *Waited for you until nine o'clock* (A.M.)
> *and have gone to father.*

After a few horrible minutes he decided to call Malone. While the call was being put through, he tried to realize that he had lost Helene, lost her forever. He deserved it, of course, but that didn't make him feel any better.

The only thing to do was to jump off Navy Pier. No, the damn lake was frozen. The window would do. "Press agent jumps from window day following marriage to heiress." That's how the headlines would tell it. He wondered if his friends would be sorry. He wondered if Helene would be sorry.

Malone's voice was filled with incredulous surprise. "Aren't you on your way to Bermuda?"

"No. Where's Helene?"

A pause, then, "Don't you know?"

"Damn it, would I be asking you if I did? Where is she?"

"I left her at the entrance of the hotel about eleven last night. Where are you?"

"At the hotel." Jake drew a long breath and added, "I just got here."

Malone was silent for a good thirty seconds, then indignantly called on heaven to witness that he had already had enough trouble to last the average man a lifetime just getting Jake and Helene married, and from now on he was going to live his own life.

When the lawyer paused for breath Jake said unhappily, "She left me a note, and she's gone."

"I don't blame her," Malone snapped. "I wouldn't have bothered to leave a note." He hung up.

The fourth time Jake called him back the lawyer swore crossly into the phone and said, "Hold your head under the shower until I get there."

That helped a little. Not much, though. Jake examined himself in the mirror and decided that for a man who had just risen from the dead, he didn't look half bad. By the time Malone arrived he had had a shave and a shower that almost silenced the bells in his head.

"Married twenty-four hours and she goes home to father," Malone said, kicking the door shut. "A fine start!" He looked at Jake searchingly. "It must have been a big night."

"Malone, did you ever drink any real Tennessee corn liquor?"

"Once. When I woke up I found I'd been buried three days."

Jake groaned. "It's worse just after you're exhumed." He explained his meeting with Lulamay Yandry and the subsequent events. "Malone, do you think she'll ever forgive me?"

"I don't know. Hell hath no jury like—"

"Fury," Jake said automatically. "Damn it, she couldn't have gone far."

Malone muttered something incoherent about how fast women could run, and said, "What's the phone number of George Brand's club?"

After fumbling with the phone book for a full minute Jake announced that it was all in fine Chinese print, and suggested calling Information.

At the club Malone was finally able to get an outraged Partridge on the phone. The gentleman's gentleman was slightly on the frigid side. Mr. Brand and Miss Helene had left together some time ago.

"It's Mr. Justus, trying to find Mrs. Justus," Malone said.

Partridge's voice softened unexpectedly. "You might try the Drake bar, sir."

Malone hung up, turned to Jake, and said, "You don't need to worry. She'll forgive you."

He ordered breakfast and forced food on the protesting Jake. It was a bit past one o'clock when the two men went down the elevator and headed for a press-while-you-wait establishment at the corner of Division and State Streets. When they emerged it was exactly half-past one, and a thin, cold drizzle of rain had begun to fall.

Malone looked at his watch. "The travel bureau—" he began.

Jake clutched suddenly at his arm. "Malone, look. There she is!"

"You're having delusions. She's at the Drake bar."

"I don't mean Helene."

The lawyer looked in the direction Jake indicated and saw Mona McClane on the opposite corner, exquisitely dressed and furred, apparently oblivious of the rain. She too was looking at her watch, and as the two men looked she hailed a passing taxi, hopped in, and disappeared down State Street.

"A very pretty picture," Malone growled, "but what of it? If you're going to go staring after other women the day after your marriage—"

"I'm not staring after other women. That bet she made with me. You know what I mean."

Malone raised his eyes and complained bitterly about an unjust fate that had mixed him up with a lunatic, hailed a taxi, directed it to the travel bureau, and finally said, "Any more about that insane bet, and I'll leave you to face Helene alone."

By the time reservations had been made for a six o'clock plane, it was nearly half-past two. The Loop and Michigan Avenue were jammed with holiday traffic that moved with difficulty through the rain, and it was a little after three when the two men arrived at the Drake bar.

Helene and her father were sitting at a small table in the corner. George Brand rose to greet them.

"It's about time," he began in a surprisingly pleasant tone.

Helene looked up, smiling. "Hello, darling. I was just beginning to worry about you."

"Just beginning!" Suddenly Jake glared at her, eyes blazing. "Do you mean to say you haven't been worrying about me?"

"Why no. I knew you'd look me up some time."

"Fine thing!" He sat down heavily. "Think of what might have happened to me. I might have been run over by a truck. I might have had an attack of amnesia. I might have been kidnaped. Almost anything might have happened. And you didn't worry. I don't suppose you even bothered to call up the police."

Helene said acidly, "I've had enough of the police to last me for a long time." Her voice grew unexpectedly tender. "Oh Jake, I'm so sorry I didn't worry about you!"

He regarded her thoughtfully. "I forgive you. This time."

His eyes met George Brand's in a long look of sympathetic understanding, a look that said it wasn't so much of a muchness to handle these women, once you knew how it was done.

"The truth is," Jake began at last.

George Brand interrupted him. "Never tell the truth when you have a lawyer along."

Malone signaled to the waiter, ordered a round of rye and seltzer, and said, "The truth is, he was out visiting another woman."

The wonderful thing about telling the truth, Jake reflected, was that no one ever believed it. Two drinks later he felt sufficiently recovered to tell of his meeting with Lulamay Yandry. Helene immediately declared that the plane reservations would have to be canceled because she refused to leave Chicago until she'd tried out Lulamay's corn liquor in a new Confederate cocktail recipe. She even had a name for it. The Rebel Yell.

She and Malone immediately became involved in a furious argument over possible ingredients, with George Brand offering suggestions. Jake announced that as he was neither a chemist, a bartender, nor a toxicologist, he had no interest in the matter, and went out to buy a newspaper. When he returned with it, his face was three shades paler, and his eyes were flickering with excitement.

He tossed the paper on the table and pointed to the story that told of the fatal shooting of the little man in the rusty black overcoat on the corner of State and Madison Streets in the presence of hundreds of witnesses.

"You never thought she'd do it," he said to Malone. "You thought she was joking when she made that bet." His voice was deadly calm. "Well—there it is!"

## *Chapter Seven*

While Malone went for more newspapers, Jake told Helene and her father about the bet he had made with Mona McClane.

George Brand scowled heavily. "It's easy to believe almost anything fantastic of Mona. But murder—I don't know. Especially murder on a bet."

Helene muttered something about bet-time stories.

Malone returned with the newspapers. All of them told essentially the same story. An unidentified man had been shot to death on the far-famed busiest corner in the world, at the height of the Christmas-shopping rush. That was all.

"She said—" Jake paused, frowned, and went on, "she said—someone that no one will mourn for—shot down on the public streets in broad daylight. With plenty of witnesses. Well, Malone—?"

Malone was expressively silent.

"Nothing on earth but a coincidence," Helene said at last in an unconvinced and unconvincing voice.

George Brand said, "Of course that's what it is. Jake is simply going up a tree over nothing."

Jake growled, "Give me those damned papers."

There was a description of the victim, the hour of the slaying was fixed at fifteen minutes past two, the names of Policeman Gahagan and a few of the bystanders were mentioned. The *News* had a photograph of the big Boston Store clock with the caption THE SILENT WITNESS! and the *Times* had a picture of the little man lying on the sidewalk surrounded by a ring of interested spectators. The picture didn't show much of him, only that he was dead.

"Nice fast work," Jake commented with professional enthusiasm, looking at his watch and at the pictures.

No one answered.

"Helene's right," Malone said at last. "It's nothing on earth but a stupid coincidence."

"Of course it is," George Brand agreed, much too heartily.

Jake muttered, "Broad daylight on the public streets, with plenty of witnesses."

"Nuts," Malone said disgustedly.

"Mona could," Helene said suddenly. "She could make that bet, knowing everyone took it as a joke, and down in her heart mean every word of it."

"Of all the damned idiotic things," the little lawyer growled. "Jake makes a cockeyed bet with a crazy dame that she can murder someone and get away with it, and so the first murder that comes along—" he paused, gulped, and finally added inadequately, "You're full of small potatoes."

Jake said dreamily, "Just the same, it would be swell to own the Casino."

Malone snorted.

"Do you mean," Helene said firmly, addressing Jake, "that you'd try to pin a murder on someone just to win the Casino?"

"In a minute," Jake told her. "I'm a married man now, and I'm out of a job. Besides," he said thoughtfully, "I'm curious to know how she did it."

"With a gun," George Brand put in helpfully. "According to the papers."

"The corner of State and Madison Streets," Jake mused, "the busiest corner in the world, during the busiest hour of the busiest day of the Christmas-shopping rush."

"Amazingly audacious," George Brand murmured. He shook his head incredulously.

"Not at all," Malone said suddenly. He drew a long breath. "In fact, that was probably the safest place in the city of Chicago to commit a murder." He stirred his rye and stared into it as though it were a crystal ball. "Not only the most crowded corner in the world, but the noisiest. Likewise, everyone on that corner would be entirely intent on his own affairs and on where he was trying to go. The chances of the sound of the shot being heard were slim."

He sighed heavily. "If you've ever tried to walk through one of those State

Street mobs, you know how a movement of the crowd can shove you along for considerable distance, even if you're trying to go in the opposite direction. Figure how that would work in the case of a body with no movement or volition of its own. The body may have been carried along by the crowd for quite a considerable distance before it fell. Then, of course, there were a few minutes of insane confusion."

He looked at his glass, stirred it, emptied it. "All the murderer had to do was walk up behind this guy, shoot him, and walk away. In thirty seconds the murderer would be hopelessly lost in the crowd."

There was a long silence.

Helene looked at the picture in the *Times* as though it might reveal something.

"I wonder who he is," she said thoughtfully. "Who he was, I mean."

Jake rose. "That's the first thing to find out. Unidentified man. He might be anybody. Let's go look at him." He looked at his watch. "I'll go cancel those plane reservations."

Helene stared at him. "But Jake—"

"Listen, baby," he said firmly, "if I win the Casino, I'll give you the hat-check concession for a present on our first anniversary. And if I don't," he paused, and decided he wouldn't go into the more sordid possibilities of the future. "Never mind. I'll go cancel those reservations, and then we'll go over to the morgue. You too, Mr. Brand, if you don't mind. You know Mona McClane better than any of us, and there's more than a Chinaman's chance you might recognize this guy."

"Try to lose me," George Brand said happily.

"Malone too," Helene said firmly, fixing her eyes on the little lawyer. By the time Jake had returned from a phone call to the travel bureau Malone had agreed to go along, though still protesting.

The morgue attendant took their names and told them they were welcome to view the remains of the unidentified man who had been shot and killed at the corner of State and Madison Streets that afternoon.

"He looked like a bum," the attendant offered, "and still he didn't look like a bum, if you know what I mean. You can look at his clothes, if you want to."

"What were they like?" Malone asked.

"Old, and not very clean. Didn't cost much when they were new. Iron hat. Long cotton underwear."

"Anything on him?"

"Uh-uh. He had a change purse with something under a buck in it, a coupla old pencils, and a dirty handkerchief. Nothing else."

"O. K.," Jake said. "Let's have a look at him."

They followed the attendant down a shabby staircase, paused while he opened a heavy metal door, and went into a big, brilliantly lighted room smelling strongly of formaldehyde. The air out in the street had been cold, with an icy winter wind. It was colder here. Jake felt Helene's hand slip into his.

"He's number seventeen," the attendant said chummily. He led the way to one of the metal cabinets in the wall and pulled it out like a bureau drawer.

Number seventeen had been a small man, short, and exceedingly thin. There was a sharp, pinched look to his face, the corners of his mouth had been perpetually drawn up in a mocking, unpleasant grin. His lips were two bloodless lines, his nose was narrow and pointed. The wispy hair clinging to his bony skull was a yellowish gray. He looked as though, in life, he might have been a disagreeable and even downright objectionable man to know, but now there was a lonely, tired, almost wistful expression on his face.

"The poor little guy!" Helene exclaimed involuntarily.

"Know him, lady?" the morgue attendant asked.

She shook her head. "Never saw him before."

Jake Justus and George Brand shook their heads silently. Malone took one quick glance at the body of the little man.

"No," the lawyer said. "I made a mistake. He's not the man I knew."

The morgue attendant shrugged his shoulders, shut the vault, and led the way out.

"Sorry to have troubled you for nothing," Malone said.

"That's O. K., Mr. Malone. There'll be a lot of people down here to look at him until somebody does identify him, if anybody ever does."

Jake said, "Well, thanks anyway."

"That's all right," the attendant said again, "that's what I'm here for."

No one spoke on the way to Helene's car. As they reached it, Helene said suddenly, "But if we can't find out who he is, how are we going to prove that Mona McClane shot him?"

Malone didn't answer. Indeed, he didn't seem to have heard. At last he drew a long, quivering breath and said, "It's about time somebody killed that guy. But why in the name of heaven and earth should it have been Mona McClane?"

## Chapter Eight

"Damn you, Malone," Helene said crossly, "stop being mysterious and exasperating. Who was he?"

It was not Malone but George Brand who answered.

"He was the go-between in the Ellen Ogletree kidnaping."

Helene started the big car and began guiding it skillfully through the heavy early-evening traffic. "I know it's rude to ask questions," she said, "but how do you know?"

"Because I gave him the money," George Brand said simply.

Helene missed the end of a truck by an inch or two, gasped, and said, "You're insane."

"I am not insane," her father said irritably. "Wells Ogletree asked me to deliver the ransom money, and I did. Fifty thousand dollars in small bills. Ogletree said he was afraid he'd be recognized, but I think the real reason was that he couldn't bear to see that much money go out of his hands all at one time." He paused to hunt for a cigarette.

"Ogletree was fit to be tied," he went on. "I don't know which was the worst, Ellen's being kidnaped or losing the money. I've seen him almost have a nervous breakdown over dropping a quarter down a sidewalk grating."

"Never mind his personality," Helene said. "What about the kidnaping and this little guy?"

"I'm getting to that. Ogletree was scared into doing what the kidnapers demanded. So I took the money in a brief case down to the Public Library, sat down on one of the benches facing the elevators, laid the brief case on the bench beside me, and read a newspaper. A little later this man came down the elevator, sat down beside me, and began reading a book. About ten minutes later he got up and walked away, carrying the brief case. The next morning Ellen was home, safe."

"And you never told me any of this before!" Helene said indignantly.

George Brand said, "I never thought you'd care."

Helene drove on in outraged silence for a moment, suddenly slammed on the brakes, and swung into a parking lot. "I can't stand any more until I've had food," she declared. "And I need a drink to help me think clearly."

She led the way to Maurice's and a quiet corner table, and refused to talk of murder until a drink had arrived and dinner been ordered.

"Now, Malone," she said firmly as the waiter moved out of earshot, "Who was he?"

"His name," Malone said, "was Joshua Gumbril. As far as anyone knows, that was his right name. He lived at—" he consulted a little notebook, "room 514 in the Fairfax Hotel on South State Street. He had an office, God knows why, in a building at Wells and Washington."

"What do you mean—God knows why?" Jake asked.

"Because his business wasn't the sort that's usually transacted in an office," the lawyer told him. He paused to mop his face with a dingy handkerchief. "He was a sort of crooks' agent, if you can imagine such a thing. If you wanted anything done from a small job of safe-cracking to a large-scale murder, Gumbril could arrange it for you."

"Were you one of his customers?" Jake asked very politely.

Malone ignored him. "I knew him because he sent me a client now and then. He must have been stinking rich, but I doubt if he spent fifteen dollars a week on himself." He paused while the waiter brought their order. "The Ogletree kidnaping may have been something he arranged as a go-between, or it may have been his own idea."

Helene observed, "If I'd been Ellen Ogletree, I'd have offered the kidnapers damned near anything not to send me home. Not that Ellen ever had anything to offer in the monetary line. Her old man keeps her so short of spending money she has to borrow nickels to make telephone calls."

"If I'd been her old man," Jake said crossly, "I'd have told the kidnapers they could keep her. She looks like a spoiled, bad-tempered brat to me."

"That's her mother's doing," Helene told him. "Mamma Ogletree is always sympathizing with Ellen for having such a mean old so-and-so for a father. Personally I'd say having Mamma Ogletree for a mother was enough to wreck any girl's young life."

"The home life of the Ogletrees is doubtless very interesting," Malone growled, "but I don't see what it has to do with the late Joshua Gumbril, nor do I see why you're so excited about his murder."

Jake said patiently, "The Casino, Malone. Marvelous location. Famous name. Wonderful clientele."

The lawyer stared at him. "You'd go ahead and pin a murder on someone just to win the deed to a night club?"

"If Mona McClane took that bet seriously enough to go out and murder this guy," Jake said stubbornly, "I can take it seriously enough to try to win it."

"Besides," Helene put in, "it would be heavenly to have a night club in the family. Think of all the money we'd save."

"Jake's right," George Brand said, "and what's more, he's morally obligated to win that bet—or at least try."

Malone snorted. "You're all just assuming that the first murder that comes along—"

"Damn it," Jake said, "we saw her on her way to the scene of the crime."

Helene stared at him. "A husband has no business keeping secrets from his wife."

"I wasn't. I'd forgotten it. Mr. Brand, does Mona McClane keep a car?"

"Two of them," George Brand said promptly, "and a chauffeur."

"Then why would she have been taking a taxi at the corner of State and Division Streets at half-past one—just forty-five minutes before the murder—and heading down State Street in the direction of Madison?"

Dessert and coffee arrived before anyone could answer that. Malone stirred his coffee vigorously, lit a cigar, and stared thoughtfully through the smoke.

"How could Mona McClane have possibly known a guy like that well enough to murder him?"

"Maybe she didn't know him," Helene said promptly.

Jake shook his head. "That's no good. She said—someone she'd have a motive for murdering. I've got to find out what that motive was, if I'm going to prove that she did murder Joshua Gumbril."

Malone scowled. "Motives for murder fall into three big groups. Money, love, and fear. Take your pick."

"Mona McClane has about half the money in Chicago right now," Helene observed, "I can't imagine any love in her life being important enough to bring on a murder, and she certainly isn't afraid of anything on earth."

"Well damn it, there's something," Jake said crossly. He looked at his watch. "Any minute now the police will find that their unidentified man is Joshua Gumbril. Before they do, I'd like to search his room and his office, if I can get in." He looked at Malone hopefully.

The little lawyer chewed savagely on his cigar for a moment, swore under his breath, finally reached into his pocket for a handful of keys which he tossed on the table.

"Some one of those will open any door in the Fairfax Hotel. But if you get in trouble, don't expect me to get you out."

Jake stuffed the keys in his pocket. "How about Gumbril's office?"

"The janitor of the building would let me in. I know him," Malone said. He sighed deeply. "All right, I'll search Gumbril's office. But it's the last thing I'll do for you. From this point on, you're on your own."

## *Chapter Nine*

The Fairfax Hotel was a dingy, ramshackle building, a few blocks beyond the South State Street of pawnshops, cheap burlesque houses, taverns, and penny arcades. The front was a faded stucco, peeling here and there; above the entrance an electric sign with three or four missing bulbs proclaimed its name.

Jake Justus took a cautious glance through the glass doors before opening them. The small, gloomy lobby was practically deserted; the desk clerk was engrossed in a magazine. Jake went in, crossed the lobby as though he had every right to be there, stepped into the self-service elevator, and went up to room 514.

The third key he tried opened the door. He locked it behind him and shoved back the bolt as an added precaution against intrusion, and turned on the light.

It was a little, shabby room. A painted iron single bed took up most of the space; a cheap pine dresser stood in the opposite corner. One window looked down on an alley and the roof of a garage. A flimsy writing desk and a battered straight chair stood near the window. On the wall over the desk was a print of "The Lone Wolf."

There was nothing about the room to indicate that someone lived there all the time and came back to it night after night. The only personal belongings Jake could see were a comb and a nail file on the dresser top, and a mussed dark-blue necktie hanging over a doorknob.

He started with the desk. Save for a few sheets of hotel stationery and a pen, it was empty. Two drawers in the dresser were empty. The third held four inexpensive shirts, one of them new, and a suit of patched and darned underwear. There was a pair of socks in one corner.

On the washstand was a cheap safety razor, several boxes of blades, an old toothbrush—but no tooth paste—and a half-used cake of shaving soap.

Jake lit a cigarette and looked thoughtfully at the bed. A man like Gumbril might very well hide personal papers in or under a mattress. With a kind of deliberate determination he tore the bed apart, looking between the blankets, feeling carefully of the pillows, and finally ripping up the mattress.

There was nothing hidden in the bed.

He took the print of "The Lone Wolf" off the wall and pried loose the back. With a disgusted sigh he dropped the picture on the floor, shook the window curtains, pulled loose the window shade, and looked inside it, and at last lifted up the one threadbare rug.

Before investigating the closet, Jake sat down on the tumbled bed and swore. Imagine anyone living in a place like this! Malone had said the late Joshua Gumbril was stinking rich. What the hell did he do with all his dough, then?

He gave the closet door a vicious kick as he opened it. If there was nothing in the closet, he had wasted his time.

One suit was hanging there, a cheap black suit, badly worn. Jake turned the pockets inside out and found nothing save a pencil stub, an old streetcar transfer, and two rubber bands. He felt the lining carefully and found nothing. He took a faded flannel bathrobe down from its hook, shook it vigorously, and felt in its pockets. Nothing. The closet's one shelf was empty.

Jake picked up a pair of shabby carpet slippers, looked inside them, and tossed them on the floor. There was a laundry bag in the corner, he kicked at it, decided he might as well be thorough, and reached for it.

Suddenly he paused, one hand half outstretched toward the laundry bag. Had the late Joshua Gumbril used expensive perfume? Jake doubted it. He doubted too that Gumbril would have had feminine visitors who used that particular scent. Yet there was a distinct odor of perfume in the closet, delicate and faint, but recognizable.

In the days before his meeting with Helene, perfume had been just perfume to Jake. However he'd learned enough about it from her to know this particular odor was a rare, probably highly expensive, one. Certainly it was one he would recognize again if he ever met it. But how had such a perfume left its fragrance in a place like this? What did it have to do with Joshua Gumbril and, much more importantly, with Joshua Gumbril's murder?

The sight of the laundry bag on the floor at his feet recalled his mind to the task at hand. Still thinking of his curious discovery, he picked it up.

It was surprisingly heavy for a laundry bag, though it was only partly full. As

Jake carried it out into the room something hard in the bottom of the bag bumped against his ankles.

He felt a sudden sense of excitement. Damn-fool place to hide anything, but still, you never could tell. He dumped the contents onto the floor. There were a small heap of soiled linen and an oblong japanned metal box.

Jake carried the box over to the corner of the room where there was a little more light and stood turning it over in his hands. It was about the size of an ordinary dispatch box, or petty-cash box. He rattled it hopefully, but heard nothing.

Of the few belongings of the late Joshua Gumbril that were in his room, the box was the only item that looked expensive. Jake had seen similar ones, designed to hold valuables of one sort or another, and he recognized this as unusually fine. If Joshua Gumbril had gone so far as to buy an expensive box, obviously the contents must be something really worth investigating.

There was a handful of miscellaneous keys in his pockets; he tried them all unsuccessfully. Then he experimented a little with a penknife. The box declined to open.

Oh well, Malone would find a way to open it. The simplest thing to do was to carry it away with him.

He had tucked it under his arm and started for the door when the knock came. A loud voice called, "Who's in there?"

Jake stood perfectly still. The doorknob was rattled violently, he heard a key inserted in the lock, and thanked heaven he'd had the foresight to shove back the bolt.

There was a brief murmuring, and the voice called again, "Hey, you in there. Open that door!"

Another period of murmuring followed. Jake caught the words, "Get the janitor," and the sound of heavy footsteps going hastily down the hall.

The box was the problem. He could walk his way out with no trouble, he told himself confidently. The box, though, was going to create difficulties. He looked desperately around the room for a hiding place. If he could only cache it somewhere and come back for it later, everything would be all right—temporarily at least.

There wasn't a single place in the room big enough to hide a one-cent stamp.

He ran silently to the window and threw it open. Perhaps he could drop the box outside, notice where it landed, and return for it as soon as the coast was clear.

A violent pounding began on the door.

Outside the window Jake discovered an indented ledge, about ten inches wide. Reaching out, he shoved the box along as far as his arm would go, and hastily brushed snow over it. There it would be easy to find again, and there wasn't the chance that some curious person going up the alley would find and make off with it.

He closed the window softly and dusted the snow from his sleeve.

"Hey! Open that door!" The voice was a bellow this time.

Drawing a long breath, Jake crossed the room, pulled back the bolt, and opened the door.

There was a little crowd of curious onlookers in the hall. Two policemen stepped into the room and looked Jake over. One of them said, "Well, Joe, I guess we got him."

Jake ran a hand through his red hair, rubbed one eye, yawned, and said, "What the hell do you guys want?"

One of the policemen looked at him blankly and said, "Huh?" The other turned toward the door and barked, "Beat it, all of you." The group of curious bystanders moved reluctantly a few feet down the hall. The policeman bawled, "Gw'an now, beat it!" and slammed the door noisily.

Jake looked in a bewildered manner from one to the other and asked, "What's the big idea?"

The larger of the policemen, the one with the red face, stared at Jake and said, "What are you doing here?"

"Taking a nap," Jake said promptly.

The smaller one said, "Nuts. What are you doing here?"

"I told you," Jake said crossly. "I'm taking a nap—or I was until you guys came along and woke me up."

"And just how," asked the smaller policeman with nasty politeness, "do you happen to be taking this here nap in this here room?"

"I'm waiting for Mr. Gumbril. He was out when I got here, and I decided to take a nap while I was waiting for him."

"Oh, you're waiting for Mr. Gumbril, are you?" the red-faced policeman said icily.

"Yeah," Jake said. "Anything wrong with that?" He reached for a cigarette.

The larger of the two knocked Jake's hand away from his pocket in one quick move, snapping, "Cut that out!" He pinned Jake's arms down while the other policeman patted him swiftly and expertly for weapons and found none. Then they decided to leave him alone.

"What's the matter with my getting a cigarette?" Jake demanded in an injured tone. No one answered. He got one out, lighted it, flipped his match toward the wastebasket, and said irritably, "What goes on, anyway?"

"You're gonna have one hell of a long wait," the smaller policeman said. "Gumbril's dead."

Jake managed to look surprised.

"How long you been here?"

Jake said, "I don't know. I forgot to punch the time clock when I came in."

"Haven't you seen the afternoon papers?"

"No. Should I have?"

The red-faced policeman decided to make the duet a trio. "Where were you all afternoon?"

"That's my business."

"Yeah?" The cop glared at him, then glanced around the room. "Do you always take your naps on the inside of the mattress?"

Jake looked at the bed as though he were noticing for the first time that the mattress was ripped open. He didn't approve of such untidiness.

"Mice?" he suggested hopefully.

"I suppose," the cop said, "you're gonna stand there and tell us the room was all messed up like this when you got here." He cast an eloquent eye around him. "Bedclothes all over the floor. Everything pulled outa the dresser drawers. Laundry bag turned inside out. I suppose the mice done that too."

Jake shrugged his shoulders. "Well, rats then. How should I know? Maybe Gumbril was looking for something."

The cop started to speak, restrained himself, pointed to the chair, and snarled, "Sit down and shut up."

Jake sat down and smoked his cigarette while he watched the two men search the room. In spite of the jam he was in he could barely repress a grin as it went on. Searching the room of the late Joshua Gumbril was hardly a productive occupation.

He wondered what was happening to Malone.

The red-faced cop finally kicked the closet door shut, cursed, and said, "If there ever was anything here, this guy has it."

"We shoulda searched him before we started on the room," his companion said, looking at Jake. "Stand up, you."

"Got a warrant?" Jake asked pleasantly, getting to his feet.

"Warrant, hell!"

Jake agreeably allowed himself to be searched. The policemen found nothing that interested them save the plane reservations.

"Planning a getaway," one of them muttered.

Jake suggested politely that since they had searched him and found nothing even remotely incriminating, he might as well be on his way. His suggestion, as he had expected, was ignored. After that he kept discreetly silent. There were times to argue, but this wasn't one of them.

A short time later he was ushered into the presence of Dan Von Flanagan of the Homicide Bureau by the red-faced policeman.

"We found this *blitzkrieg* in Gumbril's room. He'd already tore the place apart. Probably looking for Gumbril's dough. He didn't find it, or anything else." He regarded his prisoner triumphantly.

Von Flanagan looked up with morose, weary eyes. "Well, well, Jake Justus! Nice to see you again. Did you murder Joshua Gumbril, and if so, why?"

# *Chapter Ten*

Daniel Von Flanagan of the Homicide Bureau didn't like murders. He didn't like murderers, either.

In the first place, he'd never wanted to be a policeman. He'd even gone to court and had the "Von" added to his name because just plain Flanagan sounded too much like a policeman. In the second place, he'd never wanted to reach his present position on the homicide squad. Since both things had happened to him anyway, he had a deep personal conviction that every murder in the city of Chicago was committed purely to annoy and harass him, and that murderers attempted to conceal the evidence of their crimes only to make his life a more difficult and disagreeable one.

Now the big, half-bald man gazed sourly at Jake Justus. "How the hell did you get mixed up in this?"

Jake looked deeply injured, and said nothing.

The red-faced policeman answered for him. "He says he was waiting for Gumbril. He says he didn't know Gumbril was a'ready murdered. He says he was gonna meet Gumbril in his room and Gumbril wasn't there, so he took a nap while he waited. He says the room was a'ready all tore up when he got there. He says Mickey Mouse done it. Sa-a-ay!" He turned a suspicious glare on Jake. "If nobody was there when you got there, how did you get in the room?"

"I opened the door and walked in," Jake said promptly.

The policeman blinked twice, thinking that over. "Then why did you lock the door after you got in?"

Jake yawned and said, "To keep from being disturbed by a lot of noisy cops while I was getting my beauty sleep."

Von Flanagan interrupted whatever the policeman was about to say with a wave of his hand. "Did you go there to meet Gumbril?"

Jake lit a cigarette very deliberately, stared at the match for a moment, blew it out, and flicked it in the direction of the wastebasket. "No, I didn't." He paused, looked squarely at Von Flanagan, and added, "I've never seen Gumbril in my life."

Von Flanagan gulped. "Then why did you tell Kluchetsky you were waiting for him?"

"To keep from being bothered with a lot of dumb questions," Jake said.

The policeman's red face turned cerise, then crimson, and finally purple. "I'll ask you one more dumb question while I'm about it, wise guy."

"Go ahead. Ask two," Jake said amiably.

"Where were you at fifteen minutes after two this afternoon?"

"In a tailor shop on Division Street having my pants pressed," Jake said. "If I shot Gumbril, I must have gone down to State and Madison in my underwear."

Von Flanagan said wearily, "Nobody's accusing you of anything."

"Then make this guy quit badgering me," Jake said. "He's beginning to get in my beard."

Von Flanagan nodded to the policeman. "Beat it, Kluchetsky. I'll talk to this guy."

Kluchetsky strode to the door, paused there, turned around, and said, "If you should be needing a good mousetrap—"

"Go on," Von Flanagan said. "Beat it."

The door's slam was a profane comment.

Jake selected the most comfortable chair, settled down in it, and stretched out his long legs. "He doesn't like me." He looked at Von Flanagan cheerfully. "Who shot Gumbril?"

"I wish to God you had," the officer said savagely.

Jake sighed. "I guess nobody likes me. Sorry to disappoint you, but I didn't shoot him."

"What were you doing in his room?"

"I was looking for matches. I was going down State Street and I found I was out of matches, and so—"

For a few seconds Von Flanagan was almost unnecessarily profane.

"Well," Jake said, shrugging his shoulders, "you asked me."

The officer decided to try another approach. "Now look here, Jake Justus. I'm willing to be nice about this if you are. Why can't we just be friendly and talk it over? Certainly you haven't anything against me."

"Not a damn thing," Jake said, "except keeping Helene in jail all night just after we were married. A hell of a wedding night, with my bride locked up in the hoosegow."

"That was nothing but a joke," Von Flanagan said wearily. "Forget it."

"Sure. You forget all about my being in Gumbril's room tonight, too. That was just another joke. I'll go on home, we'll drop the whole thing and call it a day."

"Are you going to answer my question or not?"

"What question?" Jake asked innocently.

"What were you doing in Gumbril's room?" Von Flanagan roared at the top of his voice.

"Oh, that," Jake said sunnily, as though he had forgotten it. "Well, you see, I'd read about the murder in the afternoon paper, and I thought I'd just gather a little material for a magazine story. I'm a married man now, you know, and I've got to start thinking about earning money. You know how those things are." He knew his voice was not convincing, but he hadn't expected it to be.

There was a brief silence. Von Flanagan rose, kicked back his chair, chewed savagely at a cigar for a moment or so, took a few steps back and forth across the room, and stood staring out the window for a while. He had the appearance of a man who was counting ten slowly to himself.

At last he sat down at his desk, with an outward air of calm.

"I never wanted to be a p'liceman. I never would of been a p'liceman if the alderman hadn't borrowed money from my uncle to set his brother-in-law up in the restaurant business. If it hadn't of been for that, I'd of been an undertaker, like I intended to be in the first place. So now here I am whether I want to be or not, and all people do is go around trying to make things hard for me."

Jake listened respectfully, trying to look as though he hadn't heard it all before.

"One of these days, by God," Von Flanagan said forcefully, "I'm going to retire and buy me one of those Georgia pecan orchards. That's the kind of a life—" He paused and realized he was wandering from the subject at hand.

"This guy Gumbril," he said suddenly, his voice rising in a slow but steady crescendo, "this guy Gumbril—there must of been a thousand people wanted to kill him. So somebody goes to work and shoots him right on the busiest corner in the city, on the busiest day of the year, when everybody is in too much of a hurry to see what's going on, shoots him and probably just walks off and goes to the movies. And when we finally get this guy identified as Gumbril, what happens? We get over to his office and find somebody's already been there and gone all through the place like a tornado, and carried off everything that might have told us something."

Jake drew a long sigh of relief. Malone had gotten there first after all.

"And now you," said the police officer wildly. He repeated it. "And now you!" He glared furiously at Jake. "Why do people have to go to work and make things harder for me than they already are?"

Jake thought it more tactful to say nothing.

Von Flanagan drew one long, slow breath. When he spoke again his voice was calm, with a kind of controlled desperation underneath.

"What—were—you—doing—in—Gumbril's—room?"

Jake looked at him with wide, wounded eyes. "I told you."

"God damn it, tell me the truth!"

"I told you everything I could."

The police officer rose to his feet again, walked to the door, and paused, one hand on the doorknob. "For the last time, will you tell me what you were doing in Gumbril's room?"

"I told you," Jake repeated quietly and stubbornly.

Von Flanagan stared at him for an angry moment, then opened the door and bellowed, "Kluchetsky!" Heavy, hurried footsteps sounded in the hall. "Hold this guy for questioning. Don't let him talk to nobody."

This time it was Jake who rose to his feet. "Oh now, Von Flanagan. Be reasonable."

"If I'd been any more reasonable," Von Flanagan growled, "it would have killed me."

"But you can't do this," Jake began desperately.

"Shut up, or I'll slap a charge of breaking and entering on you." Von Flanagan took his hat and coat from the rack by the door. "You can stay in the can until you want to talk. I don't care if you rot there. Me, I'm going home, and the hell with it all."

## *Chapter Eleven*

"There's nothing that can be done until morning, Helene," John J. Malone said for the twenty-third time. "Von Flanagan has gone home to bed, and if I bother him now, he'll only get sore. I can spring Jake tomorrow without any trouble, but in the meantime, just go to bed and curl up with a good book."

"I never thought I'd live to see the day when my daughter was married to a jailbird," George Brand said, stroking his beard meditatively. He gazed into the slender glass in his hand, closed his eyes, braced himself, shuddered, said, "Happy days," and drank.

"At least Jake didn't kick a policeman in the stomach," Helene observed acidly. "Not but what it's a neat trick. I never knew you could do it."

George Brand's face brightened. "I'll show you how it's done, if Mr. Malone—"

"Never mind," Helene said hastily. She looked appealingly at the lawyer. "Listen, Malone. Isn't there anybody besides Von Flanagan? Couldn't you call up somebody? How about the mayor? Can't you do something?"

For the twenty-fourth time Malone said wearily, "There's nothing can be done until morning. You just curl up with a good book and—"

"Do you know any book that's that good?"

Partridge, who had been sent for by George Brand ("You never know when you're going to need him"), came out from the kitchen with a new tray of highballs. He wore the expression of one who has been through a world-shaking experience and anticipated another at any moment.

Helene strolled over to the table, picked up a glass, and gazed into it as though it were a crystal ball. "If either of you had found anything, I wouldn't feel so melancholy."

"How do you know Jake didn't?" Malone growled. "I said all I found was Gumbril's bankbooks." He scowled. "It's hard to imagine anybody with all that dough living at the Fairfax Hotel. He certainly had very saving habits. He didn't collect the main take at the time of the Ogletree kidnaping, either. There were no large deposits around that time. There have been five-hundred-buck deposits at intervals since then, but nothing totaling the amount paid for the ransom."

"Maybe he spent it," Helene suggested.

Malone snorted. "Sure. On fat women and low horses. On low women and flat horses." He paused. "The hell with it." He paused again. "If he did handle the kidnaping for someone else, he didn't make much out of it. That's about the only thing I learned, except that he'd accumulated a lot more dough than anyone is entitled to in a lifetime. Too bad I decided to become a lawyer and make an honest living." He shook his head sadly.

This time Helene snorted.

"I hope this teaches Jake a lesson anyway," Malone said severely. "Maybe he'll learn not to cross his conclusions before he jumps at them."

"Do you know what you mean?" Helene demanded.

"I mean that Mona McClane, wanting to attract attention and trying to make clever conversation, thought it would be smart to bet Jake she could commit a murder and get away with it. The chances are she didn't mean it any more than I mean it when I say I'm sorry Jake's in jail."

Helene swore at him in a polite voice.

"Meanwhile somebody trails Gumbril to the corner of State and Madison Streets—or else happens to run into him there—and shoots him. Jake reads about it in the newspapers and immediately gets all steamed up. Whereas the whole thing is just a crazy coincidence.

"As for Mona McClane," the lawyer went on, draining his glass and setting it down with a magnificent gesture that rolled it off the table, "as for her, she's probably forgotten the whole conversation. She probably let everything that was said go in one ear and out the other like water off a duck's back."

"Louder, please," said George Brand.

Malone blinked once or twice and said, "In one ear and out the other like a duck on the water. Like a duck on the rocks."

He took a long breath, tried once more, and declared triumphantly, "Like duck soup."

"Malone," Helene said severely, "you're drunk."

"I wouldn't be surprised," the lawyer told her solemnly.

She gathered up the glasses, refilled them, and stood looking dreamily at the telephone. Malone looked at her anxiously.

"I never was one to sit idly by while my man languished in jail."

Malone sighed deeply. "I have a feeling that you're going to do something I'll be sorry for."

"Malone, don't you trust my judgment?"

"I only wish I could throw a house as far as I can trust your judgment."

She wrinkled her nose at him, picked up the telephone, dialed a number, waited a minute, and said, "I'd like to speak to Mona McClane, please."

"Helene!"

She ignored him. "She is? Oh, I see. No, no message." She put the telephone down. "Mona's out."

"Thank God," Malone said piously.

Helene turned to her father. "You know Mona better than I do. She's not anywhere in particular, just out. Where would she be likely to be?"

George Brand named a number of places in rapid alphabetical succession, beginning with the Alabam and ending with the Yar. Helene nodded, patted her hair, and slid into her coat.

"We'll drop in at all of them until we accidentally run into her."

"Then what?" Malone asked skeptically.

"I'll think of that when I get to it. Come on."

George Brand scowled. "I had hoped to go out and have a drink or so with Willis Sanders," he said wistfully.

"Bring him along. We'll make up a party. Then it won't look so pointed." She ushered them to the door, paused there. "We'll take Lulamay along too. I bet she'd have a wonderful time."

Before her suggestion could be overruled, she had crossed the hall and knocked on the opposite door. Lulamay Yandry greeted them enthusiastically. She was, she said, just getting terribly lonesome. No, she couldn't go out with them because she was *so* busy. But surely they'd drop in and have a drink, just to be sociable.

She refrained tactfully from inquiring after Jake.

Helene started to refuse, remembered Jake's description of real Tennessee corn liquor, and led the way into Lulamay's apartment.

It was a strange combination of comfortable disorder and insane confusion. Photographs still adorned the mantel and all the tables, but open suitcases stood on the floor, and odd bits of clothing were scattered from wall to wall.

"I'm packing," Lulamay explained apologetically.

"You're not leaving us!" Helene exclaimed.

The gray-haired woman smiled and nodded. "I'm going home, come next Monday. I like it here, but I'm going home." She added, as though some explanation had been called for, "I had a little business to attend to up North but now it's all settled—sooner than I expected—and I'm going home day after tomorrow."

Malone had been examining the photographs.

"Just some of my folks," Lulamay told him. "I like to take 'em with me wherever I go. Then I don't get so lonesome."

One photograph in particular had attracted Malone's attention.

"This one of your folks too?" he inquired politely. "Nice-looking boy."

"He was nice-looking," the woman said. A new, and not too pleasant note had crept into her voice. "That was my boy, Floyd. He was mighty nice-looking. He's dead."

Helene turned to look at her. Lulamay Yandry's face had become cold and hard and curiously pale.

"He was killed," she said, as though she were talking to herself. "Maybe he did deserve to die. But the man who killed him deserved to die too."

The room was very still. It was one of those uncomfortable pauses that come after someone has said too much. Then Lulamay laughed suddenly.

"But, my goodness, you folks don't want to hear me go on and on talking about my stupid old troubles."

The decanter appeared, Lulamay went on talking of other things, and within five minutes the incident had been forgotten by everyone, with the possible exception of Malone. Helene debated the potentialities of corn liquor in cocktail mixing, naming possible ingredients and declaring that the failures among her experiments could be sold to the army as new high explosives. George Brand telephoned to Willis Sanders and arranged a meeting place. Everybody had a wonderful time, save that Malone seemed curiously quiet and contemplative.

When at last they rose to go, he said good-by to his hostess very gravely, shaking her hand.

"Good-by, Mrs. Yandry. I'm glad your business up North turned out so satisfactorily."

Lulamay Yandry looked startled, but no more so than Helene.

"And I wish you a safe journey," the lawyer added.

Out in the hall Helene turned on him indignantly. "What the hell are you talking about?"

Malone shook his head. "You'll have to be patient for once in your life. I'm not going to tell you—or anybody—until Lulamay Yandry has gone home."

## Chapter Twelve

Mona McClane was not at the Alabam, nor Brown's, nor the Colony, Chez Paree, nor Colosimo's.

At the last-named spot Malone declared crossly that the expedition was not only expensive, but hard on the liver, and that in addition Helene's driving had already aged him in a manner from which he would probably never recover.

However he displayed no inclination to desert.

Helene drove slowly up Michigan Avenue from Colosimo's. "There's still a lot of places to go."

George Brand, in the back seat, hiccuped faintly and said, "On more sober reflection, I'm beginning to think the whole thing's insane. If Jake wants a night club this badly, I'll buy him one."

Helene sighed. "You don't understand. Besides, you couldn't buy him the Casino." Suddenly the big car swerved dangerously. "I know where she is. We're a pack of idiots. The Casino. I knew we'd left out one of the C's. Of course that's where she'd be."

She stepped on the gas and headed north. On the way they stopped to pick up Willis Sanders, after George Brand had been warned not to discuss the murder of Joshua Gumbril out loud.

Though the Casino was large and usually crowded, it still managed to convey an impression of cozy intimacy. It likewise offered variety. There was the main room, with its dance floor, its band platform, and its tables; there was the bar in another room with its own atmosphere and its own entertainment; there was the lounge bar from which one could watch the floor show, and, for those well acquainted with the management, there were the gambling rooms upstairs. The decorative scheme, Helene declared, was both quietly garish and ornate in a dignified way.

She looked around her with what Malone muttered was an indecently speculative eye.

"We'll take a table and then just wander," she announced.

"Maybe you will," George Brand said firmly, "Willis and I are going to just sit."

"Just a couple of old men," Willis Sanders added, looking hopefully at one of the hostesses.

Malone ordered something composed mostly of brandy, and reflected that Willis Sanders was a different man, seen away from his wife. Not that Fleurette Sanders wasn't a charming woman—aside from the hard, determined lines around her mouth. But somehow the big, pink-faced man was not half as dignified and restrained as he was in Fleurette's company. He seemed like a boy run away from school. More like George Brand who, for all his massive impressiveness, and his neat gray beard, always acted like a boy run away from school.

Malone was still thinking about it when Helene motioned him to take her on a tour of the whole place.

"Funny, though," Helene said unexpectedly as they walked through the corridor to the bar, "Sanders doesn't look like the henpecked type."

Malone started. "How did you know what I was thinking?"

"I didn't. I was thinking of it myself, watching him." She scowled. "There's something queer about it, too. Times when I've seen him with Fleurette, he didn't look like a man who was afraid of his wife. He just looked afraid. I didn't know it was Fleurette he was afraid of, but now when I see him away from her, I wonder."

Malone puzzled about it for a minute, finally said, "The hell with it, it's none of our business."

They paused in the bar long enough for Helene to lose forty cents matching coins with the bartender and to order one drink, not, as Helene carefully explained, because she wanted a drink but just to conceal the fact that she was looking for someone. There was no sign of Mona McClane in the bar.

Malone set down his glass with an air of sternness. "Why don't you give up this wild-goose chase and let me take you home, like a respectable matron."

"Because I'm having a wonderful time, and besides I'm not a matron. Wedded but not a wife. Malone, do you think you could possibly get Jake out of jail and have him join us here?"

"No. I told you I can't do a thing until Von Flanagan gets down in the morning."

"Call up Von Flanagan and have him get Jake and both of them join us here."

"Von Flanagan is death on night clubs. He hasn't been in one since he nearly got picked up in a raid and fled down an alley in the dressing-room maid's coat and hat."

Helene sighed. "Let's go look for Mona McClane."

They climbed the stairs to the little lounge bar and looked over the room below. The second floor show had just ended, and dancers were moving out onto the floor, a merry-go-round of colors and soft lights.

"There she is, Malone. The table in the corner. She's talking with the manager."

Malone looked. Mona McClane sat alone at a table, dressed in white, with one huge, sparkling ornament on her shoulder. Save for her mouth, there was nothing to her but black and white, he decided. White dress, white skin, black hair. From that distance the dark, heavy bang that fell over her forehead gave her face a curiously childlike look, impish, willful. She seemed very feminine, even frail. She was, he guessed, as hard as nails underneath. While he watched, the Casino's manager left her table.

"Let's go down and run into her by accident," Helene said.

By the time they had reached the Casino's main room George Brand and his companion had gone into the bar. Helene stood by their table a moment, looking around the room. Suddenly her face shone with delighted surprise. Motioning to Malone to follow, she threaded her way among the tables to where Mona McClane sat by herself.

Mona McClane was also delighted, but not surprised. Probably, Malone thought, nothing would ever surprise her.

"I'm so glad to see you," Mona McClane said brightly. "I went out because I felt lonely and bored, and only got more lonely and more bored."

Helene murmured something appropriately sympathetic, and talked about the floor show. Suddenly, apropos of nothing, she said, "Jake and Malone saw you this afternoon. They were on their way to meet me at the Drake bar and waved at you, hoping you'd join us, but you hopped in a cab and were gone."

Mona McClane frowned slightly as though she were trying to remember. "When and where?"

"At the corner of State and Division Streets, about one-thirty," Malone said.

"Oh yes." She seemed to remember in a flash. "I'd gone out for a walk, and when I got that far it began to rain a little, and I hailed a taxi. Too bad I didn't see you."

"It is too bad," Helene said lightly. "We've been having a swell time. What did you do all afternoon?"

Mona McClane glanced at her for only a fraction of a second. "Not much. I window-shopped, just for fun, all by myself. It began to rain again about ha'past two, and I went to the Telenews and sat through two shows and then came home. Nothing very exciting."

Helene remarked that the weather had been frightful, and Mona McClane agreed that it had. Malone observed that the Telenews was an ideal spot to kill an hour or so, and Helene and Mona McClane said it was indeed.

Helene gave a little shudder and said, "Why, Mona, you must have been on State Street about the time that man was murdered this afternoon."

Mona McClane lifted one eyebrow about an eighth of an inch and nodded. "I must have been." She lit a cigarette slowly and deliberately and said, "By the way, where's Mr. Justus? I hardly expected to see a bride of a day out without her husband."

"Jake?" Helene said airily. "Oh, he's in jail."

Mona McClane didn't appear surprised, but she did blink, once. "In jail! What for?"

Before Helene could answer, there was the sound of a furious row just behind her. She turned her head and saw George Brand and Willis Sanders approaching the table, engaged in a loud and vituperative argument. It was hard to discover just what the argument was about, but there could be no doubt as to its intensity.

The two men greeted Mona McClane, sat down at the table, and went on arguing.

"Well damn it," George Brand said suddenly, "I'll bet you—" he paused for only an instant. "I'll bet you my beard."

Sanders glared at him. "You're on. Your beard against my race horse in the Sanders' stable."

There was a moment's silence.

"That's a wonderful bet," Helene commented icily, "but what are you betting on?"

Both men ignored her. George Brand fixed his gaze on Mona McClane.

"Mona, you've got to settle this. Now listen. Yesterday afternoon you got into a discussion with my son-in-law about murder." He hastily moved his ankle to where Helene couldn't kick it, and went on, "You told him you were going to murder someone and dared him to find out about it. In fact you even made a wager on it."

Mona McClane nodded silently. George Brand drew a long breath and said, "Now what we want to know is—were you just joking when you made that bet, or did you mean it?"

The pause before Mona McClane answered was probably only a few seconds long, but it seemed to go on and on for hours.

"Of course I wasn't joking," she said very coolly and with perfect serenity. "I meant every single word of it."

The two men looked at each other.

"All right," George Brand said, "you win. She wasn't joking. But I think you'll look like hell in my beard." The two men rose, and bid the party good-by with all the impressive dignity of two ambassadors leaving the presence of royalty. George Brand said, "Malone, please do me the favor of seeing that my daughter gets safely home."

Helene snorted. "Where are you going?"

"I won't tell. You may be my daughter, but some things are sacred."

"They probably won't turn up for days," Malone told her consolingly.

"Days! The last time he went on one of these, he turned up three months later in Skagway, Alaska." She turned to Mona McClane. "I'm sorry I didn't hear you make that bet with Jake."

"I'm sorry too," Mona McClane said evenly. She seemed to be a little bored with the subject. "I'm giving a party tomorrow night—more of a brawl, probably—and I hope you'll come. Mr. Malone too, and your father, if he's turned up by then, and Jake too of course, if he's out of jail—" She grinned. "You still haven't told me why he's in jail."

"Nothing serious," Helene said lightly. "He's just held for questioning in connection with a murder." She rose, wrapped her furs around her shoulders, and said, "It's been so nice seeing you. And we'll love to come to your party. All of us."

## *Chapter Thirteen*

A night's sleep, and the arrival of a particularly attractive three-color advertising folder in his morning mail had noticeably mellowed Daniel Von Flanagan's outlook on life. There was an almost amiable gleam in his eye as he looked up at Helene and Malone.

"What do you know about Georgia pecan groves?" he asked by way of greeting.

The little lawyer was taken aback for only a fraction of a second. "Only that they're full of nuts," he said cheerfully. "Why?"

Von Flanagan extracted the folder from his breast pocket and spread it out on his desk. "One of these days," he announced, "I'm going to retire and raise pecans. Maybe when I get this damned Gumbril business washed up." He reached down into a desk drawer and pulled out a handful of pamphlets, permitting his gaze to linger lovingly on the brightest of them. "Do you know that all you have to do is sit around and watch your income ripening on the trees?"

"How wonderful!" Helene breathed. "Tell me more!"

Von Flanagan beamed at her. "Let bountiful nature and God's own golden sunshine earn your living for you, far away from the dirt and grime of the city," he quoted with fascinated enthusiasm.

For fifteen minutes Helene and the lawyer listened in respectful attention to a discourse on the wonders of pecan-raising in Georgia.

"Any day now," the police officer said dreamily. He sighed dreamily, suddenly sat bolt upright, and snapped, "What the hell was Jake Justus doing in that room last night, Malone?"

Malone ignored the question and said, "Look here, Von Flanagan, let's be reasonable about this."

"Don't you want me to turn him loose?"

"You know you can't keep him in jail," Malone began.

"He'll stay there until I know what he was doing in Joshua Gumbril's room last night," Von Flanagan said stubbornly.

Malone began angrily, "I can get him out in—"

A sudden wave from Helene interrupted him. She turned to the officer. "I'll tell you what Jake was doing there." She sat down on a corner of Von Flanagan's desk and looked at him with wide, confiding eyes. "It was all because of a crazy bet."

There was a curious, strangled sound from Malone.

"What the hell kind of a bet?" Von Flanagan asked.

Helene carefully avoided Malone's eyes. "It was like this." She drew a long, quavering breath. "We read about this man being murdered yesterday afternoon, and we got to talking about how the murderer could ever be found. You know how people get to talking." There was a wonderfully appealing note in her voice.

"Sure, sure, sure," Von Flanagan said. "Go on."

"Well—Jake bet that he could find out who murdered that man, and Malone bet that he couldn't. That's all." Helene was careful not to look at Malone.

There was a long, anxious pause while Von Flanagan considered it.

"Is that the truth?" he asked at last, in a half-convinced voice.

Helene looked at him with wide, injured eyes. "You don't think I'd lie to you, do you?"

If Von Flanagan had taken time to remember past encounters with Helene, he might have indignantly answered, "Yes!" But that look in Helene's eyes had paralyzed many a stronger man than he would ever be.

"I'll be damned and double damned," he breathed.

Helene turned on a smile that would have paralyzed the entire police department of the city of Chicago.

"Why the hell didn't Jake Justus tell me this last night?" the police officer asked.

Helene was ready for that one. "He'd promised he wouldn't. It was agreed the police shouldn't know anything about it until the bet was all settled one way or the other." A cloud shadowed the lovely eyes. "I know I shouldn't have told you about it, but I simply had to!"

It was, after all, a perfectly plausible story, especially backed up by Helene's voice and manner. Besides, the police officer had begun to wonder if he was going to learn anything of value from Jake Justus. Finally, he was beginning to feel a little guilty about the trick he had played on Helene two days before.

He looked up and to his horror saw two immense tears slowly rolling down her smooth cheeks.

"Oh, please," she begged, "isn't there any way you can let Jake go without his knowing I told you about the bet? It would be terrible if he did!"

With a terrific effort, Daniel Von Flanagan managed to look stern. "A wife has no business keeping secrets from her husband."

More tears appeared, and a muffled sob. With a faintly abstracted air the police officer produced a large, efficient-looking handkerchief and mopped Helene's face.

Malone decided it was time to take a hand. "How about a deal, Von Flanagan. If you agree not to let Justus know that Helene told you about the bet, we'll forget all about that little matter of a suit for false arrest."

Von Flanagan blushed. "That was nothing but a joke."

"It wouldn't be the first joke that created grounds for a suit. How about it?"

"All right, all right," the police officer said hastily. "I won't say a word. I'll tell Justus I decided not to hold him any longer and let it go at that."

Not till hours later did Von Flanagan realize that no one had discussed the possibility that he might keep Jake in custody, not after Helene's first words.

The formalities of Jake's release were brief. Brought into Von Flanagan's office, pale and drawn, his suit badly wrinkled, he had listened patiently while the officer explained it was considered unnecessary to hold him for further questioning. Besides, Von Flanagan added in a fatherly manner, far be it from him to keep a man from going on his honeymoon. Jake had thought of a number of things he wanted to say to Von Flanagan during his night in jail, but a look from Helene convinced him that this was not the time to say them. Thus the final parting from Von Flanagan was almost tearfully amiable.

Out on the steps Helene paused a moment, drawing on her gloves. "What were you muttering under your breath about deliberate and unprincipled liars, Malone?"

"I was only saying that I'd love to have you on a witness stand. As my witness, of course."

"Well I talked Jake out of jail, anyway."

Malone said, "With any reasonable luck you ought to land in jail together next time."

"If we do," Jake said crossly, "you can go home and curl up with the whole damn corpus juris."

Before he could say more, two men who had been lounging about near the building entrance suddenly stepped up.

"You—Jake Justus—"

Jake wheeled around. "What do you want?"

The speaker was a small, slender, and yet broad-shouldered man with a hard, pallid face and glossily black hair. His clothes, from the tips of his gleaming light-tan shoes to the top of his purplish-black Homburg hat, could only be described as snappy. In fact, Helene said later, snappy was a feeble understatement.

"I'd like a word with you in private," the man said. The cigarette in his mouth barely moved as he spoke.

Jake said, "This is private enough for me."

The stranger scowled. "I don't talk in front of no other people."

"Come now, Georgie," Malone said unexpectedly. "I'm Mr. Justus' lawyer. You trust me, don't you?"

The man he had addressed as Georgie stared at him, then broke into a smile. "I didn't know you for a minute, Malone." He hesitated only an instant. "The boss wants to talk with Mr. Justus. I been waiting here all morning for him to come out."

"Why?" Malone demanded.

The gangster's face was impassive. "He wants to make a deal with him."

"What kind of a deal?"

That question apparently couldn't be answered.

"Tell your boss to write to my lawyer," Jake said irritably, starting for the car. The second of the two men made a sudden move, the one called Georgie waved him back.

"Wait a minute, Mr. Justus. He said you could practically name your own price."

Jake spun around. "Price for what?"

"He said you'd know what he meant."

"I don't, and tell him to go to hell." He shoved Helene into the car and climbed in beside her. Malone followed, slamming the door.

As Helene started the car, the two men on the sidewalk seemed to be holding a hurried conference. The one called Georgie gestured toward the building from which Jake had just emerged and shook his head firmly.

"Who are your friends, Jake?" Helene asked, guiding the big car skillfully through the combination of half-darkness and softly falling snow.

"Damned if I know. Damned if I know what they want, either."

"The guy in the purple hat is Little Georgie la Cerra," Malone volunteered. "I don't know his pal. The boss is Max Hook, head of a gambling syndicate and God knows what else. Used to own the Casino. What have you been getting mixed up in, Jake?"

Jake shook his head. "I haven't the faintest idea. Should I have gone to see this Hook guy?"

"No."

Helene asked, "How come you know this handsome yegg, Malone?"

"I got him out of jail once. Something trivial—suicide, I think."

"Huh?" Jake said.

"Never mind. What did you find up in Gumbril's room?"

Jake described the finding and hiding of the box.

Helene scowled. "Everything we need to know may be locked up in that box. Now all we need to do is get it."

Jake looked thoughtful. "I'm not so sure," he said. "As I remember our pal Gumbril, he was not a sweet-scented citizen. Yet the inside of that closet of his made a pleasant impression on my nose."

"So you're turning into a beagle," said Malone. "What has that got to do with Gumbril's box?"

"Figure it out," said Jake impatiently. "Gumbril never used that perfume, and yet the smell of it was in his closet. Question: how long does a scent last?"

Helene nodded thoughtfully. She said, "What the mastermind is trying to say, Malone, is that somebody was in that room just ahead of him. And if Jake could find that box, anybody could."

Jake said, "Which adds up to the fact that it's probably empty right now and that I spent the night in jail when I definitely had other things to do."

"Keep to the subject," said Helene severely. "There's a chance that the perfumed marvel didn't find that box, and we ought to think of a way to get it."

"Let me out of here," Malone said, "before you think of a way to get it. I have clients to see and an office to go to. From now on you're on your own."

Helene said, threading her way carefully through the traffic, "Have you considered that if Mona McClane gets pinched for Gumbril's murder, you can probably defend her for an exorbitant fee?"

Malone was silent for a moment. "No, I hadn't."

"Well, think of it now. And let's get Jake shaved, and his suit pressed, and start life all over again."

Jake said, "Let's go to the bank first so I can cash a check. I lost all the money I had on me playing rummy with one of the cops."

"When I play cards with cops," Helene said acidly, "I win." She drove the big car to Jake's bank on La Salle Street and paused before the entrance. "Run in and out fast, I can't park here."

Jake pushed his way through the crowds into the bank, cashed his check, looked at the balance it left, and reflected that winning the bet he'd made with Mona McClane might not only be good clean fun, but sheer necessity.

As he started across the sidewalk the smaller of the two men who had accosted him earlier appeared from nowhere, got into Helene's car, and slammed the door. Before Jake could make a move he felt a gentle, but terribly insistent pressure against his back, and heard a voice, low-pitched but speaking with deadly intent, close to his ear.

"Never mind the car. Your friends are O.K. Just walk slowly down La Salle Street as if nothing was bothering you. You and me have to take a little ride together."

Jake hesitated for a split second, then moved. There was nothing to do but obey. At the first words he had recognized the voice as that of Little Georgie la Cerra.

## *Chapter Fourteen*

"Your friends are o.k.," the voice at Jake's ear said again in that low, hissing whisper. "They're just going to ride around the block a coupla times. You're O.K. too if you keep moving and keep your mouth shut."

Jake knew it was definitely not a time to be funny. He had a notion that Max Hook's boys didn't play that way.

"Right down La Salle Street," La Cerra whispered. "Turn right on Adams. I'll tell you when we get to the car."

Jake nodded and kept moving. The sidewalks of La Salle Street were crowded, but none of the people around him had the faintest notion that he was walking down the street with the important end of a gun shoved into his ribs. But they were Jake's ribs. He kept moving, and thinking.

"This ain't nothin' personal," came the low voice. "When the boss orders me to bring somebody to see him, I gotta bring him. See?"

Jake decided this was intended to constitute an apology for what might be considered social misconduct.

If there was a policeman in sight, something might be attempted. La Cerra would have no hesitation about firing in the midst of the crowd. That was good gangster technique. A getaway would be easy in the resulting confusion. But if a policeman's attention could be attracted first, the gunman wouldn't take the chance.

The problem was that in all La Salle Street, there wasn't a policeman in sight.

A bluff might work. If La Cerra's boss was so anxious to see him, he probably would prefer to see him alive. It was hard to bluff, though, with a gun against his back.

If there was only a way of attracting the attention of the passing crowds to himself and his companion, La Cerra wouldn't dare shoot. Once people were looking, a dozen or more witnesses would remember La Cerra, should he fire. But with everyone going down the street intent on his own affairs, La Cerra could fire and get away, and no one would remember he had been there.

Jake tried to think of how he might attract attention in such a way that the gunman couldn't shoot until it was too late for him to do so and get safely away. Jake could think of nothing more adequate than making faces. They couldn't have been very good faces, he reflected later, because no one seemed to notice them.

He was damned if he was going to be kidnaped on a public street like this. Perhaps one quick move—

*"Repent—Oh Chicago!"*

Jake was startled into jumping, ever so slightly. He felt the gun at his back jerk a little. Before he could take advantage of the move, however, he heard La Cerra's voice at his ear.

"Keep moving and don't pay no attention."

*"Oh Sodom—Oh Gomorrah—Oh Chicago, repent!"*

Jake recognized the voice. A little ahead of him in the crowd he could see a tall, ungainly figure in a shabby, not too clean Prince Albert coat. Long, silvery hair curled down over his soiled celluloid collar from under a broad-brimmed black hat. He held a Bible in his hand, and as he strode down La Salle Street with the conscious majesty of one possessed by revelation, from time to time he would hold the Bible aloft and call, in a clear, ringing voice, "Repent! Oh Chicago—repent!"

The prophet was a familiar figure on La Salle Street and had been for many years, yet people on the crowded walks always paused and turned to look at him. They were pausing to look at him now.

An insane idea began to form in Jake's mind. It was, in fact, something he had long wanted to do, under happier circumstances. He managed to feel in his inside pocket without attracting his companion's attention and drew forth a largish address book. Then he drew a long breath and waited hopefully for the prophet to speak.

He didn't have long to wait.

*"Oh Chicago—repent!"* cried the prophet.

*"Oh Chicago—repent!"* Jake repeated.

This time the crowd really stopped to look. This prophet had an echo.

The prophet stopped likewise. Here was a problem for which there was no precedent in Scripture. For the first time in his many years on the street, he had a curiously hesitant appearance.

The gun at Jake's back had wavered a trifle, now it was held firm again.

"Cut that stuff out and keep walking."

Jake dutifully kept walking, his eyes on the figure ahead. The crowd was interested all right, but in the wrong man.

*"Repent—Oh Chicago!"* The prophet tried it again.

*"Repent—Oh Chicago!"* Jake's voice was an exact echo.

The prophet stopped dead in his tracks and looked timidly over his shoulder.

About half the crowd was looking at Jake now. Suddenly the prophet wheeled around as though he had decided to ignore the whole proceedings and try something new. He raised his hand magnificently.

*"Oh Sodom—Oh Gomorrah—"*

*"Oh Sodom—Oh Gomorrah—"*

That was the last straw. The crowd began to laugh. Without turning to look back the prophet of La Salle Street made off briskly and unobtrusively in the direction of Jackson Boulevard, and was heard of no more that day.

Jake realized that the pressure was gone from his back. Little Georgie la Cerra had disappeared.

There was more than the routine appreciation that an artist gives his admiring audience in the smile that he returned to the crowd. "Little do they know!" he told himself. Yet he hadn't the faintest notion that his unwelcome mentor had gone quietly home to mother. He'd freed himself for the time being, that was all. The trick now was to get as far away as possible, and to do it fast.

He pushed his way to the edge of the sidewalk and looked around for a taxicab. Chicago's five thousand cabs had all vanished into thin air.

At that instant Helene's long, sleek car drew up alongside, the door to the front seat was opened, and he jumped in. By the time he had caught his breath, they were halfway down the next block.

"Have I married a man or a gang war?" Helene asked grimly. "Watch out for traffic cops, Malone." She simultaneously drove through a red light and made an altogether illegal left turn onto Jackson Boulevard. For an instant Jake wished he were back with La Cerra. "What shall we do with your pal, Jake?"

Jake turned around. There on the floor of the back seat was La Cerra's companion. Malone was sitting on him, placidly smoking a cigarette.

"Lie still, damn you," Malone said mildly. There was a muffled protest from the gangster.

Helene crossed Michigan Avenue and headed into Grant Park. "Sit him up, Malone, and we'll ask him some questions." She skidded the car expertly around a corner.

"Lemme out of here," the man said in a weak voice.

"Shut up till you're spoken to," Helene told him pleasantly, "or I'll take you for another nice drive."

The gangster had been pale. Now he turned fairly ashen.

"What's your name?" Malone demanded shortly.

The man murmured something that sounded like "Blunk."

Jake leaned over the back of the seat. "What does Max Hook want me for?"

The man named Blunk was silent.

"Come on, talk!"

Still no answer.

Jake reached out and landed an expert blow on the side of the gangster's face.

Helene turned into the South Drive. "There's a better way than that, Jake." She called over her shoulder, "Are you going to answer questions, or aren't you?"

No response.

Suddenly Jake had a hazy notion that the end of the world was at hand. For a terrible moment the car seemed to be spinning crazily in space. Trees, buildings, and passing cars whirled around in an insane merry-go-round. In the next moment they were proceeding south on the drive as though nothing had happened.

"Are you going to talk?" Helene asked. "Or shall I do it again?"

"Please," said Blunk in a very small and breathless voice, "don't do it again, lady. I can't tell you nothin'. I don't know nothin'. Georgie, he says to me this morning, he says, com'n, pal, we got work to do, so I goes with him and we waits for this guy to come outa the p'lice station, and I don't even know who he is except Georgie says the Hook wants to see him, and so help me, lady, that's all I know. I just went along to protect Georgie."

"You couldn't protect a canary bird from a kitten," Helene observed icily. "Malone, do you think he's telling the truth, or shall I shake him up again?"

There was an anguished howl from the little gangster.

"He's probably telling the truth," Malone said wearily. "We might as well throw him out."

Helene sighed. "Just when I was beginning to enjoy myself." She slowed down to an almost reasonable pace. "Well, my little friend, the least I can do is drive you home. Where do you live?"

"I live right here, lady," Blunk said hastily.

"This is the park, you idiot. You'll have to walk a mile—"

"I live here—I mean, I like to walk, honest, lady," said Blunk with heart-wringing sincerity.

The last they saw of him was a smallish figure trudging down the edge of the drive through the still-falling snow.

"Tell your pal I'll see him at revival meeting," Jake called after him.

"What the hell are you talking about?"

"I'm saved," Jake declared happily. "In fact I'm an assistant prophet now. But I'll do my testifying later. First, tell me how—"

Helene said, "This yegg got in the back seat and poked a gun at my neck and told me to drive him around Grant Park for a few minutes. So we drove around Grant Park. I had a notion it might be wise to get back to you, so I did."

"You leave a gap," Jake said a little weakly, "between the time when you were driving around with his gun at your neck and the time when you picked me up."

"Oh that," Helene said cheerfully. "I threw the car into a skid on Columbus Drive, and the man-killer fainted."

## *Chapter Fifteen*

"I don't want to sound complaining," Jake said, "but I spent the night in the can, and I've just put in a very busy few minutes. I'm beginning to feel like the corpus delicti in this case, and I refuse to lie down and testify until I've had a drink."

"It's not the worst idea in the world," Helene said reflectively. "Malone and I put in a busy night ourselves." While she drove in the direction of Oak Street she described the visit to the Casino and the meeting with Mona McClane.

Jake scowled. "I don't see that you've proved anything, except that the Casino is a damned nice place to own and that we'll probably get very, very rich running it."

"It proved that Mona McClane meant that bet," Helene said. "If you'd seen her face when she said so—"

Jake said, "Hell, I could have told you that. If you had any doubts, why didn't you go out to the morgue and take another look at the late Joshua Gumbril."

She wrinkled her nose at him. "Also I found out she didn't have any alibi for yesterday afternoon."

Malone said a rude word about alibis. Helene said a ruder word about Malone, swung the big car into Oak Street, and parked it in front of the Ranch.

After a secluded booth had been found, and the waitress had gone to fetch three ryes, Helene said, "Now about this business of Jake's being so popular with the underworld. Anyone care to make a guess?"

Malone lit a cigar, stared through its smoke, and said slowly, "There's two possibilities, both based on Max Hook's crediting Jake with Gumbril's murder. One is that these yeggs were pals of Gumbril's, and Jake has been elected as the leading character in a revenge murder."

"Rats," Jake said scornfully. "Are you trying to tell me that little buzzard had any pals who loved him enough to revenge his murder?"

"You never can tell," Malone told him.

"I'm going to like the other possibility better, whatever it is," Helene said. "Go on, Malone."

"The Hook believes Jake found something of value in Gumbril's room and wants to make a deal with him."

"Maybe I did find something of value," Jake said, "and it's parked on the window ledge outside Gumbril's room. The problem seems to be what to do next."

"If you're asking your lawyer's advice," Malone said, "take the first plane for Bermuda and stay there until this blows over."

Jake glared at him. "Do you have the faintest idea I'm going to leave Chicago until I find out why Max Hook's yeggs are playing tag with me?"

"You'll find that out all right," the lawyer said grimly, "if my first guess is correct. You'll end up with more holes in you than a pair of ten-cent socks."

Jake ignored him. "Besides," he said irritably, "after all I've gone through because of that damned box of Gumbril's, you aren't going to get me out of Chicago until I make sure there's nothing in it. No gunman is going to scare me out of town."

Helene cheered. "A bit on the hammy side, but a nice sentiment." She added thoughtfully, "It seems to be a question of who came first, the ham or the yegg."

"Something might be locked up in that box," Jake said, "now all we need is to get it."

"That shouldn't be so all-fired difficult," Helene hazarded. "We know right where it is."

Malone said, "Don't forget Von Flanagan probably suspects that all this sudden interest in Gumbril's room may mean something. In which case there will be a reception committee for future visitors. Of course, if you don't mind going back to jail again—"

"Von Flanagan can't keep a bunch of cops parked up there forever," Jake said. "Sooner or later room 514 in the Fairfax Hotel is going to be open to the public. I'll just have to wait until then to get the box."

"Unless I think of something," Helene said in a small but very ominous voice.

Jake and Malone both offered a fervent prayer that she wouldn't.

"In the meantime," Jake said, scowling, "I've got to do something. The question is what to do first." He paused, rubbed his forehead, and added, "I can't make up my mind, that's all."

"Maybe one of the pieces is missing," Helene said acidly.

"That's the piece he laid aside to give Von Flanagan," Malone said. "Hell, let's order lunch before those Indians painted on the wall start shooting at us instead of the deer. When that's done, I'll tell you what to do first."

Lunch and another round of rye was ordered, and Malone moved out of the Indians' line of fire.

"Now," the little lawyer said firmly, "first, you count me out. Then you go ahead and do as you damned please."

Helene glared at him. "A fine pal!"

"You forget I've got a living to earn," Malone snapped. "I can't spend my time helping Jake play games with Mona McClane."

Jake looked at him long and fixedly. "I'd just like to ask one question," he said mildly. "How much dough have you got in the kitty right now?"

The lawyer turned red. "None of your damned business."

"All right," Jake said, "it's none of my damned business. But I do know you haven't had a big client since the Nelle Brown case—which I gave you, you ungrateful so-and-so—and I also know all about the brunette girl you met at

Chez Paree. If you've paid your office rent, I'm an Indian."

"Then get up on the wall and shoot deer with the other ones," Malone said, "because I have paid it." He paused a minute, frowned, and added, "Well, for November anyway."

Jake drew a long breath. "If you'll just fix your low, grasping mind on the fee you can charge Mona McClane for defending her if I can pin this on her, you may change your attitude toward playing games."

The little lawyer chewed savagely on his cigar for a moment. "All right," he said crossly, "I'll play. Within limits. At least, I'll go along with you to her party tonight."

The waitress arrived with their order before Jake could answer. When she had gone, he said, "What's the idea of that party anyway?"

"Maybe she's going to make a confession," Helene suggested.

Jake snorted. "That would be damned unfair." His eyes began to glitter. "She might be scared I'm going to win the Casino from her, and make a quick confession to gyp me out of the bet. That would be a dirty trick." He added angrily, "But no ding-danged dirtier than choosing this particular time to murder that guy. Why couldn't she have waited till we got back from Bermuda?"

"Maybe it was something urgent," Malone said, attacking his salad. "Murder often is."

Jake finished his lunch in a gloomy silence. Then he ordered one more drink all around and waited for the waitress to clear the table before he spoke.

"The more I think about it, the madder I get," he said, looking at Helene. "If I didn't give a whoop about the Casino, I'd win this bet just to get even with Mona McClane for choosing the time she did." He turned to Malone and added wildly, "If you do get to defend her, I hope to God you lose the case. That's how I feel about it."

Helene said quietly, "You sound just like Von Flanagan. The murder was committed just to annoy you. Why don't you retire and raise mink?"

"It's pecan orchards now," Jake said morosely. "Damn it, darling. Do you realize we've been married for—" he looked at his watch, "over forty-eight hours, and I haven't been alone with you for as much as five minutes?"

"Well, if you will go around making crazy bets when my back is turned, and getting drunk with strange women and getting thrown in the can—"

"Hell's bells," Jake roared, "I'm doing it all for you—"

Malone said, "There's nothing I enjoy more than a good old-fashioned family brawl, but if that's the best you can do I'm going back to the office." He paused, and added without moving his lips, "You might look at what just came in."

"Another Indian?" Jake murmured hopefully.

His eyes followed Malone's to the doorway. Daphne Sanders stood there irresolutely, a trifle unsteadily. Her dark eyes were blazing, her cheeks flamed scarlet.

"It looks like a vendetta," Helene whispered.

The tall girl suddenly sat down at the nearest table and sent the waitress for a drink. She didn't look as if she needed it. While the three watched she got it down with one breath, banged the glass down on the table, and sat glaring at it as though it were the sole object of her wrath. It looked to Jake as though in another moment she would burst into furious and noisy tears.

Suddenly she lifted her head, as though aware that she was being observed. Her eyes roved around the room for an instant, finally found the three who had been watching her. For a divided second she seemed to hesitate, then with an air of quick decision she rose, crossed the little distance to their table, and sat down beside Helene.

When she spoke, however, she seemed to be addressing the empty air.

"Some day, by God," she said in a half-choked voice, "some day I'm going to kill her."

## *Chapter Sixteen*

Malone took his cigar from his mouth. "Not a bad idea," he told the distraught girl calmly. "If you'd like me to defend you, you can probably get away with it." He paused, and added, "By the way, whom do you mean by 'her'?"

"The little bitch!" Daphne Sanders said, as though she hadn't heard him. "I'll show her. She ought to be ashamed of herself. She knows she hasn't anything but money to offer, damn her. And when I think that I introduced them! All right, she'll be sorry."

Malone sighed, and said, "Just who are you going to kill, and how?"

"I'm going to cut her throat," Daphne Sanders told him, "I'm going to drop acid on her face just a little at a time, and then I'm going to cut off her hands, and then I'm going to cut her throat slowly so she won't miss a thing. Tell that silly waitress to bring me a drink."

Malone signaled to the waitress, and then said, "All that is very interesting and highly instructive, but *who?*"

"Ellen Ogletree," the girl said calmly, as though she were a little surprised he hadn't known it all the time. Her drink arrived and she sipped it slowly, while the crimson faded from her cheeks. After a moment or so she said, in a more normal tone, "She really has it coming to her, you know."

"Who is *he?*" Helene asked, in a vague attempt to be helpful.

The dark-eyed girl drew a long, quivering breath. "Leonard Marchmont. He's an Englishman, and he hasn't any money of his own, but—" Suddenly the color blazed in her cheeks again. "All right, he is nothing but a good-for-nothing grafter who takes expensive presents from girls. I don't care. And I hate to see Ellen Ogletree get away with anything." A hard, vicious note came into her voice. "The last couple of years she's been giving him money. She even paid for his car. He'd never look at her if she didn't have money."

"I thought Ellen Ogletree was engaged to Jay Fulton," Helene said in a mildly surprised tone. "Or doesn't that count?"

"The engagement is off," Daphne Sanders said. "She broke it last night. She's out somewhere with Len right this minute." This time her face turned really pale. "If I ever run into them together, I'll kill her."

"There's a certain sameness to this monologue," Helene murmured. "We finally get the idea that you're going to kill her."

"Better fix up an alibi first," Malone said calmly, "Having your rival out of the way won't do you any good if you're tucked away in the hoosegow." An idea seemed to strike him suddenly. "Why don't you let me take you home, and we'll talk it over on the way. Then you can take a little nap and think about it coolly and sensibly, and maybe you'll get another idea."

The girl relaxed a little, and almost smiled. "Maybe that's a good plan. I don't know why I should bother you with my troubles." Her voice was just a trifle thick.

"Because I'm a lawyer," Malone said, "and people always bother lawyers with their troubles." He rose and helped her to her feet. "Wait for me here, you two. I'll be right back."

Jake watched Malone guiding the girl toward the door. "Has Malone got another client, or is he just taking a girl home to sleep it off?"

"She's not going to do any damage," Helene said. "She won't like Ellen any better when she sobers up, but people who talk as good a murder as that seldom commit one."

"A nice sentiment," Jake said pleasantly, "and I'm glad you agree with me." For a few minutes he sat looking at her admiringly. The honey-colored silk of her dress almost matched her hair, and it fitted over her shoulders closely, revealing interesting lines and curves. "As I said a few minutes ago, we've been married more than forty-eight hours."

"I'm on a train of thought. Mona McClane—"

"Damn Mona McClane. Listen, dear. When people are married—" he paused, grinned at her, and said, "Maybe nobody ever told you."

She didn't seem to have heard him. Her blue eyes were fixed on some point far out in space. "The conditions of the bet and the conditions of the murder were the same. You saw her starting for the scene of the crime. She says she was wandering up and down State Street all afternoon." She paused, frowned. "None of that does any good if there isn't a link between her and Joshua Gumbril. And there is such a link. I don't know what it is, but I know it's there. We touched on it, I'm sure, and we didn't recognize it."

"Helene," Jake said patiently, "if you'll stop thinking about the murder for a minute—"

"I don't dare. I'm too close to something we need to know." She wrinkled her forehead. "Jake, we've overlooked something."

"You're damned right we have," Jake said soulfully, "and it's nothing to do with murder, either."

She looked at him across the table and a faint pink came into her cheeks.

"How do you expect to solve a murder case if you go chasing after women all the time?"

"I'm only chasing one," Jake said, "and if I never win the Casino—" He stopped suddenly, staring at her.

There was a blue, blazing light in her eyes. "Wait a minute. Let me think. I've almost got it. The Casino—"

Before she could say another word Malone arrived, a little out of breath, and plumped down in his chair.

"Well, she won't carve up Ellen Ogletree for a few hours, anyway. But I'd hate to have that girl take a dislike to me."

"Damn you, Malone." Helene glared. "I'd almost remembered something."

"It's about time," the lawyer said gloomily. "Sorry I interrupted you." He leaned on the table and spoke in a lower tone. "Don't look now, but I think Von Flanagan has decided he was a little previous about letting Jake go."

Jake stared at him. "What the hell?"

"Anyway, he has a couple of plain-clothes men sitting in the bar waiting for you to leave. Evidently he wants to keep you in sight."

"Why?" Jake asked wildly.

"Maybe he's planning to pick you up for murder," Malone told him quietly, lighting a cigar.

Jake declared indignantly that Daniel Von Flanagan was the unaccounted-for and irregular product of mixed parentage, part Oriental, adding furiously, "Imagine him accusing me of a murder. I'm a friend of his."

"I'd hate to offer that to a jury as defense," Malone said. "Especially when you got mixed up on the alibi you gave him."

"What in blazes are you talking about?"

"You told Von Flanagan that at the time Gumbril was being murdered, you were in a tailor shop on Division Street having your pants pressed."

"Well?"

"So Von Flanagan probably called the tailor shop and found out you left at one-thirty. I don't know how you could have made a fool slip like that, but at the time the late Mr. Gumbril was getting himself shot, you were on your way to the travel bureau."

"Oh God," Jake said. He thought for a moment. "I'll call him up and explain."

Malone snorted and wondered audibly if marriage could produce softening of the brain in two days' time.

Helene lit a cigarette, blew smoke through her slender nose, and said, "Well, that gives you an added incentive for proving who did murder Joshua Gumbril."

"How in the name of heaven am I going to get a chance to prove it, if I'm going to have a couple of cops on my tail?"

"I'll fix that," Helene said smoothly.

The two men stared at her. She looked at her watch, buttoned her gloves, rose, and pulled her furs about her shoulders.

"It's time to go home anyway," she observed, "and I don't feel like taking a brace of plain-clothes men with us. Malone—" She paused only a moment. "You're going to Mona McClane's party with us tonight. Meantime, take my car—" she handed him the key, "and park it near the hotel for me."

"Glad to, but why?"

"Because Jake and I are going to go out and lose some policemen, and that car of mine isn't any more conspicuous than a Knights Templar parade. As soon as they give up the chase, we're going home. If you'll meet us there early in the evening, we'll go in a body to Mona's party."

Malone pocketed the key. "What are you going to do in the meantime?"

"If you were a gentleman instead of a lawyer," Helene said firmly, "you wouldn't ask." She paused for a moment by the table while a small frown formed in the exact center of her forehead. "I do wish I knew where my old man was. I have a feeling he's in jail." The frown vanished. "Oh well, he'll turn up, and he never gets in jail for anything serious."

"Like homicide," Jake said with a shudder.

Malone patted his shoulder reassuringly. "Never mind. I'll defend you."

They parted at the door. As Jake and Helene stepped out to the sidewalk, two burly men in serge suits hastily left the bar and stood in the doorway, doing an unsuccessful best to look oblivious and unconcerned.

Helene hailed a taxi, said, "Marshall Field's," gave Jake's hand a squeeze, and devoted herself to staring out the window at Michigan Avenue shops. In a second taxi half a block behind, the two men debated the advisability of turning in the bar check on the expense record.

The pulse in his head reminded Jake of an inspired performance by Gene Krupa. He didn't know just what Helene had in mind, and didn't dare ask. Whatever it was, it would probably work. He felt a curious combination of alarm and pleasant excitement.

The taxi dropped them at the Randolph and Wabash entrance to the department store. Jake followed Helene through the crowded doorway as the second taxi drew up to the curb. She led the way to a stairway leading to the basement and paused one moment at the top.

"Follow me, and hope for the best."

Then she dived down the stairway like a rabbit.

Thirty minutes later Jake climbed into a taxi on Madison Street with a vague feeling that he'd been through a war, an earthquake, a riot, or a department-store basement at Christmas time. With lightning rapidity Helene had led him up and down aisles, around corners, from hats to lingerie to powder boxes to gift wrappings.

When they emerged the two plain-clothes men had disappeared. Jake had an idea they had been trampled to pieces at ladies' blouses and would be nonchalantly swept out the next morning in a welter of Christmas wrappings.

As soon as he had caught his breath he said, "Of course all they have to do to pick us up again is wait in the hotel lobby until we show up."

"That's all right. I just wanted to prove something. Now let's go home."

"Mona McClane—" Jake began, without much conviction in his voice.

"Later," Helene said firmly.

There was no sign of the police in the hotel lobby or in the hall upstairs. Helene closed the apartment door and let her furs slide into a heap on the floor.

"Malone will be here in a few hours to go to Mona's party with us. But not for a few hours—" She didn't finish the sentence.

Jake slid his hands down her shoulders. Funny how satin could feel like skin, even have the same magnetic warmth.

There was a thundering knock on the door.

Helene lifted her finger to her lips. "Whoever it is will go quietly away if we don't make a sound."

It became obvious in the next few minutes that this was wishful thinking. The knocking ceased. It was followed, however, by the sound of a large and heavy object exerting considerable pressure on the echoing wood. Helene's eyes met Jake's in one long, significant look. Then she shook her head sadly and opened the door.

There stood George Brand and Willis Sanders, arm in arm and beaming. Jake stared at them blankly for a minute. There was something very strange about them, but he couldn't quite decide what it was. Helene's eyes were like a pair of marbles.

"I always pay my bets," George Brand said happily, kicking the door shut behind him.

Then Jake realized what was strange. George Brand's face was rosily pink, newly and smoothly shaven. The neatly trimmed gray mustache and imperial were resting, incredibly, on Willis Sanders' lip and chin.

## *Chapter Seventeen*

"I made a bet with Willis," George Brand said. "I bet him my beard, and he won. So there's the beard." He sat down heavily in a large armchair and smiled happily.

"It's very beautiful," Helene said when she recovered her breath, "but how did you do it?"

"Partridge," Willis Sanders said, as though that explained everything. He added after a moment, "You can pull it, if you want to, and it won't come off. It's there to stay."

Helene looked from one to the other. "I've always thought you two looked alike, but I never realized how much alike before. It's baffling."

George Brand beamed. "We met a couple of girls last night after we left you. Today we went to take them to lunch, after I'd given Willis my beard, and they were baffled too. They were very baffled."

Jake stood staring first at George Brand and then at Willis Sanders. It was a little hard to be sure which was which.

George Brand announced that Partridge was on his way, bringing food. Helene declared that Malone had to inspect the transferred beard, and telephoned the lawyer, who arrived fifteen minutes later. By that time Jake had stated that he intended to spend all his future honeymoons in the middle of a race track where there would be more peace, quiet, and solitude. No one paid any attention to him.

Dinner made Jake feel a little better. The small, shy Partridge had achieved something of a masterpiece, despite the meager facilities of the kitchenette. Jake looked at Partridge with a new respect, a respect that mounted to admiration whenever his eye fell on Willis Sanders' realistic new beard.

After dinner Willis Sanders went away, beard and all, to take Fleurette to Mona McClane's party. There was some speculation as to the effect of the new beard on Fleurette, and everyone wished Willis Sanders luck.

Helene opened one of the suitcases packed for the Bermuda honeymoon, and changed into something long and clinging, the same pale-gold color as her sleek hair.

"Now," George Brand said, as though he'd forgotten it before, "I want to know what progress you've made with our murder."

Helene rapidly brought the developments up to date.

"You aren't getting anywhere," he complained. "I wish you'd move faster. I have a date in Havana at New Year's."

Jake thought of something he might add, but refrained.

Helene frowned. "If I could only remember—" she paused, staring at Jake. "Something about the Casino and Mona McClane."

Before anyone could offer a suggestion, there was a knock at the door. Helene opened it.

Two men stepped into the room, kicking the door shut behind them. One, a heavy-set, ugly man with a thickly freckled face, was a stranger. The other was little Georgie la Cerra, impeccably attired in a mid-night-blue suit that was just a shade on the purple side, and a bright tan polo coat. He was holding an extremely businesslike-looking gun in one hand.

"This time," said Little Georgie by way of greeting, "there won't be no funny business."

His companion grinned, displaying an incredibly wide expanse of yellow, broken teeth.

"My friend here," Little Georgie explained, "is gonna stick around here and see there's no trouble. Me and Mr. Justus have some place we gotta go."

Everyone sat very still.

"Why can't Max be businesslike about this?" Malone said very calmly. "Why don't you tell Jake why Max wants to see him? Maybe he'd be glad to go."

"Max'll tell him why he wants to see him," the gunman snapped. "He didn't tell me to talk to no lawyers. He told me to bring Mr. Justus to see him, and I gotta bring him. When Max says he wants a thing done, he means he wants it done."

Jake sat motionless, estimating the distance between himself and the gangster and wondering if he could cover it before La Cerra had a chance to fire. But the man beside La Cerra was keeping his hands ominously in his pockets. That wasn't encouraging. Still, Jake felt he had to do something. He couldn't let the gunmen quietly carry him off without offering some kind of resistance, especially before Helene.

At that moment Partridge unexpectedly appeared from the kitchenette, carrying a large tray of drinks. Apparently he failed to notice the gun in their visitor's hand.

"A drink for the gentlemen, Mr. Brand?" he suggested, in his mildest voice.

George Brand nodded silently.

La Cerra had slipped his hand in his pocket, gun and all. His eyes narrowed, but there was a smile on his lips. "Sure, I'd be glad to have a drink," he said, "before Mr. Justus and me leaves."

Partridge started across the floor toward him. It may have been that the large tray obscured his vision, or perhaps he didn't notice the rug that curled up in front of him. At any rate, without warning, he suddenly tripped and fell. The tray, with its collection of brimful glasses shot up into La Cerra's face, throwing him off balance so that he too landed on the floor. Somehow in the ensuing melee of men, glasses, and tray, Partridge found himself sitting on the hand that held La Cerra's gun.

At exactly the instant Partridge had started to fall, Jake had made a lightning dive at the feet of La Cerra's companion, and they were added to the heap of combatants on the floor. George Brand gave a whoop of joy and joined the fray. Malone saw a gun lying on the floor, grabbed it, and stood holding it. Helene had removed "Whistler's Mother" from the wall and was brandishing it menacingly over the head of La Cerra's companion.

"Now," Jake said grimly, looking down at the fallen invaders, "now, by God, we are going to have a talk."

"I got nothin' to say," La Cerra muttered.

"Partridge," Jake said, "do you know any ways of making people talk?"

"Oh yes, sir," Partridge said with what was almost enthusiasm. "I once worked in a household where there was a Japanese butler—" He paused and coughed apologetically.

La Cerra looked at the small figure of Partridge with a certain uncomfortable respect.

"Mr. Justus, nobody's lookin' for no trouble," he began plaintively.

"Shut up," Jake said, "and answer my questions. Why does Max Hook want to see me?"

La Cerra faced him with a last shred of defiance and said nothing.

Partridge coughed again. "There's a pair of pliers in the kitchen, sir, if—"

"Get them," Jake said.

The gangster turned pale.

"Well," Jake said, "I'm listening."

"Hook wants to make a deal with you," the gangster said in a low voice.

"What kind of a deal?"

"He wants to buy what you found up in Gumbril's room."

"Oh." Jake thought for less than a minute. "Listen, you dope. If I'd found anything in Gumbril's room, don't you think the police would have taken it last night?"

La Cerra looked uneasy. "You mean you didn't find nothin'?"

"Not one damn thing. Get that straight. You march right back to Hook and tell him all I found in Gumbril's room was a pair of old red-flannel drawers and Ann Sheridan's autograph. He's welcome to both of them, but I want you guys to stop bothering me. I'm a married man now, and it's liable to be embarrassing— I hope." He added the last two words in a pious whisper.

There was a puzzled frown on La Cerra's face. "You must have found something."

"There was nothing to find. Now beat it."

"If it wasn't there," La Cerra said stupidly, "where the hell is it?"

"Where the hell is *what?*"

"Don't you know?"

"No!" Jake roared.

Malone spoke up. "Are you talking about Gumbril's personal records?" As the gunman nodded, he went on, "Well, tell Hook he can't be half as anxious to get hold of them as we are."

"Is that on the level?"

"Ask Hook if I ever lied to him," the lawyer said coldly. "Tell him if he finds those records first, we'll offer him a deal."

La Cerra muttered something about mistakes.

"Out," Jake said firmly, "before I make one."

Partridge opened the door and showed the visitors out with an elaborate display of politeness.

"Maybe I'm being rude," Jake said thoughtfully. "Maybe I should pay Mr. Hook a social call."

"Wait till he starts sending engraved invitations," Malone said. He made an unsuccessful attempt to straighten his tie. "At least you know why he was bothering you." He mopped his brow with a mussed and dingy handkerchief. "That leaves only Von Flanagan thinking you murdered Joshua Gumbril."

Jake said, "Tomorrow I get that box of Gumbril's if I have to climb up the side of the building."

"Meantime," Helene said, "we're due at Mona McClane's." She looked at the litter on the floor. "Nice work, Partridge. In emergency, break glass."

"Too bad all those drinks were wasted, though," Jake said.

Partridge looked up, surprised. "Nothing was wasted, sir. It was only water."

About thirty seconds later Jake repeated, "Water?" in what he realized was a very feeble voice.

"What the hell do you mean?" George Brand growled.

"It was water in the glasses, sir. When I heard the gentlemen come in, there wasn't time to fill the glasses with anything but water." He rose to his feet, a tray of broken glassware on his arm. "I do hope I did right, sir."

The last look he gave George Brand as he left the room expressed his intense disapproval at being mixed up with such people.

## *Chapter Eighteen*

"Don't look now," Helene said as her big car turned off Rush Street, "but I think that man is here again." She glanced in her rear-view mirror and said, "At least, we seem to be leading a parade."

Jake looked back. A long, black car was less than half a block behind. As he watched it, Helene suddenly turned left, drove for a block, and turned left again. The black car followed discreetly. She stopped. The black car stopped. She started again and drove very slowly, so did the car behind.

"Maybe it's done with mirrors," George Brand suggested.

Helene turned into a darkened side street, the black car close behind now. For a few blocks she drove with a blissful disregard for speed limits while the other car managed to keep up the pace. Then she stepped on the brakes suddenly, and at the same time, pulled over to the curb with a jerk that set Jake's teeth rattling in his head.

The driver of the black car evidently tried to stop some distance behind Helene, but failed. There was a banshee wailing of brakes and the whine of tires sliding on moist pavement, and when the pursuing car did stop, it was directly alongside Helene's.

There appeared to be a moment's hesitation on the part of the driver over the

delicate problem of whether to back up or drive on. Helene took advantage of it
to open her window wide, and Jake recognized little Georgie la Cerra beside the
driver. He leaned across Helene and shouted.

"Hey you! I think I hear your mamma calling you home!"

A conference seemed to be going on in the other car. Jake withdrew from the
window and slid one hand into the pocket where La Cerra's gun still remained.
Then the door of the other car opened and Little Georgie, both hands tactfully in
sight, came over to the window.

"If you're looking for a job as a bodyguard," Jake began nastily.

"Lookahere," the gangster said unhappily. "I gotta do what I'm told, don't I?
I don't want to bother nobody. I ain't lookin' for no trouble. But I gotta do like
I'm told."

"Sure," Jake said, "and I'm telling you to get back on your horse and ride
away."

"The Hook told me," little Georgie said, "maybe you was telling the truth
about you didn't find nothin' in Gumbril's room. He told me he wasn't doubting
but what you was telling the truth. But just the same he told me I shouldn't let
you outa my sight, just for safety's sake, and so I ain't lettin' you outa my sight.
See?"

Jake glared at him savagely for a minute. "All right. Don't let me out of your
sight. Except that I'm damned if I'm going to let you sleep under my bed."

He leaned back in his seat, and Helene started the car with a jerk.

"I have an idea," she observed coolly, "that when you start climbing up the
side of the Fairfax Hotel to get that box, Little Georgie is going to hold the
landing net."

She turned the car in the direction of Mona McClane's.

"In the meantime," she said suddenly, "that guy gave me a few bad minutes
earlier in the evening. An eye for a tooth, that's what I always say." With that she
pressed down on the accelerator.

The next fifteen minutes was something Jake hoped he would be able to forget, and knew would come back to haunt him in his more terrible nightmares.
Helene drove the big, powerful car everywhere except up the sides of buildings,
and her passengers expected that at any moment. It wasn't, however, until she
began to play in-and-out-the-window with the huge concrete pillars in the underpass below Wacker Drive that Jake decided it was time to be masterful. Tactfully he reminded her that they were overdue at Mona McClane's.

With a regretful sigh she slowed down and headed once more in the direction
of the Drive.

As soon as Jake felt that he could turn his head without its falling off his neck,
he looked back. The gangster's car was still following, a little farther behind,
but there. Jake decided to take back fifty per cent of everything he had thought
about Little Georgie la Cerra. Or at least, his driver.

Helene said, "There's a bottle of Bacardi somewhere in the back seat, in case any of you big, strong men feel faint."

By the time the bottle had been passed around, her passengers were able to speak again.

"I hope Little Georgie has a drink," John J. Malone said soulfully. "I never felt so sorry for a guy in my life. And as far as the driver of that car goes, he's probably earned the city safety council's reckless-driving award." He paused, thought a moment, and said, "That don't sound right, but I must have meant it."

Helene prepared to make a left turn off the Drive. "Hope our friends don't mind waiting for us outside Mona McClane's."

"Mind!" Jake indignantly. "They'll probably be grateful for the chance to sit still!" He looked back as Helene slowed down in front of the McClane driveway and saw the big black car edge into a parking place.

The old McClane house on Lake Shore Drive had always excited Jake Justus' curiosity. It was an enormous, ugly, square house, built of some kind of brownish stone, and set in almost a block of ground surrounded by a magnificent iron fence. For fifty weeks of every year it stood empty, blinds drawn tight at every window, the once famous lawn going to seed. It had always had a haunted look to Jake.

Now he saw it through a veil of swirling snow as Helene's big car turned up the driveway. Only a few windows showed; the rest were still tightly curtained. Snow clung to the edges of the roof and the window sills, and lay in great drifts on the lawn.

A plump colored maid showed them into a softly lighted, comfortable room full of big, cushiony furniture. Jake sank into a chair with a feeling of never wanting to rise again. Tables, desks, and bookcases were huge, heavy affairs, yet the room itself was so large that they didn't make a dent in its vast space.

In that room, Mona McClane seemed tiny, fragile, yet far from insignificant. Jake guessed roughly it was about half the size of Soldiers' Field, but five feet of Mona McClane dominated it from wall to wall.

She was, Jake observed, the least spectacularly dressed woman in the room, and the most spectacular. He remembered that had been true at the wedding party, too. She wore black tonight, a dress that was extremely simple and, he guessed, extremely expensive. It clung to her just a little as she walked. The single, unadorned ruby that she wore on a long, slender chain was so perfectly plain in its setting that he decided at once it must be real.

He looked around the room. There was Daphne Sanders, apparently recovered from her state of mind of the afternoon. She seemed a little pale, but exceedingly calm, and nearly sober.

Beside Daphne, Fleurette Sanders was delicate, bird-like, perfect. Jake admired her dress, extreme in cut, made of some strange, exotic, printed stuff. Those two women ought never to sit near each other, he decided. Taken by

themselves, both Daphne Sanders and Fleurette were reasonably interesting speci-
mens to look at, but side by side they seemed to bring out all of each other's
worst points. Neither of them looked particularly happy at the moment, either.
Fleurette Sanders had a distinctly displeased expression on her small face. Jake
wondered if she hadn't appreciated her husband's new beard.

The transfer of the beard had made a sensation, in a small way, and George
Brand and Willis Sanders were wandering about together, showing off, very
pleased with themselves.

Jake finished his drink, the plump colored maid removed his glass and substi-
tuted a filled one. He sipped it, sighed, leaned back in his chair, and closed his
eyes. It wasn't a bad party, taken on the whole. Everyone seemed to be having a
good time. Under other circumstances, he would probably be having a good
time himself. He opened his eyes long enough to notice Helene across the room,
talking vivaciously with a brown-haired, undistinguished-looking woman, and
closed them again. The chair was wonderfully comfortable. He wondered if he
could manage just a tiny nap without being noticed.

Detached phrases from the room's conversation came vaguely to his ears,
without making much impression. Someone casually mentioned the murder at
State and Madison Streets the day before. And then Fleurette Sanders' reedy
voice brought Jake wide-awake in an instant.

"I saw that murder."

The incredible sentence echoed in the breathless quiet that followed it.

Then Malone said, "Don't speak too rashly, Mrs. Sanders, or you'll find yourself a material witness."

She shrugged her shoulders delicately. "I didn't really see enough to be a
material witness. I was quite a distance away. Besides," she laughed a little
shrilly, "I'm among friends."

"Where were you?" Mona McClane asked lightly.

"Of all the silly places," Fleurette Sanders said, "I was in the dentist's chair.
My dentist's office is right on the southwest corner, on the third floor. I was
sitting there waiting for him to attack me with some new devilish instrument,
and looking out the window while I waited, and I saw—everything that happened." She frowned as though the recollection was faintly repugnant to her,
not horrible, just distasteful.

Jake started to speak, saw that Malone was concentrating on getting the ash
from his cigar into the ash tray, and kept quiet.

"Probably," the little lawyer said, clearing his throat, "the only way anyone
could see what happened there was by looking down from a window. Possibly
you're the only real witness."

She shook her head, smiling deprecatingly. "I didn't see enough to testify to
anything." She went back to chatting with Wells Ogletree about something else,
and the subject seemed to be closed.

Jake sighed. Helene's pale-gold hair was like a beacon, beckoning him across the room. Or was it a beckon beaconing? He felt a little vague about it. With a heroic effort he rose and walked to her side.

Helene introduced him to Mrs. Ogletree.

Wells Ogletree's wife was a small, harassed-looking woman with unmanageable brown-gray hair and peering, inquisitive eyes behind heavy glasses. Her tan-colored print dress looked expensive and dowdy. Jake felt immediately she was the sort of woman who was always one sentence behind in the conversation and trying desperately to catch up. At the moment she was a little drunk.

She giggled at him. "Your bride has just been telling me that four gunmen tried to kidnap you, and you beat them off single-handed."

"Helene underexaggerated." He wondered if that was the right word. "There were ten of them."

Mrs. Ogletree looked impressed.

"I have many enemies," Jake assured her. Somehow an extra syllable crept in and it came out as "many enenemies."

"Oh," Mrs. Ogletree said. Fifteen seconds later she giggled again and said, "Oh, then you're a gardener."

Jake had a profound conviction that the conversation wasn't getting anywhere.

"This is really an engagement-breaking party for me," the woman said confidingly, laying a plump, freckled hand on Jake's arm. He had a momentary terror that she was going to rest her head on his shoulder. "My dear little girl's engagement. She was engaged to the most awful man, with a lot of money, but she broke it off last night. I'm so happy!"

Jake followed the direction of Mrs. Ogletree's gaze to where Ellen Ogletree sat. The girl looked highly pleased with herself. Her small, weakish mouth was curved in a half-feline manner, her little, pointed chin was held high.

"Is that the man she was engaged to?" Jake asked politely.

Mrs. Ogletree squeezed his arm and said, "Of course not, silly boy. He was an awful man, really awful."

"That man over there looks awful to me," Jake said.

The man with Ellen was tall and slender, with thinning blonde hair, a concave chest, and stooped shoulders. He had a narrow, razorlike nose, pale blue eyes, and a slightly receding chin. His apparently permanent expression was that of one who has just heard an incredible but well-verified fact for the first time.

"That's Leonard Marchmont," Mrs. Ogletree said. "Ellen's wild about him. So is Daphne Sanders. Isn't it wonderful?"

Jake looked again, more closely, remembering what Daphne Sanders had said about the man earlier in the evening. He felt a little bewildered. The English were truly a wonderful race, if they could overcome handicaps like that.

"He'll never marry Ellen," Mrs. Ogletree confided. "She hasn't enough money." Suddenly she clasped Jake's hands. Her own were warm and unpleasantly damp. "I don't want Ellen to marry. I don't want my dear little girl to go away and leave me alone."

Jake looked her straight in the eye, said very solemnly, "I promise I'll never, never try to take her away from you," gently disengaged his hands, and fled.

He wondered where Helene had gone. People seemed to be wandering about all over the house. Probably if he explored a little he could find her. But perhaps he ought to mark his trail as he went. There seemed to be such a lot of downstairs to the old McClane house.

One room had been fitted up as a miniature bar, complete even to the half-pint enameled piano. Jake stood in the doorway an instant, reflecting that if he did win the Casino, and if he ever did become very rich, he would build Helene a house with just such a built-in bar. Helene would love that. Still, if he won the Casino, she would never be home anyway.

There were half a dozen people in the room, clustered around the piano. Daphne Sanders stood alone at the far end of the bar, staring vindictively into a glass. Jake ambled over to her. She seemed to be getting that look in her eyes again.

"It isn't that I care a snap about him," she said as though she were picking up the conversation where it had been left off that afternoon, "but I hate to see her get away with anything."

Jake nodded gravely. It seemed to him that he ought to offer advice, but he couldn't think of any.

"The little bitch," Daphne Sanders added, "she's almost as bad as Fleurette."

"It seems to me you take dislikes to people," Jake said.

She looked at him indignantly. "I have plenty of reason." She added after a moment, "Go away."

He decided it was just as well to obey. He wasn't here to find out anything about Daphne Sanders, anyway. This wasn't just an evening's fun, he reminded himself.

At the far end of the shadowy hall, a door stood open. He decided to investigate, and walked into a library, a pleasant, soft-lighted room at the front of the house. No one was there, and he sank down on the big cushioned davenport happily. It seemed to him he had wanted to be alone for a long time now.

He felt in his pocket for matches and found none. There was an ash tray at his elbow, but no matches. He rose, searched the other ash trays and the top of the table. No matches anywhere. A hell of a way to run a house, he reflected.

The drawer of the big library table was just slightly open, enough so that he could see a couple of bright-covered match folders. He gave the drawer a little jerk, helped himself to matches, and lit his cigarette.

As he started to push the drawer shut, a gleam of light on metal caught his eye. He pulled the drawer open another inch or two.

There was an ugly, efficient-looking little gun in the drawer.

He took it out and shut the drawer. A series of small electric shocks went up and down his spine.

Jake had no doubts. In his hand was the gun that had killed Joshua Gumbril.

## *Chapter Nineteen*

The problem was entirely a moral one. On the one hand, Jake reminded himself, the gun was a valuable piece of evidence that he ought to have in his possession. On the other, it distinctly was not the correct thing to pinch a lady's gun when you were a guest in her house.

He thought over all the arguments on both sides, without reaching any conclusion. He wondered what Helene or Malone would do. He wondered what Emily Post would do.

Suddenly he remembered that he was still carrying the gun taken from little Georgie la Cerra earlier in the evening. There, that would solve everything. A fair exchange was no breach of good behavior. He slipped La Cerra's gun into the library table drawer and closed it softly.

Now to get a word to Helene and Malone and inform them of his great discovery. No, there was a better way. He'd just say nothing about it, and surprise them with the gun at some opportune time.

He put the gun in his pocket, finished the drink he had carried into the library with him, set the glass down on the table, and stretched out on the big davenport that faced the windows to enjoy what he considered a very well-earned rest.

Just a short nap, or even a doze, was going to make him feel much better. He yawned, settled himself comfortably, and admired the snow that was falling past the windows like a veil. Like a bridal veil. He wondered where Helene was, his bride. He began to feel very sorry for himself.

Voices by the library door roused him from his reverie. After the first moment or so he identified them as belonging to Fleurette and Willis Sanders.

The small woman whose name had once been Flossie seemed very angry about something. "You must have had some good reason for telling her you'd do it," she was saying indignantly. "I want to know what it is."

Willis Sanders mumbled something indistinguishable.

"She must be blackmailing you," Fleurette said. Her voice was low, but nastily insistent. "And I think I know why. Don't you know what you let yourself in for when you agree to something like that?"

Jake heard something that sounded like "couldn't help it."

"You should have come to me," the woman said. "I'd have known how to handle it. And I still do." She paused and said furiously, "Fool! Idiot! Imbecile!"

The voices drifted away again. Jake sat up and ran a hand through his hair. This was a hell of a house in which to take a quiet little nap. Just as soon as you

were comfortable, someone came in and had a fight. He felt that the conversation he had overheard must be important, but he preferred not to think about it
now.

He rose, straightened his tie, and gazed out the window. Through the snow he
could make out the figure of little Georgie la Cerra standing unhappily in the
shelter of the immense gatepost.

Suddenly an idea came to him. (He claimed later that it came to him straight
from heaven.) Opening the window a trifle, he whistled softly.

The gangster looked up and saw him. Jake beckoned frantically. After an
instant's hesitation Little Georgie came over to the window, somewhat skeptically.

"This is a swell party," Jake said enthusiastically. "Come on in."

"What the hell's the idea?"

"Don't get me wrong," Jake said in an injured tone. "I don't know any of
these people, and I'm bored. Come on in."

Little Georgie la Cerra glanced in through the lighted window. "I can't," he
said unhappily, "I ain't got on my tux."

"The hell with it," Jake said, "neither have I. Here, I'll give you a hand."

The gangster hesitated only an instant. "No tricks now—" He decided to al-
low Jake to haul him in through the window. They deposited the new visitor's
hat and topcoat in the hall and brushed the snow from his shoes. Then Jake led
him in the direction of the little bar.

"There's a swell girl here," Jake confided, "just your type."

He beamed happily at Daphne Sanders.

"Miss Sanders, want you to meet a friend of mine, just dropped in. Name's—
Mr. Cherry."

"Charmed," Daphne said politely. "What do you drink, Mr. Cherry?"

"Gin," La Cerra said, "and call me George."

Jake thought he detected a faint look of admiration in the girl's eyes as Little
Georgie la Cerra downed an ordinary water tumbler of gin.

"Do you ride?" she asked, as though she might as well make the best of things.

"Horses? No."

"Golf?"

"Uh-uh."

"Sail?"

"You mean boats? Naw."

"Shoot?"

"And how," said little Georgie with enthusiasm, "and I don't mean pool."

Five minutes later Little Georgie was giving a creditable imitation of the to-
bacco auctioneer and confiding his ambition to get on the radio. Ten minutes
later he was showing Daphne his good-luck charm, which Jake recognized as a
genuine white jade Buddha. Fifteen minutes later, when Georgie started demon-

strating wrestling holds, Jake decided that it was the dawn of a beautiful friendship and tiptoed off with the feeling of a good deed done. Not only had he provided Daphne Sanders with a new interest in life, but he'd quite possibly saved Ellen Ogletree from violent and possibly homicidal attack.

The big living room seemed much as he had left it. Fleurette and Willis Sanders had returned. Jake sank down in an easy chair near Helene and wondered how soon they could go home.

Through a pleasant haze he heard Malone's voice speaking near him. Then suddenly he was wide awake as Mona McClane said, "But murder is so often justified."

Jake sat bolt upright. Malone, cuddling a glass in his hand, was preparing to speak in his best lecture-hall manner.

"Everyone has the makings of one good murder in him," the little lawyer said. "Probably everyone is entitled to one good murder. Whether the supply of murderees would keep up with the demand—" he paused reflectively.

Wells Ogletree's long, thin, aristocratic nose fairly quivered with an excess of righteousness.

"That, it seems to me," he said harshly, "is an attitude that practically condones murder."

Malone didn't appear to have heard him. "Of course," he twirled his glass thoughtfully, "there is such a thing as unrequited murder. Cupid too often fires from ambush, because love, like murder, does not always wait upon the consent of the victim."

"Love," said Wells Ogletree, "is something that I, for one, have always been accustomed to believe the most intimate—"

"Precisely," Malone went on smoothly, as though a prosecuting attorney had raised an unreasonable objection. "Like love, murder is the most intimate of human relationships. And, like everything that is intimate, it is strictly a private matter between the murderee and the murderer. Murder becomes justified when, for example, the existence of another person becomes sufficiently obnoxious to warrant the risks involved in removing him. The lover says, 'I cannot live without you.' And the murderer says, 'I cannot live with you.' The trouble with murder—" Malone paused, as if a new note had crept into his thought, a doubtful note.

"The trouble with murder is that so often it leads to the commission of more serious crimes."

That was too much for Wells Ogletree.

"That," he observed icily, "is an attitude that practically condones lawbreaking."

"You forget," Malone said, with no trace of apology in his voice, "I earn my living by defending lawbreakers before a court of justice."

Wells Ogletree said coldly, "One cannot but consider it a reprehensible occupation," and let it go at that.

"It's also true," Malone was saying, "that everyone alive deserves, at some time in his or her life, to be murdered." He added, "A few people I know deserve to be murdered at regular intervals."

Mona McClane said sharply, "And a number of people deserve to be murdered very early in life—but better late than never."

Jake thought Helene was a little pale. The atmosphere of the room seemed alive, fairly crackling with cross-currents of hatred. He thought it was almost possible to hear it, like static on a cheap radio. Different people hating each other for different reasons. It gave a strange, electric quality to everything that was said, a quality that threatened at any moment to burst into verbal flames.

But it was Fleurette Sanders who inadvertently set off the holocaust.

"Really," she said, crushing out her cigarette fastidiously, as though there were something faintly objectionable about it. "All this talk about murder seems to me to be in the worst possible taste."

There was an instant's pause. In it, Jake looked up and saw Daphne Sanders framed in the doorway. The shadow in the hall behind her was, he guessed, Little Georgie la Cerra. The girl's face had suddenly gone dead white.

"You shouldn't object to talk about murder, Fleurette." There was no emotion in her voice. "After all, you murdered my mother."

The situation wasn't relieved by Fleurette Sanders' laugh.

Mona McClane swung around in her chair and said, "Really, Daphne!"

"She shouldn't mind its being said," Daphne Sanders said coldly. "Everyone's been thinking it for years."

Jake wondered if anyone else noticed that Willis Sanders' face had turned a mottled gray-white, and that its expression seemed curiously incongruous with the new beard. He thought too that if anyone ever looked at him the way Daphne Sanders looked at her stepmother, he'd be afraid to go to sleep at night.

"If your accusations weren't so utterly absurd, Daphne," Fleurette Sanders said pleasantly, "I'd insist on your being more specific. But I'm sure that no one takes it seriously."

"I do," the girl said coolly.

Willis Sanders spoke with sudden sternness. "Daphne, I forbid you to say another word."

She flashed him a single, burning, malevolent glance, and was silent.

## *Chapter Twenty*

Helene's big car was barely out of the driveway before she said, "Malone, do you think Fleurette Sanders really killed the first Mrs. Sanders?"

"I don't know," Malone said. "Somebody did."

"If you ask me," Jake muttered, "that girl Daphne is nothing but a murder walking around looking for a place to happen." Speaking of Daphne reminded him of Little Georgie, and he looked around for the gangster's car. There was no sign of it anywhere. "Two birds with one stone are worth two in the bush," he said happily.

Before Helene had a chance to ask questions, there was a sudden interruption. She had turned off Lake Shore Drive onto a side street, and a long, low-slung roadster came up beside them, all but forcing them to the curb. Ellen Ogletree's voice called from the roadster.

"I'm sorry to stop you this way," she said breathlessly, "but I want to—I have to—talk to you people, and I didn't want anyone there at Mona's to know. Except Len. He's with me."

Jake couldn't see the little lawyer's face, but he knew Malone's eyebrows must be raised in two questioning curves.

"Sounds urgent," he said quietly.

"It is," Ellen Ogletree said. "At least I think it is. It's about—about that man who was murdered—the one Fleurette saw—" She caught her breath and said, "Is there some place we can talk?"

Jake held his watch to the light and said, "There's a little bar on the west side of Rush Street just above Chicago Avenue that's still open. We'll meet you in a booth there in five minutes."

Helene started the car and murmured, "As you mentioned this afternoon, when people are married—"

Jake said hastily, "It won't take ten minutes to talk with her, and the night is still young."

"What the devil do you suppose the Ogletree girl wants?" Malone said crossly.

"Maybe she wants to tell us she saw Mona McClane shooting Mr. Gumbril," Jake muttered. He was trying hard to remember something. It was something he'd learned at Mona McClane's. Important, too. He shook his head and sighed heavily.

"What the hell's the matter?" the lawyer growled.

"There was something I wanted to tell you, but it's gone," Jake said. He thought a minute longer, finally said, "Oh well, it'll come to me."

Malone grunted. "If I had it to do over again, I'd have been a doctor instead of a lawyer. There wouldn't have been so many emergency calls keeping me from my sleep."

They found Ellen Ogletree and friend waiting in a secluded booth in the little bar.

"Are you sure this is a good place to talk?" the girl asked anxiously.

"Sure," Jake said confidently. "The only place to hold a strictly private conversation is in a public bar. It's the one place where you won't be overheard." He gave the bartender a bill, said, "Go on bringing us gin until this gives out, and don't listen to anything you hear."

Helene said, "You mean, don't hear anything you listen to."

Malone ignored them both, turned to Ellen Ogletree, and said, simply, "Well?"

The girl frowned. "It's serious. Really serious, I mean."

"Sure," Jake said. "Murder is always serious."

Leonard Marchmont laughed heartily, displaying an amazing number of large, horselike teeth. Evidently he had a vague idea that Jake had made a joke. Ellen Ogletree frowned at him, opened her lips to speak, and then thought better of it.

George Brand decided to help. "I suppose you're afraid you'll be mixed up in this murder because Gumbril took part in your kidnaping."

Ellen Ogletree looked at him gratefully. "That's exactly it." She shuddered. "I don't know why it should worry me, except that it was such an awful experience and I don't think I could stand having it all brought up again." Her little chin wobbled as though she might weep.

Marchmont laid a hand on her arm. "Frightful thing being kidnaped, you know."

Malone nodded sympathetically. "Still, I don't see why you need to worry about it, Miss Ogletree. After all, who knows Gumbril was part of the kidnap gang? Part of it, or head of it," he added.

"Head of it," Ellen said almost automatically. "I know, and Len knows, and you people. And father."

"But not the police," Malone said in his most reassuring voice. "And as Gumbril's murder must have been a gang murder—" he ended on a half-questioning note.

"If it was," Ellen Ogletree said.

Malone appeared to inhale his glass of gin. "Was it Gumbril who did the actual—" he cleared his throat delicately, "snatching?"

Ellen Ogletree paled. "No. There were two men. One of them just drove the car. I don't know who he was. The other one—the man who seemed to be running things—was an Italian, I think. His pal called him Little Georgie."

Jake had a strange notion that all the flesh on his body had moved an inch or so away from his bones. Maybe, he told himself reassuringly, it was just the gin. He rather wished Daphne Sanders had decided to bring her new boy friend into the living room before Ellen had gone. The resulting commotion would have been worth seeing. He wondered how Little Georgie was making out with her.

"Do you know who he is?" Ellen Ogletree asked.

The lawyer shook his head. "Never heard of him. You just forget it and everyone else will. Nothing to worry about."

A little color had returned to the girl's face. Jake noticed that her complexion, under its heavy make-up, was far from perfect.

"I hope you're right. The murder did give me a nasty shock, though."

"The poor little girl has been through so much," Leonard Marchmont said sympathetically.

The poor little girl looked extremely pathetic and said, "It really was frightfully hard on me, really it was." Jake noticed a faintly English intonation in her speech which could only have come there by association.

"It couldn't have been good clean fun for your father, either," Helene said. "Fifty thousand bucks is fifty thousand bucks."

Ellen opened her eyes wide and said, "Oh, but it wasn't his money."

The lawyer spilled only a little of the gin on his tie. "Louder, please."

"It was my money. I guess you don't understand."

"No," Malone said. "I guess I don't."

"My grandfather left it to me," Ellen said. "The money, I mean. But father is in charge of it until I'm thirty. He can do just as he pleases with it until then. He pays my bills and gives me an allowance," she laughed a little harshly, "a nickel at a time. So when the kidnaping happened, the money was paid out of my estate. It didn't cost him anything." She added the last words in a faintly spiteful tone.

Jake waited until the bartender had come and gone away before he murmured, "That's very interesting." He wondered vaguely why the girl had lied about why she wanted to see them.

"If he'd had to dig it up himself," Ellen Ogletree said nastily, "he'd have told the kidnapers they could keep me." She paused, looked embarrassed, and said, "Please, let's not talk about it any more. Why on earth do you suppose Mrs. Sanders said that about seeing the murder?"

"Because she did see it, I suppose," Jake said. "I'd have mentioned it myself."

Leonard Marchmont said lightly, "You'd almost think the woman meant it as a warning."

"Oh, people will say anything to make a sensation," Malone murmured, gazing into his empty glass.

"Do you suppose she really saw anything?" Ellen Ogletree asked. "I mean, more than just the commotion in the crowd?"

"Possibly," the little lawyer said. "In fact, as I remarked at the time, the only way anyone could have actually seen what did happen would have been from a window somewhere above the corner. Looking down on the crowd, one could have seen the murderer move up behind his victim and move away again, seen the murdered man carried along by the crowd until he fell, in fact—" he paused to relight his cigar, "if the murderer had been anyone easily recognized by the person in the window"—he seemed to be having trouble with his cigar—"recognized by some distinctive headgear, for instance, Mrs. Sanders may even know the identity of the murderer." He expelled a great cloud of smoke like a battleship laying down a smoke screen.

"But why on earth would she say such a thing?" Ellen Ogletree persisted.

Jake shrugged his shoulders. "Making a sensation. Just as Mona McClane was making a sensation when she made that bet with me day before yesterday."

Leonard Marchmont laughed again. Jake decided it was the first time he'd ever heard what could be properly called a guffaw. "I say," he said, "If Mona McClane was in earnest about that bet, you know, and if this murder yesterday had—" He seemed a little embarrassed. "I mean to say, if she'd done it, you know, Mrs. Sanders might have been warning her she'd seen it."

"Quite possibly," Jake said, as though it didn't matter. "Nice of her, if that was it."

Ellen Ogletree rose. "I'm afraid I've bothered you for nothing."

"Not at all," Jake said gallantly. "It's been a pleasure."

He waited until the girl and her escort were out of earshot before he said, "Now why the hell does she hate Mona McClane?"

"How do you know she does?" Helene asked.

"She must, or she wouldn't have gone to all this trouble to make sure I linked up Mona McClane with the murder of Joshua Gumbril. Not too skillfully, either." He paused. "And to make sure that Fleurette Sanders must have seen the murder."

"I'm not sure that's it," Helene said thoughtfully. "I bet she's smelling out the ground to see if the murder could possibly be pinned on her old man. Ellen would love to see someone else handing out her allowance."

Jake said incredulously, "Do you think she'd pin a murder on her own old man just for money?"

"After living with Wells Ogletree all her life," Helene said tartly, "I bet she'd pin a murder on him for peanuts."

"Fleurette Sanders—" Jake began.

A loud snore interrupted him. George Brand had laid his head on the table and was sleeping peacefully as a child.

"Get his head out of the ash tray," Helene said, "and send for Partridge."

While they waited, Malone sank into what seemed to be a long spell of almost trancelike thought. At last he lifted his head.

"The first Mrs. Sanders. It's a funny coincidence. I remember now."

Jake growled, "Whatever it is, it's a coincidence that picked a helluva time to happen." He felt for Helene's hand under the table. "What do you remember?"

"I told you I knew Gumbril because he sent me a client now and then. I just recalled one of them, that's all."

"Who, damn you?" Helene demanded.

The lawyer took a long breath. "The man who fired the shot that killed the first Mrs. Sanders," he said proudly.

At that moment Partridge arrived, a little pale, more than a little scandalized.

"I have a taxi waiting for Mr. Brand," he reported. He seemed to hesitate a minute. "Mr. Justus, the apartment building is full of policemen. *Full* of them."

Jake blinked. "Policemen? Why? What are they doing there?"

Partridge looked down his nose and said, "They appeared to be waiting for someone, sir. That's all I know."

With the help of a sympathetic bartender he conveyed George Brand to the waiting taxi and was gone.

"I'm trying to solve a murder, not go to jail for one," Jake said crossly. "Now I can't even go home. Damn Mona McClane anyway."

Helene said, "Hush. I want to find out something. Malone, go on about the first Mrs. Sanders."

"Why?" Jake asked.

"Because it has something to do with Mona McClane," Helene told him, "and don't interrupt. Go on, Malone. Wasn't she killed in a holdup or some such thing?"

"That's right," the little lawyer said. "It was five or six years ago—something like that. The Sanders were coming home from the theater, as I recall. In front of the apartment building where they lived, they were held up by two armed bandits who took everything they had on them." He paused for thought and went on, "There has always been some doubt as to just what did happen. The most popular version is that Mrs. Sanders screamed, whereupon one of the holdup men shot and killed her. At least that was Sanders' story, which was accepted by the police on the face of the available evidence. The holdup man who did the shooting got clean away, with all the swag. The other one was my client."

"What happened to him?" Jake asked.

"I got him off on a technicality. His name was Gus Schenk. He runs a tavern on the South Side now."

"That's all I wanted to know," Helene said. She rose, picked up her gloves and bag, and said, "I've always wanted to meet a man named Gus. And let's get out of here and into the car before Von Flanagan's cops begin searching the North Side bars."

## Chapter Twenty-One

Out in the car Malone growled, "All right, I'll go with you. But why the hell do you want to talk to Gus?"

"To find out more about how the first Mrs. Sanders was killed," Helene said serenely. "It's the first hint of any link between Mona McClane and Joshua Gumbril."

"Louder," Malone said.

"Mona McClane is a friend of the Sanders. The first Mrs. Sanders was shot by a holdup man whose pal was sent to you as a client by Joshua Gumbril after the shooting."

"It's about as far-flung a connection as the Atlantic cable," Malone complained.

He told Helene to take the outer drive south. "I hope you know what you're doing."

Jake thought of one last objection. "Do you realize it's past midnight?"

"All the better," Helene told him, "there's a better chance that we can talk to Gus in private."

Passing the Field Museum Malone said, "I still don't think any of this has to do with Mona McClane."

They had gone by Soldiers' Field before Helene answered, "As far as I know, it doesn't."

Going through the Thirty-first Street underpass, Jake complained, "If it doesn't have anything to do with Mona McClane, then why are we bothering with it at all?"

"Because," Helene said crossly, "it's time to buy a drink, and I always believe in patronizing Malone's old clients, and I can't think of another one who keeps his bar open all night. Now sit back and admire my driving, and don't bother me."

Despite Helene's total disregard for the traffic regulations of the city of Chicago, it was a little past three before she parked the car in front of a lighted window whose painted sign announced, simply, "Gus's."

"Now that we're here," Jake began.

"Wait a minute," Helene said. "Malone, you know this guy. You ask the questions."

The lawyer sighed. "I'll have to. What do you want me to find out?"

"Find out why Mona McClane murdered Joshua Gumbril."

"I'll ask him that first," Malone said icily. "Come on in, and let me do the talking. These guys scare easily if you don't know how to handle them."

Gus's place was small, and far from ornate. There was a brown-wood bar with about a dozen bar stools, six booths in the rear of the long narrow room, a small table with a checkerboard, an upright piano that had once been painted an unpleasant green, and a nickel phonograph.

Helene paused for a moment at the door, looking in. "How can a place as small as this one afford to stay open all night?"

Malone snapped, "Remember you're a lady, and don't ask questions." He added after a thoughtful pause, "Didn't I tell you he was one of my clients?"

Save for an affectionate couple in the farthest booth, Gus's place was empty. A tiny radio back of the bar played very faint dance music. Gus himself sat beside it, reading a magazine. He was a thoughtful, plumpish, middle-aged man, slightly bald. At the sound of the door closing he laid down his magazine with almost an air of regret, took the toothpick he had been chewing out of his mouth, looked at his visitors, and immediately broke into a wide, broken-toothed and heart-warming smile.

"Glad t'see ya, Malone. Been a long time since you was out."

Malone introduced his companions. Gus shook hands with both of them warmly and enthusiastically.

"I'm sure glad t'see ya. Any friend of Malone's is more'n a friend of mine."

Helene said, "That goes for me, double," and gave him a smile that promptly won his lifelong affection.

From that point on, however, conversational progress was maddeningly slow. Malone ordered a drink. Jake ordered a second. The house bought one. Then that ritual was repeated, in the same order.

There was discussion of the weather, the races, mutual friends and acquaintances, slot machines, and the hard time a bookie had making an honest living for himself. At last when almost every conceivable subject had been exhausted, Malone brought up the subject of the sudden death of the late Joshua Gumbril.

"I read about it," Gus said. A note of sincere admiration crept into his voice. "Imagine pickin' the corner of State and Madison Streets. That was a smart stunt. Now I'd never a'thought of that myself."

There was a brief discussion of the manner of Mr. Gumbril's abrupt taking off, and the subsequent bafflement of the police.

"I can't say I'm sorry," Gus said at last, shaking his head sadly. "I never was one to speak ill of the dead, and I never had no trouble with Gumbril. He never done me no harm, and he maybe done me some good. But I never could feel no liking for him. I guess there ain't nobody to mourn for him."

A phrase of that insane conversation with Mona McClane flashed momentarily through Jake's mind. "Somebody that no one will mourn for—"

Malone lit a cigar and said very casually, "Remember that Sanders holdup, Gus—speaking of Gumbril—and the way it came out?"

Almost holding his breath, Jake watched the man for the faintest sign of wariness. There was none.

"Yeah," Gus said, wiping off the top of the bar and gathering the glasses for another drink on the house. "Yeah, I remember. I was perfectly in the clear, though. Not a single thing anyone could pin on me." He looked at the lawyer, "Hell, I wasn't even there, was I?"

"No," Malone told him.

"That was a funny thing," Gus said reminiscently, setting out the refilled glasses. "A very funny thing." A new light came into his eyes, not wariness, but anxiety. "Say, that old business hasn't anything to do with Gumbril getting shot, has it, Malone?"

"I don't see how it could," Malone reassured him. "Hell no, Gus. That was years ago."

Gus looked relieved. He wiped the top of the bar again. "That's what I thought. But it was kinda funny just the same."

"What was kind of funny?" Malone asked.

No one who didn't know him as well as Jake would have heard and recognized the faint quiver of excitement in his voice.

"That you're the second person this week that's spoke to me about the same thing." He began chewing on his toothpick. "Coming almost the same time as this Gumbril guy getting shot, it struck me as kinda coincidental."

"It's funny how these things happen," Jake said lightly.

"Yeah," Gus said. He threw his toothpick on the floor. "I remember once when my sister-in-law was down in Kansas City—"

Fifteen minutes later he ended the story about his sister-in-law and Malone asked very casually, "Who else was it said something to you about the Sanders killing, Gus?"

"She didn't say nothing to me, she asked me," Gus said. He grinned broadly. "I didn't tell her a thing. It was that big, warm-looking Sanders babe. Daphne I guess her name is."

Jake had an uncomfortable feeling that he might die of old age before Malone answered.

"Daphne Sanders, eh?" the little lawyer said at last, with an air of quiet amusement. "What did she want to know?"

"If the dame who married Sanders later didn't frame the whole thing. She wanted it two grand worth. Maybe if she'd come up to five—" he paused, sighed, shook his head, and said, "Why the hell should I stick my neck out?"

"Why indeed," Malone agreed. "What did you tell her?"

"I told her I didn't know nothing about it. She wanted proof anyway. What the hell kind of proof could I give her?"

"None whatever," Malone said agreeably.

Gus scratched his right ear thoughtfully. "Say, Malone, how high do you think she'd go?"

"Not high enough," the lawyer assured him. "Not anywhere near high enough."

"I s'pose not." The bartender sighed regretfully. "I could use the dough. Still, as I just said, why should I stick my neck out?" He scratched the other ear. "Funny, though, Malone. What d'ya s'pose she wanted to know for, anyway?"

Malone said vaguely, "I guess she doesn't like her stepmother any too well." He added casually, "Just between ourselves, Gus, how much did you get out of it?"

"No more than the dough Gumbril give me. Five hundred lousy bucks, plus what I had to pay you, for all the risk I took." He became suddenly vehement and impassioned, leaned heavily on the bar with one hand, and gestured dangerously close to Malone's nose with the other.

"If I had of known what I was getting into, believe me, Malone, I never would of went into it."

Malone lifted an eyebrow and said, "You mean you didn't know what the layout was before you saw it sprung?"

"Hell no," Gus said.

"Come on now, Gus," the lawyer said contemptuously. "Save your kidding for your customers."

"Honest, Malone. I didn't know Gumbril had anything to do with it, either. I thought the whole thing was Joe's idea. Hell, it was just another stickup to me." He paused, looked embarrassed, and said to Helene, "This was all a long time ago, lady. I didn't really know what I was doing. Believe me, I'm a reformed man."

"Don't mind us," Helene informed him brightly. "My husband here just beat a burglary rap with Malone's help."

"Tch-tch-tch," the bartender said reprovingly. He looked solemnly at Jake. "You hadn't ought to live that kind of a life, married to a nice girl like her. It not only ain't right, but it don't get you no place. Why don't you open a tavern?"

"I've been thinking of it seriously ever since I met her," Jake said, very gravely. He shoved a handful of coins across the bar. "Let's have a drink."

"Sure," Gus said, gathering the glasses. "If you ever decide to do that, I can give you a lot of good advice."

"It's all past history and nobody gives a damn now," Malone said almost dreamily, "but I always thought Gumbril put you next to that Sanders business."

"Hell no," Gus said again, busy with the glasses. "It was Joe's doing. I didn't expect no gunwork. I never would of went along if I had." He shoved the re-filled glasses across the bar.

"Well you live and learn," Malone said platitudinously. He added, looking into his glass, "Just what ever did happen there, anyway—between ourselves and strictly off the record?"

"Malone, I ain't even sure." Gus leaned confidingly on the bar. "So help me, Malone, and that's the truth. All of a sudden, see, without no warning, Joe he just opened up and let the old dame have it. Wham, just like that. I never knew what he done it for." He shook his head sadly. "It wasn't like Joe."

"I understand she let out a yell," Malone said idly.

"Uh-uh. There wasn't a yip. Not a single yip out of her. We scrammed in the car. Joe, he let me out at the Grand Avenue El station just like we'd arranged. When he let me out he just said, 'See Gumbril.' " He shook his head again and sighed, "You know, that's the last I ever seen of Joe."

"Funny," Malone commented. He paused. "So Joe got the whole take, huh?"

"That's right, Malone. Gumbril, he gimme the five hundred. Near as I can figger it, that was the setup from the start. Joe, he was to get whatever we took off the Sanders. Maybe Gumbril gave him some extra, I don't know. Me, I was to get the five hundred."

"What the hell did Gumbril get?" the lawyer asked.

"That's the damn funny thing, Malone. As near as I see it, he didn't get nothing."

Malone looked at him scornfully and said. "Go on, Gus. What d'ya take me for, anyway?"

"I wouldn't kid you," Gus assured him earnestly. "Gumbril, he give me the five hundred, see, and says in that wheezy voice of his that Joe has beat it with what was took off the Sanders, and I'm to go to you if there's any trouble, which there was a little, but you took care of it very nicely." He beamed at the lawyer.

"Thanks," Malone murmured appreciatively.

"And he says I should send him your bill when it come in, which it did, and believe me—" he turned to Jake and Helene, "when I seen it, I knew right away I was on the wrong end of the racket. I wished I'd gone to school like my old lady wanted me to. But anyway, I says to him, 'Gumbril, what are you getting out of this?' and he gives me that funny grin of his and says, 'Not a red cent.' "

"I can't believe it," Malone said, almost faintly.

"Gumbril had his faults," Gus said firmly, "but he never was one to lie. He said he wasn't getting a cent, he was just discharging his family obligations."

Malone seemed to be having considerable trouble with his cigar, and his voice was a shade too casual.

"What did he mean by family obligations?" he said at last.

"Search me. That's all he said. He give me that funny grin and says he was just discharging the last of his family obligations, and that was all he said. So I signed his paper and took my dough and didn't ask no more questions."

"Paper?" Malone asked almost lazily.

"Yeah." Gus grinned widely. "You know, Malone. Every time you did any business with Gumbril, the old guy put it all down in writing and made you sign it. Said he did it for self-protection." He spat a piece of toothpick on the floor. "Self-protection, hell. He waited to see if you hung onto any dough, and then put the bite on you. As soon as you were broke, or he'd got all he could, he'd tear up the paper." He grinned again. "The way to queer that was to act broke. But you had to watch yourself. He was a wary guy."

Malone nodded. "I'd heard something of the sort. Wonder where those papers are."

Gus shook his head. "He probably only kept the best of 'em. He was a guy who hated to have anything around, if you know what I mean. Maybe that's why he was so glad to see the last of his family obligations."

Malone drew a smoke ring, regarded it for a moment, and said, "Well, it was a damned queer mess from start to finish. I never knew Gumbril had any family."

"Me neither," Gus said. He gathered up the glasses again. "I never knew nothing about him. He was a funny little guy." He sighed, lifted his glass, and added reverentially, "Well, we all have to die some time."

Malone said solemnly, "You never can tell."

The bartender set his glass down hard. "Say, Malone, do you know if Gumbril left any dough?"

The little lawyer caught his breath before he said, "Why?"

"Oh—well, nothing. I mean—it's like this, Malone. A guy, I mean a guy like Gumbril, he can pile up a hunk of dough while he's on the make, and still not have a scratch of it left when he kicks out." He rubbed his nose and began again. "Look, Malone, it's tough to think of a little guy like Gumbril getting his like that, no doubt when he least expected it, and him having no friends and no family, and if on top of that he didn't have no dough left, and the city has to bury him—" Gus paused for breath, his face the color of an early June peony, "What I mean is, Malone, if the little guy didn't have no dough left when he was took so sudden, I'd like to kick in towards giving him a swell funeral, and I know a lot of the boys would feel the same way."

It was a moment or so before Malone could trust himself to speak. "Don't worry, Gus. Gumbril left enough cash on hand to cast a shadow on the national debt."

Gus looked a little vague, but relieved.

It appeared to be time for Malone to buy a drink. Everyone seemed content to drop the subject of the late Mr. Gumbril. Jake asked for and received some valuable advice on running a tavern and making it pay; Gus held forth at length on the fact that his sister-in-law (the one who had had the coincidence in Kansas City) believed that when you died you were born all over again as someone else, which Gus didn't believe altogether though he added, to be on the safe side, that you never could tell. Helene closed the conversation by stating that she didn't know what she had been before her present existence, but she certainly hadn't been a camel, and Gus congratulated Jake on having married such a bright little girl.

As they were about to leave, Malone said very carelessly, "Gus, did you ever hear of Mona McClane?"

Gus was very thoughtful for a moment. "Mona McClane. Yeah, the name is familiar. Wait a minute."

Jake held his breath and concentrated on the painting of a lone deer between two pinkish mountains that hung over the bar, on the labels on the bottles, on the sign that read, IF RED STAR SHOWS ON REGISTER, YOUR NEXT DRINK FREE.

"Mona McClane," Gus said, as though to himself. A light like sunrise broke over his face. "Sure, I remember her. She's the dame who flew the Atlantic in an evening dress."

That was when they decided to go home. Gus bid them an affectionate farewell, extracted a solemn promise to come again, and finally, on parting, clasped Helene's hand.

"It's been a pleasure meeting you, ma'am. If I believed like my sister-in-law from Kansas City, I'd say I must of known you in a previous incarceration."

## *Chapter Twenty-Two*

"We keep on finding plenty of people who had reasons for murdering Joshua Gumbril," Helene observed, starting the car, "but none of them turn out to be Mona McClane."

"She had a reason," Jake said stubbornly, "and I'm going to find it."

"Starting when?" Malone asked icily.

"No time like the present," Jake told him. "Here we are at the beginning of a beautiful new day." He gave an unconvincing imitation of birds chirruping.

The sky was a cold, dismal gray, not light enough to presage the coming of dawn, but enough to indicate that dawn had arrived in some other not very distant place. Driving north, Helene turned into Jackson Park where dark, bare trees stood desolately in the mist and soot-covered snow.

"You don't suppose," Helene began a little wistfully, "that the hotel is still crawling with cops."

"It's easy enough to find out," Malone said. "I'll go in and see if the coast is clear, and if it is, I'll leave you there and go quietly away. After all, I do need to sleep some time."

Jake sighed deeply. "As I remember, we started home hours ago. Maybe this time we can get there."

The outer drive was all but deserted, and for a few minutes the two men were too fascinated by Helene's driving to consider anything else. Forty blocks and an amazingly short time later she rounded the Field Museum and entered Grant Park. The sky had been lighting up by slow degrees and now was a sickish white; to their left the buildings of the Loop were misty and desolate as a city of the dead, to their right the leaden gray lake hurled great cakes of dirty ice against the shore.

Helene slackened her speed a little and Jake recovered his breath enough to speak.

"Malone, what do you think about the Sanders holdup now?"

The lawyer spoke slowly and deliberately, "Looks uncannily as though someone wanted the first Mrs. Sanders out of the way."

"I gathered that all by myself, but who?"

"Maybe the present Mrs. Sanders. Maybe Willis Sanders. Maybe some other person who just didn't like the first Mrs. Sanders. Maybe Joshua Gumbril."

"Why Joshua Gumbril?"

"I don't know," Malone said, his voice sounding as if he didn't give a hoot, either.

"Do you think that had anything to do with his being murdered?"

"Possibly."

"Do you think Mona McClane could have been involved in the Sanders affair?"

"Maybe."

"Do you think Daphne Sanders managed to find out anything about what really happened?"

"She might have."

Jake swore softly, and tried once more. "Do you think, for enough money, Gus would reveal that Gumbril arranged for the murder of the first Mrs. Sanders?"

"For enough money," Malone said crossly, "Gus would swear he was the corpus delicti. Leave me alone, I want to think."

Jake muttered something about uncommunicative so-and-sos, and was silent the rest of the way.

Helene parked the car in front of the hotel. "Malone, you take a look around, and if it's all clear, we'll go in."

Malone didn't appear to have heard. He was staring fixedly at a dark-blue car that had stopped at the curb in front of them. "Huh?"

She repeated her suggestion. He nodded, said, "No doubt," in an absent-minded tone, and continued staring at the car ahead.

"Do you think he could be going into a trance?" Helene asked Jake anxiously.

Several men had emerged from the car, a second, similar car had stopped in front of it. A brief conference appeared to be going on at the curb.

"Malone, what the hell?"

The little lawyer woke to sudden action. "We're all going in together. Come on, and hurry up."

Malone grabbed her by one arm and Jake by the other, and led them across the sidewalk. For all his apparent haste, he crossed the walk in an unconcerned, almost leisurely manner. The instant they were inside the lobby he rushed them toward the self-service elevator, shoved them in, slammed the doors shut, and pressed the button that started the elevator moving upward.

"But, Malone, the cops waiting for Jake—"

"They aren't waiting for Jake, if they're still there at all," the lawyer snapped. "No time to talk now. Do as I tell you, and don't ask questions."

The elevator stopped. He opened the door and said, "Helene, stand here and hold the door open until I signal you to let it go."

Several suitcases were standing before the door of Lulamay Yandry's apartment. The police had gone. As Malone hustled down the hall Lulamay herself stepped out, dressed for traveling.

Downstairs, someone was making frantic efforts to bring down the elevator. Helene took a firmer hold on the door.

Malone had stopped Lulamay and was speaking to her in a hurried whisper. From that distance Helene could catch only a few words. "Men—downstairs now—freight elevator—"

Lulamay's face turned very pale. Abandoning the suitcases and giving the lawyer a brief glance of gratitude and good-by, she turned and ran down the hall and around the corner. In another moment Helene heard the door of the freight elevator slam shut.

Malone signaled to Jake to unlock the door of his apartment, and then waved to Helene to let the elevator door go and hurry down the hall. As she entered the apartment and reached for the door to slam it shut, she heard the elevator starting to go down.

"Malone, who are those men downstairs?"

"The popular name for them is G-Men," Malone said grimly.

"But what do they want?"

"Lulamay. I knew her as soon as I saw her son's picture on the mantel." He scowled. "Maybe I shouldn't have tipped her off, but after all, I'd drunk her liquor."

Helene started to ask another question; Jake laid a hand on her arm.

"They'll come in here to look for her," Malone said, "and we may get messed up in this affair, and then someone may remember we were unduly interested in Gumbril's death—"

"Gumbril!" Helene gasped.

Malone didn't seem to have heard her. "If only we didn't all look so damnably as if we hadn't been to bed all night, they might not start asking questions, but—"

"I'll fix that," Helene said quickly. "Jake, get in bed, clothes and all. Throw your overcoat and hat around and mess up the bedroom a little."

From across the hall they could hear sounds at the door of Lulamay's apartment, loud and repeated knocking, at last the door being forced open. Helene ran into the bedroom, turned over the contents of a suitcase that was packed and ready to go to Bermuda, hauled a negligee from the resulting scramble, put it on over her dress, and began taking down her hair.

"Malone, take off your shoes and lie down on the couch."

The little lawyer obeyed. She threw his overcoat over him, hurried into the kitchen and brought out glasses and empty bottles which she hastily distributed around the room.

A loud knocking began at their door. She ignored it, took off her shoes and stockings, and began pulling down her hair. The knocking continued, and grew louder. Helene gave a last look around the room, saw that Jake appeared convincingly asleep, and that Malone was prepared to let go with what she hoped would be an extremely realistic snore.

She mussed her hair a little more, pulled the negligee around her, opened the door, blinked, and said, sleepily, "Huh?"

The two men at the door paid no attention to her. One of them pushed past her, walked to the bedroom, peered in, walked across the living room, and looked in the kitchenette.

The snore from Malone was a masterpiece of realism.

Helene, by the door, began a sleepy and profane tirade, punctuated with indignant questions. One of the men interrupted her to ask about the neighbor across the hall. She shook her head blankly and went on sputtering.

From the hall she caught the words "Freight elevator." The two men wheeled around and were gone. Helene slammed the door after them, shoved back the bolt, and stood leaning wearily against the wall.

Malone stopped in the middle of a snore, ran to the window, and looked out. Jake and Helene followed him.

Half a block down the street a taxicab was moving south. One of the cars Malone had noticed drew away from the curb and followed. Suddenly a shot rang out, and then another, almost unbearably loud in the early-morning hush. The taxicab careened insanely across the street and stopped abruptly against the curb; its driver leaped out and ran like a rabbit for shelter.

The first shot appeared to have come from the taxicab. It was followed by others. There was a sound of brakes screaming as the pursuing car stopped, and the sound of deeper, more roaring gunfire. The roar continued for a few deafening moments, punctuated by those lone, desperate shots from the barricaded taxicab.

In the distance they could hear a siren, growing steadily louder. It was joined in an instant by another.

Somewhere in a window a woman began screaming.

Jake put his arms around Helene and held her tight. The wailing sirens were very close now.

Suddenly the sound of gunfire ceased. The silence that followed was enormous, overwhelming.

Jake drew Helene away from the window; Malone followed them. For a minute they stood silently in the center of the room.

At last Malone closed his eyes for an instant, opened them again, and said very quietly, "Well, maybe she'll have a chance now to settle accounts with Joshua Gumbril in hell."

## Chapter Twenty-Three

Malone's face had turned a strange, terrible gray.

"If she hadn't expected them, she might have surrendered peaceably, and saved her life, at least for the present." He spoke as though it were extremely hard to form the words. "By warning her, I sent her to her death."

Before either Jake or Helene could speak, he had turned suddenly and walked into the kitchen. After a moment they could hear the sound of water running into a coffeepot.

"Jake—"

"Leave him alone."

She leaned against him, burying her face in his shoulder. "Jake, why? Who was she?"

"Malone will tell us. Give him a little time."

He stroked her pale-gold hair very gently. They stood there for a long time, listening to the faint sounds of the coffee percolator, and to Malone's footsteps as he paced up and down within the narrow confines of the kitchenette.

At last the footsteps stopped. There was a faint rattling of china, then Malone's voice raised in an angry roar.

"Where the hell's the cream?"

Jake felt Helene suddenly relax in his arms. She drew a long, quivering breath.

"There isn't any cream. The coffee just happened to be there, left over from Papa's party."

Malone muttered something unintelligible.

Helene held Jake's hand tight. "That party! Our wedding day! Jake, how long ago was it?"

"We're practically ready to plan a celebration for our golden-wedding anniversary. And I still haven't seen you alone long enough to tell you—"

"That you still love me," she finished for him. She began singing, "Put on your old gray bonnet," in a rather pleasant, slightly off-pitch voice as Malone emerged from the kitchenette with a tray on which reposed a coffeepot and three cups.

The coffee was strong and black and hot. It revived them and warmed them a little. When it was gone, Helene disappeared to change her dress and repair the damage to her hair.

At last she returned, exquisitely dressed and groomed, nothing about her to indicate that she had missed a night's sleep, save perhaps the faint pallor under her fresh make-up. By that time the cold, gray light of early morning had changed to the equally cold, still grayish light of day. Malone, his hands in his pockets and a cigar in the corner of his mouth, stood staring out the window, watching occasional lonesome snowflakes that fluttered down on the wind.

When the little lawyer did speak, his voice seemed normal again, with no trace of emotion, though he went on staring out the window.

"I suppose you're wondering what it was all about," he said evenly.

Helene reached for a cigarette and broke a match loose from a folder before she spoke. "Who was Lulamay Yandry, Malone?"

"Head of a gang of criminals and bank robbers, at one time."

She dropped the cigarette in the act of lighting it. "That little gray-haired lady!"

Mimicking her voice, he repeated, "That little gray-haired lady."

"You said 'at one time,' " Jake said thoughtfully. "What did you mean by that, Malone?"

"Because the gang is history now. One by one its members were wiped out— killed, sent to jail, or executed. There weren't many crimes the gang wasn't credited with; bank robbery was their specialty, but they also went in for a number of sidelines. Kidnaping, stealing cars, and assorted brands of just plain banditry. Lulamay was the brains and she outlasted all the others. A popular name for her was Mother of Criminals. As a matter of actual fact, she was only the mother of two. The oldest is in Alcatraz for life. The younger—Floyd—was Lulamay's favorite."

"It was his picture you recognized over in her apartment night before last, wasn't it?" Helene remembered.

The lawyer nodded. "That was Floyd. Leaving his picture around where anybody could see it wasn't the smartest thing in the world to do. But Lulamay had reached the point where she simply didn't care any more."

He walked away from the window long enough to aim his cigar ash at the nearest tray, missing it by a good three inches. Then he resumed his staring at the sky, somehow managing not to look down at the street where a little crowd of curious bystanders had already gathered.

"What happened to Floyd?" Helene asked at last.

"He was executed by the state of Illinois," Malone told her, "for the shooting of a bank guard in a holdup. That was about six months ago."

Jake said suddenly, "I admit that I was a backward child in school, but I still don't see what any of this has to do with Joshua Gumbril."

"He supplied the information on which Lulamay's boy was arrested, convicted, and executed," Malone said quietly.

"Knowing Gumbril," said Jake, "I have a hunch that was the prize double-cross of the season."

"I gathered," Malone said, "that Gumbril had found Floyd useful at one time, but later thought it wiser to have him out of the way. It probably was a difficulty over a division of money. Gumbril was able to turn Floyd in and keep comfortably in the clear. But he figured without Lulamay. If Mona had waited a day or so longer, Lulamay would have beaten her to it. That was the business that brought her to Chicago."

Helene was deep in thought for a few minutes. "Was that why they were after her this morning—Gumbril's murder?"

"No. Lulamay was wanted for—well, quite a number of things, such as a jailbreak she personally arranged for Floyd a few years ago. Several officers were shot, a deputy sheriff was kidnaped and carried across a state line in a stolen car. Another time—"

The little lawyer drew a picture of Lulamay's life. She had been a farm girl in Tennessee, always ambitious for the ownership of more and better things. Marriage to a moderately poor farmer hadn't toned down her ambition in the least. By the time her two sons were going to the district school, she had transferred her ambitions to them.

Her husband discovered that the making and selling of corn liquor added considerably to the income of the farm, and helped to satisfy Lulamay's demands for continually better clothes and mail-order furniture. The two boys were entering their teens when Lulamay's husband shot it out with revenue men, and lost.

She, considerably more successful in avoiding trouble, carried on his business profitably. By the time repeal came the boys were full-grown, and their mother decided to branch out into other, more fertile fields. In 1936 she and her boys beat a strategic retreat when the Tennessee farm that was their base of operations was raided. Besides a quantity of arms and ammunition, the raiders found stacks of fashion magazines and a copy of Emily Post's *Etiquette.* In 1937, at a time when FBI men were combing the nation for her, she took a leisurely tourist trip to Europe; the means by which she obtained a passport are still a mystery<??p-182>

The year her oldest boy ended up in Alcatraz—that was 1938—she took a large frame house on the edge of a small Indiana town and settled there, becoming immediately popular in the community. The neighborly, gray-haired widow joined the leading church society and the Federated Women's Clubs, thereby making her commodious house an even safer hide-out for unfortunate lawbreakers who were taking it on the lam. Some ten months later citizens of the town were astonished to find their neighbor's face on front pages from coast to coast, after the justly famous and spectacular jailbreak and delivery of Floyd.

"They were bound to catch up with her sooner or later," Malone said very slowly. "And deservedly. I wouldn't have handled her defense for any money. But I'd been her guest, and drunk her liquor. Warning her was a matter of good manners, not morals—not such a delicate distinction in this case."

"Besides," Jake added, "she was a nice old girl, regardless."

It was Lulamay's only obituary.

When Malone spoke again, his voice was slow, almost dreamy. "If I hadn't warned her, they'd have taken her by surprise. There wouldn't have been a chance for any gunplay." He drew a long breath and repeated, "If I hadn't warned her—"

Helene interrupted him quickly. "She'd have been tried and convicted, Malone. Somehow I think if she'd had her choice, she'd have preferred to end it the way she did. It was quicker. Easier."

Malone's silence was long and eloquent.

"Thanks, Helene," he said at last. He struggled into his coat, pulled on his hat. "There may be unexpected repercussions from this business. I'm off to make sure about that now."

"What do you mean?" Helene demanded.

"I'm not just sure what I mean, that's why I'm going to find out. Stay here till you hear from me, just to be on the safe side."

He was gone without any further explanation.

Jake sighed, shook his head, gathered up the empty coffee cups and carried them into the kitchenette. From the kitchenette window he could see the morning sun doing its best to break through the clouds that still blanketed the sky. Fat chance, he told the sun morosely. Just as he had a fat chance of learning why Mona McClane—oh well, the hell with that. Right now—

He walked back into the living room. Helene lay on the sofa, one arm curved around her head, her pale-gold hair loose on the pillow, her long lashes curved against her cheeks. She was very lovely. She was also fast asleep.

## *Chapter Twenty-Four*

After a long time spent watching Helene, Jake began to get tired of waiting for her to wake up. For a while he debated what to do. Perhaps she wanted him to waken her. On the other hand, she hadn't been asleep all night. For that matter, he'd lost a night's sleep himself.

He dozed a little, there in the easy chair. When he looked at Helene again, she hadn't stirred. Maybe if he waited a little longer, she'd wake up of her own accord. But he had a horrible conviction that she'd sleep for hours more, if nothing disturbed her.

Perhaps if she were wakened accidentally. He dropped a book on the floor experimentally. Nothing happened. He opened the window wide and banged it down loudly as he could. It didn't work. At last he noticed a collection of glasses on the table nearest her, and swept them off with one magnificent gesture. She didn't stir.

Well, there was nothing to do but go ahead and wake her. He drew a long breath. After all—

Before he could carry out his intention the telephone rang. He answered it automatically, watching Helene hopefully. The bell hadn't disturbed her in the least.

It was Ellen Ogletree. "I'm sorry to disturb you, Mr. Justus, but something's happened. I must see you."

He scowled heavily at the telephone. "Where are you?"

She was down in the lobby. He scowled again, told her he'd be right down, and banged the telephone on its hook. Oh well, perhaps when he returned, Helene would be awake. He took one last look at her as he went out.

The door of what had been Lulamay's apartment stood open, through it he could see two men going relentlessly through her pitifully scattered belongings. He told himself sternly that the sight didn't unnerve him in the least. All that ailed him was a slight hangover and the loss of a night's sleep. A glance in the elevator mirror confirmed this diagnosis. Everything from his badly mussed red hair to his muddy shoes seemed definitely the worse for wear. His eyes were a trifle swollen and faintly pink. He needed a shave.

Ellen Ogletree and Leonard Marchmont rose from a davenport in the lobby as the elevator door opened. The Englishman looked at him sympathetically.

"You look frightful, Mr. Justus! What's happened to you?"

"I was eaten by cannibals," Jake told him briefly, "and I didn't agree with them. Well, Miss Ogletree—?"

The girl seemed a little uncertain and anxious. "The lobby is unusually full of people, isn't it?"

Jake nodded calmly. "There was a shooting here this morning. Nothing serious, but it drew a crowd. What can I do for you?"

She blinked a minute, decided he was joking, and let it go at that. "I'm looking for Daphne Sanders."

Jake shook his head. "You're asking the wrong guy. She wasn't the girl I took home last night."

Ellen Ogletree frowned. "This is serious, Mr. Justus. She's disappeared." She hesitated a moment, looked around again. "This isn't a very good place to talk."

"Have you had breakfast?" Jake asked.

The girl shook her head. He led the way into the coffee shop and found a table that was reasonably secluded. The thought of breakfast was faintly revolting to him, but Jake couldn't pass up this chance to find out if Marchmont would order tea. He didn't. He sent out to the bar for brandy and soda.

Jake shuddered slightly and waited until his coffee arrived before he spoke. The thought that he might be responsible for Daphne Sanders' disappearance worried him. If Little Georgie was still in the snatch racket, possibly the well-meant introduction had been the wrong move.

Ellen Ogletree's next words put his mind at rest. "She had a frightful row with her family when she got home last night, and she left home."

"Is that all?" Jake said disgustedly. "People are leaving home all the time."

The girl lit a cigarette. Jake noticed that her fingers trembled ever so little. "Her father is almost losing his mind."

"As long as he doesn't lose his beard," Jake said calmly, "he should worry. What was the row about, or do you know?"

"Over—what Daphne said last night. About Fleurette, I mean."

Jake nodded gravely. "Statements like that do bring on family arguments."

"Daphne's very excitable," Leonard Marchmont put in. "It's hard to tell just what she might do."

Jake agreed with that, but he kept his thoughts to himself. "Just what am I supposed to do? Find her?"

The girl smiled wanly, and shook her head. "We thought maybe you'd seen her. We've been out looking for her all morning."

"Sorry, I haven't. Any idea where she might have gone?"

Marchmont said, "She went back to Mona McClane's and spent the night there. But she left there about nine this morning. Ellen thought she might have come here."

"She'll turn up," Jake said reassuringly. "Forget it. Maybe Helene will have some bright ideas when she wakes up."

Ellen Ogletree looked at her watch. "I'll have to forget it for the time being. I'm meeting Mona and Fleurette for lunch and I don't want to be late." She made an appointment to meet Marchmont later and said to Jake, "If you do see her, try and persuade her to go home, won't you? I'm terribly sorry for poor Mr. Sanders."

"I'll do my best," Jake said, "but persuading girls to go home is rather the reverse of my specialty."

Leonard Marchmont was still puzzling over that five minutes after Ellen had gone. At last he gave it up.

"Women are the devil," he said gloomily. "But I suppose you know that."

Jake said, "I'm beginning to suspect it. Why is it any of Ellen's business whether the Sanders girl leaves home or not?"

"Dashed if I know. Let's go into the bar, I can think better there."

Jake finished his coffee, accompanied the Englishman into the bar, ordered a lemonade and felt very heroic about it, took one sip of it and called for rye.

"How do you figure in this, or is it impolite to ask?"

Evidently it wasn't. "I don't. I used to go about with Daphne a bit. Really you know, I didn't want to come along this morning because of that, but when Ellen got the phone call she insisted on my helping look for the girl."

"Either you're a little mixed up, or I am," Jake said. "What call do you mean?"

"From Mr. Sanders," Marchmont said. He reached for one of the drinks, said, "Thanks awfully," and went on. "You see, it was just a bit late when I brought Ellen home. She suggested that since it was so late perhaps I'd best linger about and explain that I'd just arrived to take her shopping. So I lingered about and Ellen popped up the backstairs and changed her frock, and came popping down again by the front stairs and told me she'd found a message from Mr. Sanders asking her to call and that we must duck right out to the corner pharmacist's and call him back." Being completely out of breath he ended with a gesture indicating that the call had been made.

Jake took a gulp of his rye and said, "It's still a little confusing to me."

"Mr. Sanders wanted Ellen to help find Daphne," Marchmont explained slowly, mopping his high, domed forehead. "So we went out to search the neighborhood. Sanders seemed to be frightfully upset. That's quite understandable, but Ellen—" He shrugged his shoulders.

Jake shook his head. "I don't see why she should be so concerned about the Sanders' troubles."

"No more do I," the Englishman said, "unless Ellen's grateful to Mr. Sanders about the position."

"Position?" Jake repeated stupidly. He wondered if he'd slept through something.

Marchmont nodded. "My position. Ellen talked Mr. Sanders into giving it to me. Frightfully good of him, really, you know. All I have to do is to meet a few out-of-town people now and then and take them to lunch. Quite a decent remuneration, too." He sat staring gloomily into his brandy.

"You know," Marchmont said confidingly, "when I came over here five years ago, I really thought I'd have no trouble in finding a good position. I do know a bit about motorcars, you know. Spent a good many years at it. But it seemed to be so frightfully difficult to find anything. Everything was so infernally strange here, you know. I couldn't go home because I knew there wasn't an earthly thing there either. There was really nothing to do but stay on here, and that's frightfully hard when you've no money you know."

Jake felt a moment's sympathy for the Englishman. He could especially understand the money part.

"Ellen spoke to Mr. Sanders last night," Marchmont said suddenly. Jake had a notion the Englishman wasn't talking to him, but to himself. "Curious Mr. Sanders never thought of engaging me himself, when I spoke to him. Ellen turned the trick somehow. Nothing to do with motorcars, though. Something to do with advertising. I'm not sure just what. Mr. Sanders assured me I didn't need to know much about it." He looked faintly puzzled.

"It's something no one knows much about," Jake assured him.

Marchmont smiled at him gratefully. "I really am most appreciative of the position. I presume marriage with Ellen goes with it, but that's not so bad, even with her parents thrown in. Her father's all right if you never ask him for money, and her mother's easy to get along with if you let her win from you at cards now and then, and if you pass along all the gossip you hear to her."

Jake said, "I guessed the latter about Mrs. Ogletree, but not the first."

"She's a passionate gambler," Marchmont told him, emphasizing the words. "But she invariably loses unless you let her win." He sighed. "Oh well, it isn't so bad. I could have done much worse." Suddenly he looked speculatively at Jake. "I say, you haven't done badly yourself, not half badly."

The reason for Leonard Marchmont's friendly acceptance of him, what had seemed to be a sense of kinship in Marchmont's attitude, suddenly became clear to Jake. They were in the same line, but working different territory.

That explanation flashed through Jake's mind in half of a second. In the other half second a punch, brought all the way up from the floor, landed on Leonard Marchmont's aristocratic English nose. Into it went not only Jake's rage at the Englishman, but his past rage at everyone and everything that had irritated him in days. As it landed, sending Leonard Marchmont toppling off his bar stool, Jake realized that for a long time he had wanted to punch someone, damned near anyone, in the nose.

He flung a bill at the bartender and went out, letting the door slam behind him. It seemed to him that his feet didn't come within hailing distance of the floor all the way to the elevator. Indeed, he was so exultantly happy that he had reached the door of the apartment before he began wondering what the morning's events really meant.

Helene still slept, one arm curved around her blonde head, her face childlike, exquisite, a little pale. Jake forgot Ellen Ogletree and her Englishman, Daphne Sanders, and everything else.

As he stood looking at her, deciding just how she should be wakened, her eyes suddenly flew open, like the eyes of a doll. She stared at him for an instant, blinked, and sat up.

"The Casino! That's the link?"

"You're still dreaming," Jake said. "Do you know where you are? Do you know who I am?"

She paid no attention to him. "The link we've been looking for. The missing link. That's it."

"You're thinking of bonds," Jake said patiently. "The bonds of wedlock. Remember?"

There was a knock at the door, and a voice called, "It's me. Malone."

Jake sighed. "All right, damn it. That clergyman was just kidding me along. But tonight, murder or no murder—"

He opened the door and let the little lawyer in.

## *Chapter Twenty-Five*

John J. Malone looked a little more disheveled than usual. Jake suspected, not unjustly, that he had been sleeping in his clothes.

He pulled a newspaper from his overcoat pocket, unfolded it, pointed to the front page, and said, "That's what I expected. I thought you'd like to know."

With the death of Lulamay Yandry, the case of the Gumbril slaying had been brought to a satisfactory conclusion, according to Daniel Von Flanagan. Another paragraph told of the execution six months before of Lulamay's younger son. There was a rehash of his trial, with the news, now printed for the first time, that the information leading to his arrest and conviction had been provided by the late Mr. Gumbril. The Gumbril murder was described in detail. A highly sentimental story, headlined "Mountain Justice" and written by a well-known woman reporter, built a colorful picture of the gray-haired Lulamay coming to Chicago to avenge the death of her boy.

Jake glanced rapidly over the page, tossed the paper on the table, and said, "I wondered why I'd lost my popularity with Little Georgie and Von Flanagan's cops. In fact I was beginning to wonder if it's true what they say in the advertisements. Now I see it's just that I'm in the clear again."

Helene looked at the paper and then at Malone. "Is that what you went tearing off to find out about this morning?"

"No, it wasn't," the lawyer said. He tossed his overcoat inaccurately at the arm of a chair, lit a cigar, and sat down. "I've just been checking up on the early history of Joshua Gumbril, not overlooking his family obligations." He paused, looked at the cigar, and said, "I thought it might be important, and maybe it is."

"Whether it is or it isn't," Helene said, "tell us quick."

Malone cleared his throat. "Joshua Gumbril was born in Waukegan. His father was a harness maker. He had one sister, quite a bit younger, and no brothers. Both his parents have been dead about twenty years. He was considered exceptionally bright in school. So was the sister. She was a little thing, evidently pretty, and very talented."

"How the hell did you find out all this?" Jake demanded.

"If you must know, I've been to Waukegan and back," the lawyer snapped. He puffed at his cigar and went on, "The sister's name was Flora, but everyone called her Flossie. She grew up to be a chorus girl. While Joshua Gumbril didn't seem to have much affection for his family he did have a certain sense of obligation. Enough, at least, to arrange for the death of the first Mrs. Sanders at what must have been some financial loss to himself."

He was looking at the floor, not at their faces.

"After the death of the first Mrs. Sanders," he continued, "Joshua Gumbril's sister, whose name had now become Fleurette, married Willis Sanders as soon as it was decently possible, thus disposing of Mr. Gumbril's family obligations for all time." He knocked the ash from his cigar. "Is there a drink in the house?"

While Jake stared speechlessly at the lawyer, Helene went into the kitchenette, mixed a drink, came back, and handed it to Malone. "I always suspected Fleurette Sanders had been a chorus girl. She was much too well bred and well mannered and conservatively dressed to have been anything else. These days the only women who have what my great-aunt used to call refinement are chorus girls and night-club hostesses."

Jake said, "That's all very well. But you didn't find Mona McClane sitting on one of the branches of the Gumbril family tree."

"I had fun," the little lawyer said moodily. "I always wanted to see what Waukegan looked like in the daytime."

Helene looked at the newspaper again. "Of all the collections of coincidences—"

"There were others," Malone said. He chewed on his cigar for a moment. "It's a curious thing that when Mona McClane made that bet, no one knew the prospective victim she had in mind. Yet of that little group present, outside of ourselves there was hardly one person who didn't have a perfectly good motive for murdering the same man."

He appeared, as he went on, to be talking to some invisible jury. "Take Wells Ogletree," he mused.

"All right, I'll take him," Helene said briskly. "Did he get the fifty-grand ransom money that was paid to Gumbril?" As the two men stared at her she went on, "Yes, I noticed what Ellen Ogletree said. That money came out of her own fortune which was under her old man's trusteeship. Would Wells Ogletree kidnap his own daughter for fifty thousand bucks?"

"For anything over six bits," Jake said promptly, "Wells Ogletree would kidnap the Statue of Liberty."

"It's probable," Malone said absently, "and not impossible. How about Ellen herself?"

"She might have had a motive for murdering Gumbril," Jake said. "It depends on what happened to her while she was in the hands of the kidnapers."

"If you mean what I think you do," Helene commented, "I doubt if Ellen would consider that a motive for murder."

Jake ignored that and said, "How about Daffy Sanders?" He went on to tell of the morning's events. Malone listened, scowling.

"Daphne may just be a little tetched, or she may actually have learned something about her mother's death," the lawyer said. "We can't tell which. We can count her in, though. Willis Sanders likewise. He might have been blackmailed by Gumbril after the slaying, or been afraid that he would be. That's true of Fleurette, too."

"Do you think Gumbril would actually have blackmailed his own sister?" Helene asked incredulously.

"If he had a dual personality," Malone said, "he probably blackmailed himself."

Jake scowled. "Almost everyone there seemed to have a motive for murdering Joshua Gumbril—except Mona McClane."

"There's some link between Gumbril and Mona McClane, all right," the lawyer said savagely, "but what the ding-danged hell is it?"

"It's something to do with the Casino," Helene declared. "I don't know just what it is, but I know it's there, and if you two don't heckle me too much, I'll find it."

Malone sighed. "The question is," he said, "do you want to find her motive?"

"Damn you, Malone," Jake said, "are you going to back out now?"

The little lawyer rose and walked back and forth across the room a few times, his hands in his pockets. "I'm not an officer of the law," he said grimly. "My profession has always put me on the other side of the fence. I've never served the cause of justice," he added gravely, "but rather the cause of injustice."

"If that's your real reason," Helene said smoothly, "I'm a monkey's aunt."

Malone glared at her, took a long draw on his cigar, stamped it out very slowly and deliberately, and said, "Every girl I've considered calling up for a date in the past three days looks like Mona McClane, if that tells you anything at all. The only reason I have for helping pin this crime on her is to win a damn silly bet that never should have been made in the first place."

"All right," Jake said angrily, "forget it."

Malone put on his overcoat, adjusted his muffler, and stood fingering his hat. "Just what are you going to do next?"

"Get the box," Jake said. "It looks like our last hope."

"Look here, Malone," Helene began earnestly, "you can't desert us this way—" Jake waved her to silence.

The lawyer gave his hat one last twirl, finally put it on. "Well, don't get into trouble."

"If I do, I'll get out," Jake said.

"O. K.," Malone said. "I'm sorry."

"Forget it," Jake said miserably.

"Well, I'm sorry anyway," Malone said. He slammed the door on his way out.

The clock above the elevators said two-thirty when the lawyer arrived at his office building. He paused at the drugstore to replenish his supply of cigars and went on up to his office.

He wondered what Jake and Helene were doing.

Suddenly he felt very tired and lonely. Life was all at once very meaningless and very full. Perhaps, he decided, he was getting old.

He opened the door of his office and saw Willis Sanders, very pale and heavy-eyed from lack of sleep, sitting in the anteroom. He was still wearing the neatly trimmed false gray beard.

## *Chapter Twenty-Six*

Willis Sanders rose to greet Malone with a well-managed but unconvincing air of calm. "Your secretary here said she hadn't the faintest idea when you'd be in, but I decided I'd wait just the same—on the chance that you might come along any time."

Malone said, "I seem to be a little late getting down this morning." He opened the door to his private office and added, "Go right in. I'll be with you in a minute."

He turned to the pretty brunette who sat at the typewriter. "Any calls?"

"Nothing of importance, Mr. Malone, except this." She reached for a pad of paper and wrote on it rapidly, "Mrs. Sanders telephoned you a little past noon, asking for an appointment at two o'clock. I didn't mention this to Mr. Sanders when he came in. It's now two-thirty and she hasn't come in or telephoned again."

The lawyer said, "Nice work, dear," and gave her shoulder an affectionate pat. "If she should come in, handle it tactfully." He went on into his office, closed the door, tossed his hat and coat inaccurately at the brown-leather davenport, and said, "Nice to see you. Will you join me in a drink?"

"Thanks," Sanders said. He looked as though he needed one badly.

Malone rummaged through the office for a bottle of rye, finally found it in a file drawer marked UNANSWERED CORRESPONDENCE, located two glasses under an old hat in the closet, dusted them, and poured two drinks before he spoke again. "I see you're still wearing your beard."

Willis Sanders turned faintly pink. "I can't get it off. Not until I locate Partridge and find out how." He finished his drink quickly, spilling a little on his hand, and gratefully accepted a second.

By the time Malone was comfortably settled behind his desk and had lighted a cigar, Sanders had made up his mind to speak.

"That was a damned silly bet Mona made with your friend, wasn't it?"

Malone smiled. "Yes, it was. I'd practically forgotten it."

Sanders smiled weakly in return. "Had you?" He mopped his brow.

"Of course." The lawyer stared fixedly at the end of his cigar. "It was nothing but a joke."

His visitor laughed hollowly. "That's what I thought." He lit a cigarette. "I felt very disturbed, though, by that idiotic remark Daphne made last night. I hope nobody took it seriously."

"Surely no one did," Malone said vaguely and comfortingly.

"I'd hoped not," Sanders said a little too brightly. "Daphne is a strange girl. No telling what she's going to say."

"I don't think anyone paid any attention to her," the lawyer said.

Willis Sanders coughed, clearing his throat. "Amazing, though, about that little Southern woman—what was her name?"

"Yandry, wasn't it?"

"That's it. To think we all sat there making bad jokes about murder, and the very next day she went out and—" He paused, clearing his throat again in an embarrassed manner. "It's just amazing, when you come to think about it, isn't it?"

"Very," Malone said dryly. He knocked the ashes from his cigar. "Very coincidental, as Gus Schenck would say."

"Gus Schenck?"

Malone nodded. "Client of mine."

"Oh," Willis Sanders said. That seemed to be all he had to say.

Malone waited as long as he thought Sanders could stand it before he asked, in his most unconcerned manner, "Did you know in advance that your wife was going to be shot, or did Fleurette tell you about it afterward?"

"Afterward," Sanders answered automatically, "but—" He stopped suddenly and said, "What do you mean?" with a very unconvincing air of indignation.

Malone coughed and said, "Nothing. I just like to know where I stand." He looked thoughtfully at his cigar and said, "One of us has to ask the questions, and it might as well be me. You didn't shoot Joshua Gumbril yourself, did you?"

"Of course not," Sanders said. He added stiffly, "This doesn't seem to be getting us anywhere."

"No, it doesn't," Malone agreed. "Where do you want to get? What the hell brought you up here, anyway?"

Willis Sanders said, "Well—" stopped, and looked embarrassed.

Malone rose, refilled Sanders' glass, and sat down again.

"This is the way it happened," he said thoughtfully. "You started running around with Fleurette. Before you knew it, she had her hooks in you so you couldn't get away. Then she told you she intended to marry you, and that she'd make you a free man in a way you couldn't raise a squawk about." He paused, mopped his face, and said, "Don't mind me, I'm only thinking it over. Maybe you didn't take Fleurette's threat seriously. But the night your wife was killed, you knew what it was all about—no, don't misunderstand me, you didn't know it in advance. But when it happened, you realized right away what was going on. You were just scared enough that when you were questioned, you testified that your wife had screamed and the holdup man lost his head and fired."

He paused, looked at Sanders, and said, "Don't feel embarrassed, I'd have done the same thing myself."

He wondered if Fleurette Sanders had arrived to keep her appointment and how the girl in the anteroom was dealing with the situation if she had.

"You married Fleurette as soon as you decently could," he continued, "because you knew that if you didn't, she'd see to it you were accused of arranging the murder of the first Mrs. Sanders. When you got over the shock of what had happened, you settled down to an existence that was bad, but not damned bad. Fleurette was clever, and people accepted her. Then Daphne began getting a lot of notions in her head. There wasn't a thing you could do. So you hoped for the best and waited to see what would happen next."

He shook his head and murmured, "How I do run on!" In exactly the same tone of voice he asked, "Did you know Fleurette was Joshua Gumbril's sister?"

Sanders looked uncomfortable and said, "Yes. But not till later. Not till after we were married."

Malone shook his head again and said sympathetically, "You must have had a bad hour or so when you learned he'd been murdered."

Willis Sanders said miserably, "I was afraid Daphne had done it. I knew she'd been trying to find out the truth—and—well, then there was that bet, you know— Mona's bet with Jake Justus—and of course when I read about the murder that was the first thing I thought, but then Daphne, and—" He rested his forehead on his hand and said, "I don't know what to do. That's why I came here to talk to you."

"Glad you did," Malone said quietly. "Talk never hurt anybody." He rose, strode to the window, and stood looking across a dismal vista of downtown roofs. "Well, it's a good thing it all turned out as it did. I don't mind admitting I wondered a little about Gumbril's murder myself. But of course it's all cleared up now. The Southern woman certainly was justified, and she's gone beyond the reach of murder trials now."

Willis Sanders leaned forward. "She really did shoot him?"

Malone turned around and said very reproachfully, "You don't think the police department would make a mistake, do you?" turned back to the window, and went on, "Of the people involved in your first wife's murder, Fleurette is in no position to talk. Gumbril is dead, the man who actually fired the shot is gone, God knows where, Gus Schenck is the last man on earth who wants the whole mess stirred up again, and why the hell you want to see a lawyer, I don't know." He turned back from the window to the distraught man, with the friendliest and most reassuring of smiles.

Willis Sanders managed to smile back faintly, and said, "I guess I don't. But when I got to thinking about it, and adding everything up in my mind, it just got me down, and I thought I'd better talk it over with you. Because Mona—" he paused, scowled, and said, "she meant that bet, you know. She said so. And when I read about the Gumbril murder, and it seemed to fit in so perfectly, and then I got to thinking about everything all at once, and—" He stood up suddenly and said, "Oh well, the hell with it. I'm glad I came to see you."

There was a gentle knock at the door. Malone bawled, "Come in," the door opened, and Jake Justus walked in, kicking the door shut behind him.

The tall, red-haired man was unusually pale, there was a heavy frown on his face, and he appeared to be out of breath. Sanders' presence seemed to startle him a little, he greeted him briefly, nodded to Malone, and stood silently by the desk, folding and unfolding the newspaper he had been carrying under his arm.

"Well?" Malone growled. "What kind of a mess are you in now?"

Jake didn't answer. He glanced again at Sanders, then at Malone. Suddenly he unfolded the newspaper and tossed it on the lawyer's desk.

Malone looked at it for a long time without comment, without the faintest flicker of expression on his face.

At last he turned to Willis Sanders and said, "I'd rather you read about it in the papers than tell you myself," and handed him the newspaper. Screaming headlines told of the fatal shooting of Fleurette Sanders at the corner of State and Madison Streets at one forty-five that afternoon.

# *Chapter Twenty-Seven*

Fleurette Sanders had been shot and killed at the northwest corner of State and Madison Streets at precisely one forty-five by the big clock on the corner of the Boston Store. It appeared that she had been going south on State Street and was turning the corner to go west on Madison Street when the shot was fired.

As in the shooting of Joshua Gumbril on the same corner three days before, there was no trace of the killer. Fleurette Sanders' small, fragile body had been carried a little distance by the closely packed crowd of holiday shoppers before she fell. No one had heard the sound of the shot.

There were no details given in the newspaper story, which was confined to a screaming headline and a hasty, last-minute paragraph.

Jake tried hard not to look at Willis Sanders' face as he read. Malone sat by his desk, apparently completely absorbed in the minute examination of a fingernail.

Though the newspaper account of the slaying was not long, it seemed to take a very long time to read. Jake had a feeling that Sanders was reading it over and over slowly, word by word, trying first to realize the import of what it said, and then to believe that what it told was true. At last the big man folded the paper carefully and meticulously along its original creases, and laid it on Malone's desk, without comment and almost without a change of expression.

Jake wished that someone would speak. He couldn't think of anything to say himself.

Malone rose, poured whisky into Willis Sanders' glass and handed it to him without a word. He held the bottle toward Jake, raising one eyebrow in a question. Jake shook his head, then changed his mind, nodded, and held out his hand.

"Where's Helene?" the lawyer asked.

"She's on her way here. She went out looking for her father."

Very slowly and deliberately Malone screwed the cap back on the bottle after Jake had returned it to him, stood it on the desk, looked at it, looked up at Sanders, looked quickly back at the bottle, and said casually, "Did you shoot her?"

Willis Sanders turned pale, said, "Of course not," paused, began to turn a purplish red, and said angrily, "Are you accusing me of—"

"Don't get sore," Malone said quietly. "Nobody's accusing anybody." He added, "It just looked as though I might have you for a client, and I wanted to know whether or not you did shoot her, so I'd be sure where I stand."

"I didn't," Willis Sanders said.

Malone said calmly, "You may have to prove that."

Sanders started to speak, stopped, stared at the lawyer, and then said slowly, "Yes, that's right. I suppose I will be accused of killing Fleurette. But I didn't."

"A man can have one wife murdered without attracting much attention," Malone said, "but when it happens twice, it's liable to arouse suspicion, especially among such imaginative people as policemen. What time did you get here this afternoon?"

"It was—around two o'clock, I guess."

"Where had you been before that?"

"I'd been to lunch at the Palmer House bar."

"What time did you leave there?"

"About one fifteen."

The lawyer swore softly to himself, chewed savagely on his cigar, and, with an I'm-not-gonna-believe-it-anyway note in his voice, said, "Did it take you forty-five minutes to get here from the Palmer House?"

"I guess it must have. I wasn't in any hurry. I hadn't quite made up my mind about coming to see you. I walked about a bit, thinking it over."

"Where did you walk?"

"Let me think. The Palmer House is at Monroe Street. I went out on the Wabash Avenue side and walked west on Monroe Street. When I got to La Salle, I started up here, and then I decided to think it over a little more. So I walked up to Wacker Drive and over to Clark Street, and then I came back here. It was just about two when I arrived."

"A hell of an alibi," Malone growled, "but that's all right." He lifted his head and bellowed loudly, "Maggie!"

The door opened and the pretty, black-haired secretary came in. "Yes, Mr. Malone?"

"Listen, sweetheart, I want you to make a note of this. It was one thirty when Mr. Sanders came to the office, and he stayed until I got here."

"Yes, Mr. Malone."

"What time did Mr. Sanders get here?"

"One thirty, Mr. Malone."

"Did he leave the anteroom at any time?"

"No, Mr. Malone. He sat right there until you came in."

"How do you know it was one thirty when he arrived?"

"Because I'd just called Cathedral eight thousand on the phone to get the correct time to set my watch, and I was listening on the phone when Mr. Sanders walked in. It was exactly one thirty-two, to be strictly accurate."

"Nice work, darling," Malone said. "That's all."

She paused at the door, said, "The buzzer on your desk is working if you need me again," and went out.

"Well," Malone said thoughtfully, "that takes care of that."

"I'm not so sure," Jake interrupted. "That one thirty alibi depends on sweetheart's phone call to Cathedral eight thousand."

"You seem to have the situation well in hand," said Malone. "So what?"

"So the police are not so dumb," said Jake. "They'll check that call, find it was never made, and that's the end of a beautiful alibi."

A happy smile appeared on Malone's face. "That bright thought occurred to me before you were born," he said. "Why do you suppose I pay sweetheart out there a salary?"

Jake smirked. "You could sue me for libel if I told you."

"That's something else again," said Malone smugly, "and we don't call it salary. But one of her jobs is to call Cathedral eight thousand every half-hour. Nine working hours every day. Six working days every week. One hundred and eight potential little alibis."

"Well I'll be damned," said Jake with awe.

Malone nodded. "A few of my clients would have been if I hadn't thought of that simple scheme. But so far as Mr. Sanders is concerned, we're not in the clear yet. If some dope turns up who knows you and who happened to see you wandering around the streets at five minutes to two, we may have to think fast. But I've thought fast before."

"Not fast enough," Jake said. "Anybody who ran into him on the street at five to two would have thought he was George Brand. You're forgetting the beard."

Willis Sanders started, blinked, put one hand up to his chin, and felt uncertainly of the false hair.

"Of course," Malone said, "of course!" His voice was a nice mixture of awe and wonder. "That beard is almost providential." He looked searchingly at his new client. "The trick now is to keep you out of harm's way until you've gathered your wits enough to talk."

Before he could offer any suggestions, Helene arrived. She started to speak, saw Willis Sanders, turned a shade paler than she was already, finally said, "Well!" and sat down.

Sanders looked up at her. "I didn't do it."

Helene said soothingly and absent-mindedly, "Of course not," sat down and lit a cigarette with white, nervous fingers.

"Helene," Malone asked suddenly, "where's your father?"

"Downstairs in the car."

"Awake?"

"Reasonably."

"Run down and bring him up here."

She rose, smiled at him wanly, and went out.

"Sanders, how well do you know George Brand?" Malone asked gently.

"He's as good a friend as I have," Sanders said.

"That's lucky," Malone said. He looked at his watch and remarked comfortingly, "There's plenty of time, don't worry."

A moment later Helene arrived with George Brand. Malone handed him the newspaper, he read it silently, dropped it on the desk, stared at Sanders and then at Malone.

"You don't think he'll be accused, do you?" he demanded indignantly.

The lawyer's only answer was to shrug his shoulders.

"That's utter rot," George Brand said. "People like Sanders don't go around murdering their wives."

"That's what you think," Malone said agreeably. "But it might be hard to get the police to accept your opinion as evidence. I want you to look after Sanders for a while." He turned to the unhappy man. "Did you drive downtown?"

"Yes."

"Where's your car?"

"In a parking lot on Wacker Drive."

"You and Brand go up there and get it," Malone said, "and drive straight home. Let the news be broken to you when you get there. Don't talk to anybody." He paused and said very firmly, "Get this straight now. You came downtown this morning, had lunch at the Palmer House, came straight to my office, waited for me about an hour, talked with me about a personal matter which you are not required to divulge to anybody, met Brand here, and went home. Understand?"

Sanders nodded.

"Good," the lawyer said. "Now tell me exactly where you went and what you did."

Sanders cleared his throat nervously, looked hesitantly at George Brand, and repeated exactly what Malone had told him.

"Very nice," Malone said. "You'll do. As far as what may come up next, I'll meet it as it comes. That's what I'm here for. So go home now, and relax. Mr. Brand, keep him from talking to anyone. And for the love of Mike, shift that interchangeable beard back to its original owner."

George Brand nodded. "Don't worry, I will. I'll take care of everything."

Sanders rose, fastened his overcoat, picked up his hat, started toward the door, stopped, and said, "But who did kill Fleurette?"

"Don't look at me," Malone said crossly. "I've been too busy."

"Of course. I only thought—" He paused, dropped his hat, and picked it up again. "Somebody did."

"Evidently," Malone agreed. "That's not for you to worry about. Let the police do the worrying. That's what you pay taxes for."

"Mona—" Sanders said suddenly. His voice stopped as though it had been cut off somewhere deep in his throat.

"This does coincide with the terms of her bet, doesn't it?" Malone said easily and unconcernedly. "Assuming of course that she wasn't joking when she made it."

"She wasn't joking," Sanders said.

"Did Mona McClane have any reason for murdering your wife?" Malone asked without looking up.

"No. Not as far as I know."

"Forget the bet," the little lawyer advised. "If anything unexpected turns up, you'll hear from me. And don't worry."

At the door Sanders paused again, his hand on the knob. He hesitated a moment, finally said, "Thanks," very awkwardly and in a low voice, and was gone. George Brand waved reassuringly to Malone and followed him out.

Malone sat motionless until he heard the corridor door open and shut. Then he bawled loudly, "Maggie!"

She came in, muttered something about the buzzer being in working order.

Malone said patiently, "When Fleurette Sanders phoned for an appointment, where did she call from, or do you know?"

"From a telephone booth. I know because when I told her you weren't in and I didn't know where you were, and asked if I could call her back when I did hear from you, she said that she was calling from a phone booth and I couldn't call back."

"Wonderful," Malone said.

The girl strolled over to the desk, picked up the newspaper, glanced quickly through the account of the murder of Fleurette Sanders without a sign of surprise, put the paper down, and commented, "Mr. Sanders didn't act like a man who had just shot his wife."

"He hadn't," Malone told her.

She shrugged her shoulders, said, "You don't have to practice your act on me," and went out, slamming the door.

Malone looked at his watch, rose, and turned on the little radio that stood on the bookcase. "There's a news broadcast in a few minutes. It may have some later dope."

He fiddled with the dial until sweet Hawaiian music came from the loudspeaker, then returned to his desk and sat staring moodily at the half-empty bottle of rye.

"I seem to be back in this damned mess whether I like it or not."

"You didn't have to take Sanders as a client," Jake said indignantly.

"Hell," the lawyer said, "he's the only client I could get." He frowned angrily at the bottle.

Jake said, "Sanders' story sounded fishy as hell to me."

Malone nodded. "Me too. That's why I believe it. No man as smart as Willis Sanders would deliberately make up that story."

"Very pretty reasoning," Helene commented, "but it won't count for much in court."

Malone started to answer, halted, and turned his attention to the radio. The Hawaiian music had ended, and an anonymous voice had begun to speak, faintly and indistinguishably. Malone bounded across the room, turned a knob, and the voice suddenly became loud and full.

". . . slaying at the corner of State and Madison Streets this afternoon . . ."

"That's it," Malone said quickly.

"Officer Garrity, who drove the police ambulance, stated that when the ambulance arrived at the morgue, and he and officer Lally went to remove the body from the ambulance—" the voice paused and for a moment appeared to be having trouble "—the body appeared to be in a completely unclad condition." The voice paused again unexpectedly.

"What the hell?" Jake asked of the anonymous voice.

"Police Officer Garrity stated that he was completely mystified. He said, quote,

I've been on the force for twenty years and I've never known such a thing to happen before. I don't believe it. Unquote. Witnesses and the traffic officer who saw the body placed in the police ambulance stated clearly that the body was, at that time, completely dressed. Both officers Garrity and Lally are positive in their statements that the ambulance made no stops at all between the corner of State and Madison Streets and the morgue. Neither of them is able to offer any explanation for the condition of the body on its arrival at the morgue. . . . La Porte, Indiana. School-board authorities here stated today that the student strike was under—"

Malone bounded up and shut off the anonymous voice.

Helene started to ask a question. The little lawyer waved at her to be quiet, picked up the telephone and began calling various numbers, until at last he found the policeman who had driven the ambulance. The policeman, it seemed, was an old friend. Malone carried on a long conversation with him, alternating brief questions with, "You don't say so!" and, "Well I'll be damned!" Then he hung up.

"Garrity says," the little lawyer said in a curiously weak voice, as though he didn't believe it himself, "he says that the body of Fleurette Sanders was put into the ambulance at State and Madison Streets fully dressed, and that he and his pal drove direct to the morgue, without a stop. When they got there and went to remove the body, they found it in what the radio announcer referred to so delicately as an unclad condition. Garrity's own phrase was, 'It was as naked as a worm.' "

## *Chapter Twenty-Eight*

Jake stamped out his cigarette and said, "Would you mind telling me just why the clothes were taken off Fleurette Sanders' body between State and Madison Streets and the morgue?"

"I'll go you one better," Malone said. "Will somebody please tell me how they were taken off?"

Helene said, "Send that one to 'Information, Please!' and it'll get you an encyclopedia. Just what Jake and I need for those long winter evenings."

"Someone's insane," Jake said, "and I hope it's the police department, but I'm not sure."

Malone shook his head. "Things that look as mad as this seldom are. When someone appears to be completely insane, that's the time to look for a very logical, fixed, and usually diabolical purpose."

"Forgetting the strip tease, for the moment," Jake said, "who murdered Fleurette Sanders?"

"Don't look at me," Malone said, shrugging his shoulders. "I wasn't even there."

"Mona McClane?" Helene asked, "or am I getting a fixation neurosis?"

"Either Mona McClane," the lawyer answered, "or someone trying to look like Mona McClane." He clasped his hands behind his head and leaned perilously far back in his chair. "Someone wanted to murder Fleurette. That person heard Mona McClane make that damned bet. Then the murder of Joshua Gumbril showed the way. If Fleurette met her death in the same manner and at the same place, Mona would get the credit for both corpses. Not a bad idea, either."

He paused and counted on his fingers. "Besides ourselves, Willis, Sanders, Daphne, Ellen Ogletree, Wells Ogletree, and Mrs. Ogletree listened in on that bet. And of course there was Mona McClane—" He paused and scowled.

"Why the hell would Mona McClane want to murder Fleurette?" Helene asked.

"Why would she want to murder Joshua Gumbril?" the lawyer asked in return. "There simply isn't any motive. No matter where you turn, there's no trace of a motive." He groaned, leaned his forehead on his hands, and said, "It's like barking your shins against a stone wall."

"You mean it's like barking up the wrong shin," Helene said acidly.

Malone ignored her. He rose, walked to the window, and looked out across the snow-covered roofs.

"I still believe," he said at last, addressing himself solely to the roofs, "that this is a case of motive and not of method. Why did Mona McClane want to murder Fleurette Sanders?" Apparently the roofs refused to answer. He went on, "When that bet was made, it was Fleurette Sanders who said, 'By all means, Mona, pick someone who won't be mourned.' She laughed as she said it. Mona McClane said 'I can think of any number of people who wouldn't be mourned in the least.' And she didn't laugh. The motive for the murder of Fleurette Sanders might lead to the motive for the murder of Joshua Gumbril. It's far easier to imagine Mona McClane having a motive for murdering Fleurette. At least we know they'd *met* each other." He drew a long, almost sighing breath and turned away from the window. "It's easier to imagine that such a motive exists. It may not be easier to find it."

He returned to the desk, sat down heavily in his chair, uncapped the bottle and drank from it, shoved it across the desk, and said, "Help yourselves."

Helene carefully filled the two glasses to exactly the same point, handed one to Jake, emptied the other, and said, "The link between Mona McClane and Joshua Gumbril is Max Hook. That's what I've been trying to tell you."

Malone said to Jake in a sympathetic tone, "It's a shame, having your wife lose her mind. And on your honeymoon, too."

"I have not lost my mind," Helene said firmly. "And if this is a honeymoon, Elinor Glyn has been badly misquoted."

Jake nodded grimly and said, "There's plenty of connection between Max Hook and Joshua Gumbril."

"There is," Malone said, "but—"

"Mona McClane owns the Casino," Helene reminded him. "Who used to own the Casino?"

Malone thought for a moment, and said, "Max Hook," in a very low voice.

Helene turned to Jake. "It's too bad," she observed, "having your best friend lose his memory—"

"Damn it," Malone said. "How do we know how many hands the Casino may have passed through before Mona McClane got it?"

"We don't," Helene said calmly. "But it's the first hint of any connection between Mona McClane and the murdered man."

There was a discreet knock at the door before Malone could answer, and the black-haired secretary came in, carrying a large package wrapped in brown paper.

"For you, Mr. Justus. A Mr. Partridge brought it. He said a messenger boy brought it to your hotel, and he thought it might be important."

"Who from?"

"He didn't know. He just left it for you and went away." She laid the package on the desk and was gone.

Jake reached for the package, turned it over several times, and shook it.

"It doesn't tick, by any chance?" Malone asked interestedly.

"No," Jake growled. "If it did, I'd let you open it." He reached for his pocket-knife, cut the string, threw it at the wastebasket, and began unwrapping layers of brown paper.

"Maybe it's liquor," Helene said hopefully.

Jake ignored her, let the wrapping paper slip to the floor, and looked curiously at a gaily colored gift box from a Loop department store.

"Maybe I shouldn't open it before Christmas," he said thoughtfully.

"You shouldn't, but you will," Helene predicted.

He sighed, lifted the cover of the box, dropped it on the floor, and said, "What the hell?"

"What *is* it, Jake?"

By way of answer he took from the box what was probably one of the most perfect platinum fox muffs in the civilized world. Helene gasped.

"Why would anybody send me a muff?" Jake demanded. "Do I look like a piano player?"

Helene was staring at the muff, her eyes blazing. "Jake! That muff! It's Mona McClane's!"

"Are you sure?"

She nodded. "I'm positive. It's the only one in Chicago." She caught her breath and added, "It's famous. There are only two or three others anywhere in the world."

Malone growled, "Let me see it," examined the muff, felt of it, said, "There's something inside it," lifted it up by one end and shook it gently. Something small and heavy and metallic fell to the desk top with a startlingly loud sound. It was a flat, compact, black, and ugly gun.

"That tells exactly how it was done," Malone said. His voice was curiously hoarse. He picked up the gleaming blob of fur and turned it over and over in his hands.

"The sound of the shot," Helene began. She stopped, seeing the lawyer's rapt face.

He didn't seem to have heard her. "The simplest thing in the world. Just walk down the street carrying a muff. The gun is in one hand, inside the muff." He picked up the gun in his right hand, slipped it inside the fur, and held the muff with both hands. It looked strange and incongruous against his wrinkled blue suit. "Then get right up behind your victim in the crowd, and shove one end of the muff against him, like this—" He suddenly held the open end of the muff against Jake, who jumped.

"Then simply fire, with the gun still in the muff," the lawyer mused.

"Damn it," Jake said indignantly. "Stop using me for a model. It makes me nervous."

Malone sat down at his desk and continued in the same meditative vein. "Any sound of the shot—and especially surrounded as it was by the terrific racket of State and Madison Street traffic at that hour of the day—would unquestionably be most effectively muffled."

"Use a muff to muffle with," Helene commented. "It sounds like an advertising slogan."

"It's a swell muff," the lawyer said admiringly. He leaned back in his chair, his hands still tucked into the fur. "Yes, it's a lovely muff. I wonder if Jake is legally entitled to keep it."

"Whether I am or not, I wish you'd put it down," Jake complained. "It's damned unbecoming to you."

"It feels so nice and soft and warm," Malone said wistfully. He laid the muff back on his desk with an air of regret and sat stroking the fur with his short-fingered hands. "So that was how it was done," he said again, almost to himself. "A gun in the muff is worth two in the hand."

Helene sat down on a corner of the desk and lit a cigarette. "Evidently Mona didn't credit Jake with enough intelligence to figure that out for himself."

"Sending this to me is something in the nature of a challenge," Jake said. He grinned and added, "Mona McClane has definitely thrown down the muff."

"Maybe if you just sit around and wait long enough," Helene said coldly, "she'll send you the motive, too."

"Possibly," Jake said. "But I'd rather not wait. Malone, I want to know if the bullet that killed Fleurette came from the same gun that killed Joshua Gumbril."

By way of answer, the little lawyer picked up the telephone and put a call through to Daniel Von Flanagan of the Homicide Squad. The ensuing conversation was, in turn, amiable, cajoling, demanding, vituperative, and profane. It ended with Von Flanagan giving the requested information but not until Malone had asked him, in the most innocent of tones, whether he'd ever told his wife about the twelve hundred dollars he'd won on that horse at Arlington Park.

Malone put down the telephone. "It has already been established that the bullet that killed Joshua Gumbril and the bullet that killed Fleurette Sanders came from the same gun."

"What does that mean?" Helene asked.

"It means that the two bullets came from the same gun," Malone said crossly. "Don't bother me." He went back to his post at the window. "I had thought I was decently out of this. Now I seem to be in it up to my neck. If I have Sanders as a client, I'll probably have to find out who killed his wife."

He scowled heavily and said, apparently to the window, "We ought to get that damned box from the ledge outside Gumbril's room."

"If you can think of a better way than burning down the Fairfax Hotel," Helene began. "Jake, what is it?"

"Gun," Jake said. His eyes were blank. He didn't seem to be addressing anybody.

"Yes, dear," Helene said soothingly. "Gun. It shoots. Goes bang-bang. Just keep quiet for a minute and you'll feel better."

He waved at her as though she were a particularly noisy mosquito. "Wait a minute. That particular gun." He rubbed the palm of his hand over his forehead. "It's something terribly important, but I've forgotten it."

Helene and the little lawyer stared at him anxiously.

"Were you drunk or sober when you thought of it?" Helene began.

"Drunk," Jake said, as though he were speaking in a trance. "But I didn't think of it. I found it. Found—it. Wait a minute, don't tell me—" A yellowish light began to flicker in his eyes.

Helene filled the water glass about one third full of rye and handed it to him. He took it from her, emptied it almost automatically, and went on staring into space. "Gun," he said again. His eyes suddenly seemed to be the color of the paper that is wrapped around absorbent cotton.

Malone had begun counting under his breath.

Suddenly Jake reached in his pocket, drew out the twin to the gun on Malone's desk, and tossed it down before the little lawyer. "I found that in Mona McClane's library table drawer last night," he said calmly.

Helene stared at the two guns. "They're Ike and Mike," she said feebly.

"A pair," Malone agreed.

Jake told briefly of finding the gun and putting Little Georgie's in its place. He remembered and added the conversation he had heard between Willis and Fleurette Sanders, in which there had been talk of blackmail.

"So that's what you were doing all the time you were missing from the living room," Helene exclaimed.

"What did you think I was doing?"

"If I told you," she said, "Malone would save it for divorce evidence." She turned to the lawyer. "What do you think now about the guns?"

"I think Mona McClane owned them," Malone said. He picked up a piece of ribbon that had been tied around the Christmas box, tied it with a decorative bow around the gun Jake had taken from his pocket, murmured. "For identification purposes only," and dropped that gun in his desk drawer.

"The question is," he began, slamming the drawer shut. A ring on the telephone interrupted him.

Malone answered it, said, "Yes he is," handed the telephone to Jake, and said, "For you. A woman."

Jake carried on a brief conversation consisting mostly on his side of, "Yes," and, "Yes, we'd be delighted." He ended with, "In fifteen minutes." He put the receiver down and said, "We're joining Mona McClane in a drink at the Drake bar in fifteen minutes."

They stared at him. "What's the idea?" Malone asked.

"You know as much as I do," Jake said.

The lawyer shook his head. "Maybe she's just lonesome." He repacked the muff in its box with loving care, retied it in the brown-paper wrapping, put it in the bottom left-hand drawer, and locked the drawer. He looked thoughtfully at the gun that had been inside it, finally slipped it into his own coat pocket.

"Why take that along?" Jake asked.

"I don't know. I might want to use it for a paperweight. Come on, get your coats on."

"Malone," Helene demanded sternly, "what are you going to do with that gun?"

He looked at her irritably. "If you must know, I'm going to give it to Von Flanagan. Now stop badgering me, and come on."

## *Chapter Twenty-Nine*

"*So* nice to see you," Mona McClane said. She stretched her shoulders, slid a great mass of pale beige furs onto the leather seat next to her, curled her fingers around the slender stem of her cocktail glass, and closed her eyes for just one instant. "*So* nice to be here, after shopping all day in the snow and the slush and the horrid weather."

"Shopping?" Jake inquired politely.

She nodded. "For Christmas. It's just a few days away. Remember?"

"Oh yes," Jake said, as though he had forgotten it. "I've had one Christmas present already. It came this afternoon."

"Have you?" she said, lifting her brows ever so little. "How wonderful!"

Conversation lagged. Jake sat looking at Helene and thinking that she was easily the most alluring female within the corporate limits of the city of Chicago. He wondered when he'd ever be able to do anything about it. Her skin, delicately pale from lack of sleep, seemed fragile and soft as a moth's wing. Her eyes were very large and luminous. Two or three snowflakes were still clinging audaciously to the pale gold of her hair, sparkling there like crystal.

"Too bad about Fleurette, wasn't it?" Mona McClane said unexpectedly. There was nothing even remotely like regret in her voice, her little pointed face was bland and unconcerned.

"Yes indeed," Jake said calmly.

"I wonder how Willis is taking it."

"Probably very well," Malone said.

She nodded and said, "I would imagine so. I always rather suspected she either bullied or blackmailed him into marrying her."

"So?" Helene said, raising one eyebrow.

"He must feel rather relieved," Mona said, twirling her cocktail glass in her small hands, liking the coolness of its touch.

"Possibly he does," Malone agreed, "unless of course he should be arrested for the murder."

She set the glass down sharply. "Surely there's no danger of that."

"You never can tell. When it's publicly assumed that a man feels rather relieved when his wife is killed, the police are apt to jump to conclusions and make no end of silly mistakes. Especially when he's already had one wife killed under highly suspicious circumstances."

With only the faintest shadow of a frown she said, "That would be tragic, wouldn't it?"

Malone said, "It could be."

There was a little pause before Mona McClane said, "Did you hear that absurd story about her body arriving at the morgue without its clothes?"

"I did," Jake said, nodding. "Absurd or not, it's undoubtedly true."

She laughed. "Even if it's true, I don't believe it. Things like that just can't happen."

Jake shrugged his shoulders. "Things like that just do happen. The true things are usually the unbelievable ones."

"But"—she frowned again—"unless the policemen are lying, or having hallucinations—"

"A lot of policemen are liars," Jake told her, "but very few of them ever have hallucinations. And there would be no reason for the police to lie about this."

She shook her head, signaled to the bartender, and said, "The police don't always need a reason."

Helene asked, "Did you know the first Mrs. Sanders?"

"Not very well. No, not well at all. Oh, of course I'd met her a number of times. But I was away so much during the years Willis was married to her that we really never got acquainted. She was a Boston girl, rather dull, I understand. I don't think he was happy with her." She added, "Willis and I were next-door neighbors when we were children. I'm very fond of him. That's why I put up with Fleurette myself and encouraged other people to do the same thing."

"You lunched with her only today, didn't you?" Malone asked in an offhand, unconcerned manner.

"Yes, I did. Just before it—happened." She gave the faintest little gesture of displeasure, nothing more than that. "She and Ellen Ogletree. Daphne Sanders has left home, you know."

"She has?" Jake said, giving an almost perfect imitation of wide-eyed innocence. "When did that happen?"

"After last night's row. Really, publicly accusing your stepmother of murder is bound to bring on a family upheaval of some sort. Mrs. Ogletree told me about it at lunch. She always knows all the gossip, true and untrue."

"Don't tell me she told you about it in front of Fleurette!"

"Oh no. Molly Ogletree is tactless, but not that tactless. Fleurette had gone to make a phone call. Ellen had left the table—gone to the washroom, I guess. The minute they were out of hearing, Mrs. Ogletree told me all about it." She laughed, a tinkling, silvery little laugh. "It would have broken Mrs. Ogletree's heart if I'd told her I'd known it all the time."

Jake murmured, "Do you train little birds, or are you psychic?"

"Neither. Daphne stayed at my house last night." She laughed again. "I run a house of refuge for fugitives from family rows. Ellen had a quarrel with her father Friday night and spent the night with me. Last night, I had Daphne." She paused to light a cigarette, and said, "You can't possibly be interested in all that."

Jake assured her, "The impossible is my specialty."

Helene held his hand tight under the table and said very lightly, "What have you been doing all day, Mona?"

Mona McClane shrugged her shoulders wearily. "Oh—shopping and running around. After lunch I felt terribly tired of stores and crowds and Christmas decorations and I thought I'd go to the Art Institute. We all separated after lunch. I walked down to the Institute, but when I got there I didn't feel like going in, so I walked about on the avenue and went back to Field's. Mrs. Ogletree went off to some dull lecture, Ellen went off somewhere—shopping, I guess—and Fleurette—" she paused delicately for just an instant and said, "went to her death."

"Don't!" Helene said. It was almost a gasp.

Mona McClane looked at her quickly. "My dear! I'm so sorry. I didn't mean to startle you." She smiled thoughtfully, put her head on one side, and said, "Yet after all—if Daphne Sanders' accusation was correct, and Fleurette did have something to do with the death of the first Mrs. Sanders, this could be called a kind of divine retribution, couldn't it?"

"It could," Malone said gravely, "but the police have a peculiar habit of calling that murder in the first degree."

"I suppose that's true," she said gravely. "Let's have one more drink before we go, and talk of pleasanter things."

They finished the drink to an accompaniment of talk about the current ballet season. Then Mona McClane fastened her caramel-colored furs about her throat.

"I wish I didn't have to go, but I must." She smiled at Jake. "How are you getting on with your bet?"

"I'm working on it," Jake assured her gravely. He felt Helene's fingers stiffen in his own.

Malone said unexpectedly, "Are you going to be at home this evening?"

She nodded. "Yes, all evening. Why?"

"I just wanted to know where to reach you," the lawyer said. "It's just remotely possible Jake may have something to tell you before the night's over."

She tossed her head and laughed. "I'll expect you with a pair of handcuffs in your hand." Suddenly her smooth, calm voice took on an intent, electric quality. "Yes, I'll be at home all evening. Good luck, Mr. Justus, and good hunting." She waved a farewell.

The little lawyer stood staring after her as though he had been stricken with paralysis. Helene shivered. Jake put on his hat, shoved it on the back of his head, and looked thoughtful. Suddenly he said, almost to himself, "Now why the hell did she say that?"

"I don't know," Malone said grimly, "but I do know that she meant it." He tucked an arm through Helene's. "Let's go deliver her pretty little gun to Von Flanagan."

Jake glared at the lawyer. "What the hell's the idea? Are you trying to do me out of a bet?"

"I'm trying to help, you idiot. Isn't that what you wanted me to do?"

"It's no help if you tip off the cops before I have a chance to prove this thing myself."

Malone sighed. "We're not tipping off the cops," he said wearily, "if you'll keep your mouth shut and let me do the talking. We're just going to find out one very important thing that we can't find out for ourselves. And it may be the one thing that you need to know."

## Chapter Thirty

"I'm an honest cop, and I do my duty," Daniel Von Flanagan growled. He caught

Malone's eye, looked away quickly, and added, "Maybe I've made a few mistakes in my life, but show me a guy who hasn't. I never wanted to be a cop. I
never should of been a cop. But I do the best I can, and why people should go
out of their way just to make life hard for me, I don't know."

He glared at his three visitors as though they, personally, were responsible for
all his troubles.

"That woman came up here from the South just to kill Joshua Gumbril," he
roared. "She came up here to kill him and he got killed and she was starting
back home when the FBI men got her. I ask you, did it look like she done it?
Now this Sanders dame goes to work and gets herself killed in the same way
with exactly the same gun, so now it looks like it was somebody else killed
Gumbril too. The Lord only knows who'll get killed next. It's getting so it's not
safe for citizens to walk around on the public streets."

He paused, reached in his desk drawer, and pulled out the pamphlets advertising the joys of Georgia pecan-raising, looked at them wistfully for a moment,
thrust the papers back in the drawer, and slammed it shut.

"State and Madison Streets, of all places," he muttered in disgust. His voice
rose to an angry bellow. "And who took her clothes off, that's what I want to
know. Who took her clothes off?"

"Don't look at me," Malone said mildly, "I didn't do it." He lighted a cigar,
looked at it thoughtfully for a moment, and said, "Personally, I think you boys
cooked up that story."

"You do, huh," said the police officer, his face slowly turning purple. "You
think it's a fake, huh!" Suddenly he pounded violently at a buzzer on his desk
and bawled, "Garrity!" at the top of his voice.

Malone said, "There's a limit to what I believe, that's all."

Von Flanagan glared at him. It seemed entirely possible that he was beyond
speech.

The door opened and a tall, thin policeman walked in. There was a puzzled
look on his face. It seemed to have been there for a long time.

"Garrity," Von Flanagan said a shade more quietly, "what was the condition
of Mrs. Sanders' body when you put it in the police ambulance?"

"It was dead," the policeman said promptly.

"No, no, *no*," Von Flanagan shouted. He drew a quick breath and asked, "What
was the condition of the body as regards its clothing?"

"Oh," said Garrity. "It had it on. What I mean to say is, the body was dressed."
He looked at Malone almost plaintively.

"Was anyone in the ambulance besides Lally and yourself up in the front
seat?"

"No. Except the corpse."

"Did you make any stops between State and Madison Streets and the morgue?"

"No. We didn't stop no place."

Von Flanagan drew another, slower breath, looked fixedly at the unhappy policeman, and snapped, "What happened when you got to the morgue?"

Garrity looked up with a puzzled frown. "We stops the ambulance and me and Lally goes around to the back of the ambulance, and he opens the door and looks in and hollers, 'My God, Garrity, she ain't got no clothes on.' " He paused and added, "She hadn't, neither. Not a stitch on her." He looked appealingly at Malone. "I don't see how it could of happened. I don't believe it could of happened. I been on the force for twenty years, and I never heard of no corpse undressing itself on the way to the morgue." He paused again, scowled, and said, "I tell you, it ain't my fault."

"All right, Garrity," Von Flanagan said wearily. "You've said that before. Now beat it."

Policeman Garrity strode to the door, opened it, paused for a moment there, finally roared, "It ain't my fault!" and slammed the door by way of emphasis.

"There you are," Von Flanagan said. "That's the way it was. You explain it."

"Sure," Malone said easily. "The body was robbed."

The officer stared at him. "Sure. The body was robbed. Just like that. Somebody liked the clothes, I suppose. You wouldn't like to suggest how the body was robbed, would you?" His face was slowly turning purple again. "This is the sort of thing that makes me mad. Why people should go out of their way to make life hard for me—" He stopped, suddenly looked at his visitors as though he had just noticed they were there. "And now what the hell do you want?"

"I came up here to do you a favor," Malone said coldly. "If you don't want to be bothered, forget it."

Von Flanagan looked at him gloomily. "All right, damn you, I'm sorry. What is it?"

Malone slipped his right hand in his pocket, kept it there. "It isn't exactly a favor, it's a trade." He cleared his throat and spoke in his most persuasive tone. "Von Flanagan, if I could locate a certain gun and turn it over to you, would you have it tested to find out if it's the one that shot both Gumbril and the woman, and let me know the result of the test?"

"Sure," Von Flanagan said quickly, "sure, sure, sure. Where's the gun?"

"Hold on a minute. Will you agree not to ask me where I got the gun for a period of twenty-four hours?"

Von Flanagan stared at him sourly. "I can't do that. It's allowing you to withhold evidence."

Malone shrugged his shoulders. "O. K. Forget I mentioned it." He began fastening his overcoat.

"Wait a minute," the police officer said. "Don't be in such a rush." He scowled and said, "Twenty-four hours. I might do it. Yes, maybe I might do that." He looked up at Malone. "Where is this here gun?"

Malone drew the gun from his pocket and laid it on Von Flanagan's desk. "There you are."

Von Flanagan stared at the gun, at Malone, and back at the gun. Then he picked it up gingerly. "It could be the one," he said almost grudgingly. "Yes, it could be. It won't be hard to find out." He looked at the lawyer with a sudden expression of gleeful triumph. "You didn't say anything about not having the ownership traced."

Malone said, "Go as far as you like. And let me know what you find out, will you? I don't know myself who owns it."

Von Flanagan grinned. "I will, before your twenty-four hours are up." He looked at the gun again and then at his watch. "Better than that, I'll bet you two quarts of gin that if it was bought in Chicago, I'll have it traced before midnight."

"Done," Malone said coldly. "I'll take you on that. Not because I doubt you can do it, but because I know you'll do it quicker if there's two quarts of gin in it for you."

Jake started to speak, stopped himself. What in blazes was Malone doing?

Von Flanagan was still regarding the gun very thoughtfully. "Malone, who's your client?"

"I have none in connection with this case," the lawyer said promptly.

The police officer sighed. "I won't call you a liar, but by God, I don't believe you. Listen here," he said suddenly, a suspicious note creeping into his voice. "You told me you didn't know who this gun belongs to."

"I don't," Malone said.

"Then how," Von Flanagan asked, his voice again rising steadily toward a roar, "how did you get hold of it if you don't know who it belongs to?" He reached the climax of the roar as he demanded, "Where did you get it?"

Malone said, "From Santa Claus."

The harassed police officer leaned back in his chair and delivered a tirade in which he described John J. Malone as a prevaricator of the most disreputable nature and habits, with an origin that was not only illegal and immoral but otherwise highly irregular. He ended it with a colorful blush and an apology to Helene.

Helene said, "Don't apologize. It's not only interesting, but it's probably accurate."

Von Flanagan gave her the grateful smile of an artist whose talents are appreciated, turned to glare again at Malone, and said patiently, "If you don't know who the gun belongs to, where did you get it from?"

"Damn it," Malone said in an exasperated tone, "I don't know."

The police officer drew a long breath and began, even more patiently, "If you don't know who—"

Malone snapped, "I tell you I don't know where I got it from and I don't. It came in a pretty bright red box with Merry Christmas printed all over it, and that's all I know."

Von Flanagan opened his mouth and closed it again without uttering a sound.

"I'm not trying to hold out on you, you dumb cop," Malone went on. "I didn't bring that gun over here to do you a favor. I brought it over here because I wanted to find out if it was used in those two killings and I knew you could find out for me. After all, by God, the Homicide Bureau ought to be good for something."

"All right," Von Flanagan said wearily, "all right, all right. I'll find out about your damned gun." He went to the door and yelled something unintelligible down the corridor, came back to his desk, and muttered, "It'd serve you right if I refused to tell you a thing about what I find out."

Malone said, "For two cents I'd take my pretty gun and go home."

"For two cents," Von Flanagan said, "I'd tell you to stick—" He interrupted himself hastily, just as the door opened and the red-faced policeman came in. His eyes went quickly around the room, noted Jake's presence, and looked hopefully at Von Flanagan.

Von Flanagan jerked his head toward Malone and said calmly, "Charge this man with carrying concealed weapons and throw him in the can. He came here with a pistol in his pocket."

Helene gasped. Jake said, "Why you—" and shut his mouth quickly. The little lawyer sat down on a corner of Von Flanagan's desk, took a cigar from his pocket, unwrapped it slowly and deliberately and lighted it, before he spoke.

"Von Flanagan," he said casually, and in the friendliest of tones, "will you ever forget that time you and Joe Flynn and that guy from Milwaukee went out to the Wheaton roadhouse with the babes from the Star and Garter, and how the guy from Milwaukee—"

That was as far as his idle reminiscences went before the police officer hastily interrupted him. "Beat it, Kluchetsky," he snapped.

The red-faced cop looked a little puzzled. "Don't you want—"

Von Flanagan shook his head vehemently. "It was just a joke. Forget it. He didn't have any gun."

Kluchetsky blinked, scratched his right ear, finally said, "O. K.," and went way. As he shut the door, Von Flanagan mopped his brow.

"You oughta know better than to start something like that," he said reproachfully. "You could get me in a lot of trouble. That guy goes out with my wife's kid sister." He mopped his brow again. "I just went along that time as a favor to Joe Flynn, but you could get me into a lot of trouble just the same."

"I've forgotten the whole thing," Malone promised smoothly. He knocked the ashes from his cigar and buttoned his overcoat before he asked, "How soon do you think you can get a report on that gun?"

"Is there a rush?" Von Flanagan asked.

"There is," Malone assured him.

Von Flanagan looked at his watch and said, "I'll have it some time this evening."

Malone nodded. "Phone me at my office. I'll be there until I hear from you." He opened the door, paused to say, "Make it as quick as you can." He motioned to Jake and Helene who followed him into the hall.

"I'll phone the minute I get a report," Von Flanagan said. "And—" he paused, "and thanks, damn you, Malone."

## *Chapter Thirty-One*

They were barely out of the building before Jake turned furiously on the little lawyer.

"What's the idea? Von Flanagan may succeed in tracing the ownership of that gun."

"I wouldn't be surprised," Malone said.

"But if he does, and if the gun belongs to Mona McClane—"

"Then he'll find out that it belongs to Mona McClane," Malone said calmly. "What the hell of it?"

"Suppose the ballistics tests show it's the gun that was used in shooting Joshua Gumbril and Fleurette Sanders."

"Suppose it does," the lawyer said complacently.

"Damn you, Malone. If I'm going to win that bet—"

Malone said crossly, "I know what I'm doing."

Jake muttered something indignant under his breath.

"Besides," Malone pointed out, "even if Von Flanagan does all that—and I imagine he will—he won't know anything about the motive for the murders. No more than we do. And as I've pointed out before, this is a crime of motive, not method."

"Very pretty," Jake growled, "but he'll think he has enough to make a pinch. Probably he'll have it before midnight. Unless I can uncover that motive in the meantime, I'm out of the ownership of a very nice night club."

Helene started the big car moving down the street. "Speaking of night clubs, I want to call on the ex-owner of one. Do you boys care to go along?"

"Max Hook?" Malone asked.

"Right. I'd like to ask him just what is in that little box of Gumbril's. He must know, or he wouldn't have been so all-fired anxious to get it."

The two men were eloquently silent for half a block. "Well damn it," Jake said finally, "I can't think of everything. Where does this Hook hang himself, Malone?"

Malone named an address on Lake Shore Drive.

"Not that building!" Helene said with a little gasp.

"Why not?" Malone snapped. "He owns it."

Five minutes later Helene parked the car before the Lake Shore Drive building whose address appeared on the society pages at least four times a week. They walked through the lobby and got in the elevator.

"Twenty-three," Malone said.

The elevator boy hesitated a moment, coughed delicately. "What floor, sir?"

"Twenty-three," Malone said grimly, "and no stops."

The elevator shot upward. Helene noticed the back of the boy's neck was pale. On the twenty-third floor Malone tapped lightly on a door, called out, "It's John J. Malone and friends." The door opened and they stepped into what was probably the most ornately decorated apartment in the city of Chicago.

The living room was immense, rose-carpeted, filled with delicately carved, satin-upholstered furniture, with innumerable little decorative lamps, pink-shaded, and with what seemed to be hundreds upon hundreds of small silk pillows. At the windows feminine printed draperies were held back by enormous satin ribbon bows. Everywhere there were painted china boxes, cut crystal ash trays, tiny vases and statuettes, and enameled clocks. Against one wall stood a huge roll-top desk, of some brown-painted wood, badly nicked and scarred. Behind it sat Max Hook himself.

He was a mountain of a man, easily six feet tall, and such a mass of fat, quivering flesh, that he seemed, at first glance, to be completely boneless. His head, entirely bald, was egg-shaped; it was impossible to tell where it ended and his shoulders began; the whole ran together in one jellylike glob of pink flesh. From that point he spread out in a great expanse of fat shoulders and chest. Round arms ended in plump, rosy hands with fingers like little sausages.

His face seemed to be composed of a wide grin and a long black cigar.

He remained in his chair as they entered. Jake thought he probably never moved out of it. It was impossible to imagine that huge bulk being moved without the aid of a derrick.

Malone introduced Jake and Helene.

Max Hook smiled amiably. "Sure, that's all right. I know all about them." His grin widened. "You like my little place, huh?"

"I think it's beautiful," Helene breathed. Her eyes were wide with admiration.

The big man beamed at her. "I always like to have things nice. Always when I see nice things, I like to buy them. Nothing but the best. Take a cigarette." He waved to one of the china boxes.

The cigarette was, Helene discovered, not only monogrammed, but perfumed.

Those social amenities over, Max Hook became serious.

"Well, Malone, this is a pleasant surprise. What can I do for you?"

"I just thought I'd like to find out why La Cerra was so anxious to get hold of Jake the other day, that's all," Malone said smoothly.

"I'll let you ask him," the gangster said cheerfully. He raised his voice and bellowed, "Georgie!" A moment later Little Georgie la Cerra appeared. Something seemed to have happened to him since the last time they had seen him. Even Helene could tell that he was a changed man.

"The cherry, he caused your friend some annoyance. I'm sorry about that," Max Hook said apologetically to Malone. "The Cherry, he's impulsive. When I tell him he should do something, he feels like he's got to get it done, regardless. See."

Malone nodded impassively.

"So when your friend here got picked up in Gumbril's room that night, naturally it was logical to figure he might have stumbled onto something there, wasn't it? Am I right?"

The lawyer nodded again. "You are. But if Jake had found any evidence pertaining to the Ogletree snatch, you could have had it and welcome."

Hook stared at him. "He must have found something, if you know that's what I was interested in."

"He didn't. He was looking for something else, and he didn't find that either. I happened to know it was Georgie who handled the Ogletree snatch, and that it went through Gumbril. That's all."

"You are a one," the gangster said admiringly, shaking his head. "I wish I had you on my pay roll, Malone." He scowled. "I must admit I disbelieved you when you told the Cherry Mr. Justus didn't find a thing, until I learned different."

Malone took off his overcoat very slowly and deliberately, sat down on a lavender satin sofa with his elbows on his knees, leaned forward, and stared fixedly at his host.

"Max, let's talk business. I want to get everything straight. If you'll tell me all I want to know, I'll get that Ogletree evidence and turn it over to you."

"It's a deal," Hook said quickly. He added a little reproachfully, "You know I'd be straight with you anyway, Malone."

"Sure," the lawyer said blandly. "What kind of an arrangement did you have with Gumbril?"

The big gangster laid down his cigar, selected and lit, incredibly, one of the perfumed cigarettes, and leaned perilously far back in his chair. "Well, it's like this," he began reminiscently. "Way back in '27, I had a chance to make some quick dough on a big load of liquor run down from the border, only I didn't have the cash to swing it. One of my boys put me next to Gumbril, and he put up for me. After that, you might almost say we was in business together, and when repeal come in—"

The story he unfolded was a long one, the story of a little monopoly of crime and gambling, with the miserly, wizened Gumbril as business head, and the big gangster as manager of operations. The tale led slowly up to the Ogletree kidnaping.

"Did Little Georgie handle the snatch on his own?" Malone asked, "or for you, or for Gumbril?"

Max Hook put his head on one side. "Well now, it was really for Gumbril. You might say I lent the Cherry to Gumbril."

"How much did you get?" The question was like the snap of a whip.

"Not a damn—" Max Hook caught himself. "What the hell business of yours is it?"

Malone whistled. "You mean you didn't get a cut of the fifty grand?"

There was actually a faint blush on the big man's cheek. "I told you I lent the Cherry. It was a personal favor to Gumbril. I owed him a favor or two, y'understand. Gumbril, he give the Cherry a grand, which was big pay for him, considering all the Cherry done was pick up the girl and deliver her."

"Did Gumbril make him sign a receipt for the dough?"

"You know damned well he did," Little Georgie said suddenly. "He never gave anybody a dime without a receipt. Said it was his way of protecting himself. What the hell do you think I wanted out of that room, anyway?"

Max Hook suddenly said, "Where is it now? That's what I want to know. If you didn't get it, and the Sanders dame didn't have it, where is it?"

Malone waited a good thirty seconds before he asked, very casually, "What made you think she might have had it?"

"I knew you wanted something Gumbril must have had," the gangster said, "or Mr. Justus here wouldn't have cased his room. So I figured Flossie Sanders must have found it and was going to make a deal with you. If she had that, she probably had the other stuff too. I knew she must be going to make a deal with you as soon as the Ogletree dame tipped me off she had made a date with you—"

"Wait a minute," Malone said very quietly. "You mean Ellen?"

Hook stared at him. "Hell no. Mrs. Ogletree. The old lady."

"Damn it," Jake burst out suddenly, "I've had about all I can stand of this. What's it all about, anyway?"

Little Georgie said soothingly, "Let me fix you a drink, Mr. Justus. Your nerves ain't so hot."

"Look here," Max Hook said, "when I've got a good thing, I don't like to let go of it, see. But I'll tell you about the Ogletree dame. She's one of these old ladies who likes to play the wheels, see, only she can't figure so good. First thing I know, I'm stuck with a bunch of IOU's big enough to choke a pony, and no way to collect because her old man's so tight you couldn't pry a dime outa him with a cold chisel. So Gumbril suggested I make a little deal with her. I forget about the IOU's and she passes on all the society gossip to me, and to Gumbril. You'd be surprised to know how many good things I got next to that way."

"I probably would be," Malone said dryly. "Was this arrangement made before the girl was snatched, or after?"

"Before. Only the old dame didn't put the finger on her own kid, if that's what you mean. She didn't know from nothing about it. Hell, she even came to me about it and I had to get Gumbril to give her his personal assurance the kid would be O. K."

"Who did put the finger on the girl?" Malone asked.

"Flossie Sanders. She was Gumbril's sister, you know." The big gangster lit another cigarette from the glowing end of the last one. "She had plenty of reasons for wanting to get Gumbril's papers after he was bumped off. He kept all the stuff about the way the first Mrs. Sanders got hers. So I had a hunch she might have got hold of them, and I asked the Ogletree dame to keep an eye on her. Today she found out Flossie was going to see you, and she gave me a ring right away and tipped me off."

"So you had one of the boys pick her up at the entrance to Field's, and when he couldn't figure any other way to keep her from coming to me, he shot her," Malone said lightly.

"Honest to God, Malone," Little Georgie la Cerra put in unexpectedly, "you got me all wrong. We was going down State Street trying to keep her in sight in all that mob, trying to catch up with her and have a little quiet word with her."

"I know your little quiet words," Malone said, "but go on."

"Almost to Madison Street, we all of a sudden lose her in the crowd, see. We're trying to shove through when hell breaks loose up ahead. I push up in the crowd and I see the dame has been shot. But I didn't shoot her."

"Strange as it seems," Malone said, "I believe you. But I'd give a lot to know how the hell her clothes got taken off on the way to the morgue."

"You would, eh," Max Hook said suddenly. He burst into a laugh that threatened to split the pale pink walls of his apartment, opened a drawer of his desk, pulled out a heap of assorted feminine garments, and tossed them at Malone. "Well, there they are."

Malone looked at the collection, picked up a tiny, lacy affair, dropped it as though it had bitten him, and said, "How did these get there?"

"Go on, Georgie," Max Hook said amiably, "tell the gentleman."

Little Georgie la Cerra drew a long breath. "Well, it's like this. Mr. Malone, when the boss tells me he wants a thing done, he means he wants it done. He tells me he wants this Sanders dame searched for Gumbril's papers, so I know he wants her searched. So all of a sudden there she is shot, right smack on the corner of State and Madison Streets, and fifty thousand people milling around. What am I going to do?"

"Do I get three guesses?" Malone said pleasantly, "or do you tell me?"

"I'm telling you," said the gunman. "We got the car parked in a lot a few blocks off, see. Before the dead wagon pulls up, me and Louie ducks up and gets the car and drives back to the corner. By that time they got the dame inside, with two cops sitting up in the front seat, so we drive along and tails the dead wagon, trying to think what to do next. I know the Hook wants them papers, see?"

"Yes, yes, yes," Malone said. "But for the love of God—"

"She being dead already, there ain't nobody in back with her," Little Georgie said. "And those doors are easy to open. So when the dead wagon gets stalled in traffic, I hops out of the car, opens the doors, and hops in. It was as easy as that."

"The way you tell it," Malone said, "I think I've been wasting my time trying to make a living the hard way."

"Let him finish," Jake said hoarsely.

"Then I searched her. Nothing in the bag. Nothing in the pockets. I take her dress off. Nothing sewed inside it. I take the stockings off. Nothing in the stockings. By that time I know she ain't got no papers of no kind. What am I going to do?"

No one had any suggestions. When the gunman spoke again, his voice was low, curiously embarrassed. "Mr. Malone, I got to prove to the Hook I really searched the dame. How'm I gonna prove it? All of a sudden it come to me in a kind of flash. I'd just take the dame's clothes back with me. That oughta prove I searched her. So I rolls all the clothing up in a bundle, sticks it under my arm, opens the door, waits till the dead wagon slows down in traffic again, hops out, Louie picks me up in the car, away we go, and there you are."

"I wish I had been," Helene said.

The smile on Max Hook's face was one of great pride in his boys. Jake looked reverent. It was Malone who summed up the situation. He said, "You mean you got in a police ambulance on the way to the morgue, searched and undressed the body, and got clean away?"

"Sure," said little Georgie la Cerra. "The Hook told me to search her, and I searched her." He seemed to speak with effort. "I didn't like to do it. I never undressed no lady before—no dead lady."

His face, from hair to collar, was a brilliant, gorgeous crimson.

"Well, it was a nice job for an amateur," Malone said at last. He signaled to Helene, and to Jake, who was examining the dead woman's clothing, a curious frown on his face. At the door, the lawyer paused as though he had just remembered something.

"Hook, what do you know about Mona McClane?"

A look of sincere admiration came over the gangster's face. "That dame! You know what she done? She took me at my own game. Many more people like her, and every gambling house in the city would run at a loss." He sighed and shook his head. "Four times she cleaned out the bank. Then she offers to bet her winnings against the Casino, and I'm God damned if she didn't win!"

"Did she ever know Gumbril?" Malone asked unconcernedly.

Hook shook his head. "What would a swell dame like that be doing, knowing a guy like Gumbril?" He sighed again, the effect was not unlike that of a mountain caught in an earthquake. "A swell dame. But take it from me, she's a bad one to bet with!"

# *Chapter Thirty-Two*

There wasn't a word all the way down the elevator or on the way to the car. Not until Helene had started the motor did Jake speak.

"We keep finding people who should have murdered Gumbril," he said gloomily. "But not Mona McClane. Do you think Hook is telling the truth?"

"No doubt of it," Malone assured him. "He's a crook, but he's perfectly honest." He scowled. "It's easy to see why he figured that Fleurette had cleaned out Gumbril's strongbox. But if she had gone to his room—"

"She did go to his room," Jake said excitedly.

"You haven't turned clairvoyant, by any chance?" the lawyer asked scornfully.

"No, but I've got a nose," Jake said. "Perfume. I'd know it anywhere. Remember I told you how that closet smelled. There was the same perfume on her clothes. Heavy, too."

"If that's so," Malone said slowly, "and it may very easily be—if Fleurette did go to Gumbril's room—" He paused and finally said grimly, "We've got to get that box, that's all. What's more, we've got to get it right now."

Helene stepped on the accelerator and shot past a startled policeman down Michigan Avenue. "We'll have Mr. Gumbril's little box in half an hour."

"A nice sentiment," Malone growled. "Don't forget though that Von Flanagan probably still has Gumbril's room closed to the public."

"You don't discourage me in the least," she said placidly. "Jake, what was that box like?"

"It was a regular metal dispatch box," he told her, "with a very good lock and a handle on the top. It was enameled or painted dark green."

She was silent for a block or so. "Is there a hardware store anywhere near here?"

"There's Goldblatt's," Jake said; "they have a hardware department, I imagine."

"Thanks. That's all I wanted to know." She drove to Van Buren Street, over to State, and stopped the car at the corner. "Drive around the block and pick me up here on the corner." Before he could say a word she had hopped out and was lost in the sidewalk crowds.

Jake piloted the big car gingerly through the late-afternoon traffic. "Malone, what do you suppose she's up to now?"

"I don't know," the lawyer growled, "and it's probably safer not to ask. Don't worry, we'll find out."

After a few turns around the block they saw Helene on the corner and stopped next to the curb.

"Get what you wanted?" Jake asked.

"Yes. Don't bother me with questions now. Get out, you're coming too."

"You can't leave the car here," Jake complained. "We've tied up traffic for two blocks now."

"I'm not going to leave it here. Malone, you just keep driving around for a while and every five minutes go past this corner. In due course of time you can pick us up here, complete with box."

"If this is a new game, I don't like it," Malone said morosely, taking the wheel.

"Well, if we aren't here in an hour, head for the jail." She tucked her hand under Jake's arm. "Where's a telephone booth?"

He pointed across State Street to a cigar store. She picked her way delicately through the muddy melted snow to the store, looked quickly in the phone book, and dialed the number of the Fairfax Hotel.

"I want to talk to Mr. Poppenpuss."

A pause.

"But there is too. I know he lives there. Isn't this the Fairfax Hotel?" Her voice rose in rage. "Then I want to talk to Mr. Poppenpuss, P-O-P-P-E-N-P-U-S-S, in room six fourteen. I tell you there is a Mr. Poppenpuss in room six fourteen. Let me talk to room six fourteen. But I know there is." She burst into an angry tirade about the stupidity of hotel clerks, and banged the receiver on its hook.

"What the hell?" Jake asked.

"I just wanted to find out if room six fourteen is empty," she said complacently. "Thank heaven it is." She waved at a passing taxi, told the driver, "Fairfax Hotel."

"Helene," Jake said desperately, "what are you going to do?"

"Do you want to come along with me, or shall I do this myself?"

"Of course I'm coming with you."

"Then stop asking questions. To quote Malone, this is a new game and I do like it."

At the door to the Fairfax Hotel she told him, "Get a room, pay for it in advance, and try to look as if you'd never seen me until ten minutes ago."

"Helene, please—"

"And stop looking embarrassed."

Jake sighed and decided to play along. The lone, shabby bellhop showed them to a dingy room on the fourth floor, pocketed his tip and went away. He closed the door and looked at her thoughtfully.

"Since we're here, and since we've paid for the room—"

"I know what you mean," she said, "and it's a wonderful idea, but this is a business trip. I hope you still have that skeleton key Malone gave you."

"I have, but what of it? If Von Flanagan has a cop stationed in room five fourteen, the key won't do us any good."

"If it will open five fourteen, it'll open six fourteen." She opened the door and looked out. The corridor was empty. Helene started for the stairs; Jake hopefully followed.

The sixth floor corridor was just as empty. She led the way to six fourteen.

"Try the key and pray that it works."

It did. She switched on the light, closed and locked the door. Then she took a small, paper-wrapped package from her purse, woman's eighth wonder of the world, unwrapped it, and took out a long piece of heavy cord and a large hook.

"We're going fishing," she announced. She tied the cord securely to the hook and handed the apparatus to Jake. "Do I need to suggest what to do next, or do you get the idea?"

"I do," he said delightedly. "Helene, you're wonderful."

"Have it your own way," she said, "but get the box."

He opened the window and looked out. On the ledge below he could see the box, one end of it lightly frosted with snow. Luckily the snow did not cover the handle. Slowly and carefully he lowered the hook on its length of cord.

The first two tries missed the handle completely. Helene appeared beside him and looked anxiously out the window. On his third attempt the hook slipped into the handle, he gave a gentle tug, and the box moved. Helene gasped delightedly. Very carefully he hauled in the string until at last he was able to reach out with his other hand, grasp the box, and pull it over the sill.

For a moment they sat on the floor beside the open window, breathless and beaming. Then a frown began to gather on Jake's face.

"You've thought of everything except how to dispose of the body," he complained. "We've got the box, but how are we going to get it out of here? The clerk saw us come in, he saw we weren't carrying anything. What's he going to do if he sees us walking out with this?"

"You underestimate me," she said, scrambling to her feet. "I thought of that too. Come on down to the fourth floor."

They went down without meeting anybody. At the fourth floor she paused and handed him the box. "Jake, there's a corner in the corridor right at the stairs. You go on down to the second floor with the box—"

"And leave you here alone? Don't be—"

"I'll be all right, don't worry. Park yourself around that little corner out of sight of the stairs, and wait there until the clerk, and everyone else in the lobby, is out of the way."

"How are you going to get them out of the lobby?"

"That's my business. You tend to your own knitting. Whatever happens, don't pay any attention to what I may do, no matter what it is. Understand?"

He nodded, hoping for the best, but knowing he wouldn't get it.

"As soon as the coast is clear, head for the street and start as fast as you can for that corner where we're to meet Malone. I'll join you there in five minutes."

"Helene, what are you going to do?"

"You'll find out," she said ominously.

"I'm afraid I will," he said. He tucked the box under his arm, went on down the stairs, and stood in the shadows of the corner. He had barely reached its shelter when a sound froze the blood in his veins. A few floors above Helene was screaming at the top of her voice. His impulse was to drop the box and run to her aid. He didn't obey it. After the first terrible moment, he detected something just a trifle phony in the scream.

The inhabitants of the lobby, however, heard no phony note. Standing in the shadows, Jake heard the elevator shoot upward. Running footsteps sounded on the stairs. As they died away he looked around the corner, saw no one, went cautiously down the stairs to the lobby. No one was in sight. He walked quickly across the lobby and onto the sidewalk and started toward Van Buren Street.

He wanted to wait for Helene. Still, it was probably best to carry out her instructions. By the time he had covered one block, he began to worry. What if those screams had been genuine, after all? He told himself firmly they were not, and continued north. By the end of the next block he had begun to worry about how she was going to talk her way out of whatever she had screamed herself into. When he had reached the corner of State and Van Buren, he had decided to go back to the Fairfax Hotel and find out what had happened to her, come what might.

Just as he reached that decision a taxi stopped in front of him and Helene hopped out, bright-eyed and smiling.

"Darling!" Jake said, inadequately. He clung to her hand with a kind of desperation.

"How did you like my scream?"

He shuddered. "What in God's name did you do?"

She smiled happily, like a pleased child. "I ran down the stairs screaming, and when the clerk finally quieted me enough to talk, I told him you'd grabbed a twenty-dollar bill that I was carrying in my stocking and ran off with it."

"Well," Jake said grimly, thirty seconds later, "that makes one more hotel I have to stay out of in the future." He mopped his brow and added, "Suppose they'd sent for the police?"

"Idiot. I knew they wouldn't. In fact"—a look of uncomfortable embarrassment came into her eyes—"the clerk gave me a ten-dollar bill out of the cash register if I'd go quietly away and say nothing. I had to take it, but what on earth shall I do with it? It's tainted money!"

At that moment the car appeared around the corner, driven by Malone. A sudden inspiration came to Helene, she ran a few steps down the street and dropped the bill in the hand of a Volunteers-of-America Santa Claus who probably never recovered from the shock. A moment later they were in the car, driving away from the scene.

"We got the box," Helene reported. "The box and ten dollars. I think Jake got a few gray hairs too, but it was worth it."

Malone said, "Maybe you'd better not tell me how you did it. It might keep me awake nights, thinking about it. Let's see the box."

Jake held it out. "Now all we have to do is get it open."

"That's easy," Helene said. "All we need is a locksmith."

"Locksmith hell," Malone said scornfully. "Me and love, we laugh at locksmiths. I used to have a client who was a professional cracksman. Just wait till I get that box in my office!"

## *Chapter Thirty-Three*

Jake and Helene watched anxiously as the little lawyer laid the precious box on his desk, examined the lock closely, and began pawing through a desk drawer. After taking out two soiled handkerchiefs, a small pile of wastepaper, a cardboard file marked LETTERS TO ANSWER, an empty bottle, and a photograph of a plumpish young woman inscribed *"Your darling Louise,"* he found what he was looking for: a little leather kit, not unlike a manicure kit.

From it he took a handful of small, shining tools and examined them one by one. A half dozen or so he laid on the desk beside the box, the rest he put carefully back in the leather kit. Then, first with one tool and then another, he began probing the lock of the metal box, delicately and with exquisite care.

The room was deathly still. Watching Malone, Jake felt his scalp crinkling with excitement. Inside that dark-green metal box had been Mona McClane's motive for murdering Joshua Gumbril and his sister. Maybe it was still there. The gun had already come to their hands and right at this moment Von Flanagan was having it tested and its ownership traced. Any minute now Von Flanagan would telephone his findings. Any minute now Malone would get that box open. Then the case would be complete. It was almost as though that innocent-looking box held the deed to the Casino.

He tried to steel himself against disappointment. It would probably turn out that the box held nothing except an old laundry bill and a couple of mousetraps. Or Joshua Gumbril's other necktie, if he had another necktie. It might even be empty. In fact, it probably was empty. Jake was positive that it was empty. He felt that the sound of his heart beating as Malone struggled with the tools would drown out the combined Army and Navy bands.

Malone had stopped fiddling with the tools and stared indignantly at the box.

Jake said, "You thugs ought to keep in practice. Can't you get it open?"

Malone answered with a low growl. He took the rest of the tools out of the kit and experimented with them until he had tried them all. Suddenly he swept them into the desk drawer without bothering to put them in their leather kit, slammed the drawer shut, and glared at the obstinate box with a mixture of baffled rage and helplessness.

Helene cleared her throat delicately. "Try a paper clip."

The paper clip didn't work. Neither did a hairpin.

Malone said, "By God, if I have to go down and borrow an ax from the janitor and split the infernal thing in two—" his voice broke off in an incoherent and enraged gurgle.

Helene sighed, picked up the box, and examined it. Accidentally she pressed the tiny knob just above the keyhole. The box immediately sprang open, jolted out of her hands, and fell to the desk top with a horrific clatter. Helene screamed. Jake and Malone both jumped.

"Where did you learn that trick?" Malone gasped when he recovered his breath.

"It was nothing," Helene said airily. "And it's particularly easy when the box simply isn't locked."

For a moment no one dared speak. Malone looked intently and suspiciously at the box, as though at any moment it might leap up and bite him.

At last Jake said in a very weak voice, "I tried all my keys and my penknife on it that first night in Gumbril's room, because I supposed of course it was locked. I never thought of just trying to open it without unlocking it. Because you'd naturally think a box like that would be locked."

"If any of us had had any sense," Malone said peevishly, "we'd have known right away that it wasn't."

"Why?" Helene asked.

"Where was the key?"

"What key?"

"The key to the box," Malone roared, "Gumbril's key. Were there any keys found on his person or anywhere else among his possessions?"

Jake said, "No. I guess there weren't."

"You're damned right there weren't," Malone said. "If he'd kept the box locked he'd have had to have a key somewhere. Evidently he had an intense dislike of carrying anything or having anything. You saw what was in his room, Jake. You heard what was found in his pockets. The man simply didn't want possessions, except money. Not even a small key to open a metal dispatch box. He probably realized that the average person, looking at the box, would assume it to be locked, just as we did. It's even possible that the box doesn't contain anything sufficiently valuable to be locked up."

Jake groaned.

Helene said, "For the love of heaven, don't sit there talking about it, look inside it."

"Stop rushing me," Malone said crossly. He drew the box over to his side of the desk. Suddenly he dropped it as though it had stung him. He looked somewhere far beyond the walls of his office. "That was all poppycock," he said slowly.

Neither Jake nor Helene dared to interrupt him.

"The box *was* locked," he said, seeming to weigh each word against the next. "There *was* a key. The key was in Gumbril's room—not on his person, or the police would have found it. It must have been carried away by the person who opened the box."

The words, "What person?" rose to Jake's lips and died there. Malone sat staring into space, his face suddenly gray.

"If you don't open that damned box, I will," Helene said hoarsely.

Malone looked at her as though he had never seen her before. "What for?" he said, the words dragging.

He stared at the box for a long moment, finally threw open the lid and peered inside. With maddening deliberation he drew out a folded piece of paper that appeared to be an official document of some kind.

The little lawyer unfolded it and sat staring blankly at it for a long time. Then he leaned back in his chair, apparently oblivious of Jake and Helene's presence, reading the document over and over as though he were trying to memorize it.

*"Malone!"*

He didn't answer. They might have been a thousand miles away. He picked up the telephone, asked for, "Long distance," and said, "I want to speak to the county clerk of Walworth County, at Elkhorn, Wisconsin. Thank you."

At that moment Helene, her patience exhausted, snatched the document from Malone's hands, looked at it, and handed it, without a word, to Jake.

It was a certificate of marriage, dated May 21, 1914, at Elkhorn, Wisconsin, between one Mona McClane and one Joshua Gumbril.

## *Chapter Thirty-Four*

Jake felt like a small boy on Christmas morning who sees his new skates for the first time, knows they are exactly what he wanted, and can't understand why he is terribly disappointed.

Heaven only knew how he'd wanted to win that bet. He'd been willing to go to almost any lengths, take almost any risks, to uncover Mona McClane's motive for the murder of Joshua Gumbril.

Now that it had been found, now that he held it in his hand, he didn't feel excited or elated or triumphant. He didn't even feel surprised. For some inexplicable reason, he only felt disappointed.

Suddenly he realized that Malone had been talking on the telephone all that time.

". . . second person who asked that, eh?" the little lawyer was saying in a curiously flat voice. "You don't recall the other person, do you? Is that so? Well, thanks. Glad I didn't put you to any special trouble. If I can ever do anything for you here in Chicago, you'll find me in the phone book. Yes, that's right. M-A-L-O-N-E."

He put the receiver down and sat staring at the telephone. "I didn't expect to find that in the box," he said in a strange, dazed voice. "I didn't expect to find anything about Mona McClane in the box." He paused, looked at them as though their faces might offer some explanation, said at last, "That was what wasn't supposed to be there."

Suddenly he rose, walked to the window, and stood looking out across the roofs for a long time, his hands in his pockets, his shoulders hunched, his head bowed. Jake felt for Helene's soft hand and held it tight.

"Go away," Malone said unexpectedly. "Go away for half an hour and come back. Go get a drink. Go walk around the block. Go and do anything you damned well please, but leave me alone. I want to think."

Jake stared at the little lawyer's back for a full minute, then led Helene gently out to the hall and rang for the elevator. As they rode down he felt her arm trembling under his hand, and saw that her face was very pale. Out on the sidewalk she paused, looking up at him.

"Jake, what is it?"

"I don't know," he said, "and I'm not in the mood for guessing."

She frowned. "I need a drink to help me think clearly."

"Follow me," Jake said. "I'm a St. Bernard."

They walked through the softly falling snow down Madison Street to the corner of Wacker Drive, turned south for half a block, and entered a pleasantly noisy, though far from ornate, saloon.

Jake waved Helene to a secluded corner and called for, "Two double ryes, quick."

"Poor Malone," she said softly, peeling off her gloves. The rye brought a little color back to her cheeks. She lit a cigarette, looked reflectively through its smoke, and said, "Well, anyway, you've won your bet. I hope you're happy."

"I'm not," he told her. "I should be. I made the bet, I wanted to win it, but I'm not happy, and you're not either. And Malone, least of all."

"I know exactly what's in his mind," she said.

"Then you're a better mind reader than I am."

"All along," she told him, "he's been hoping he'd find proof that Mona McClane didn't mean that bet—that the whole thing was pure coincidence. Instead, when he opened the box—there was the motive he hadn't wanted to find."

"That marriage certificate doesn't mean a thing," Jake said in what he knew was an unconvincing voice.

"May, 1914," she said dreamily. "I happen to know Mona McClane was married the first time—publicly, I mean—on June 25, 1914. I'm sure of the date because it was the day I was born."

"That's impossible," Jake said. "She could never have gotten a divorce from Gumbril, or even an annulment, in that length of time."

"Maybe she didn't get one," Helene said. "Maybe she never did."

"But," Jake said, and stopped suddenly.

Helene nodded slowly. "That would mean her later marriage was bigamous. All her later marriages were bigamous."

"Well," Jake said. "There's the motive, anyway."

"But it isn't what we wanted to find," Helene wailed.

Jake frowned. "I think I know what you mean. But Malone—what the hell did he expect to find in that box?"

"He expected—" She stopped suddenly, said, "We'd better have another drink."

Jake attracted the bartender's attention, called, "Two more of the same," and said to Helene, "Go on. He expected what?"

"Wait a minute." Her eyes had suddenly grown large and dreamy, almost luminous. "He did expect to find a motive for Mona McClane's murdering Gumbril. But a different kind. Nothing like Gumbril's having an ugly blackmail hold over her. And you expected it too. I know you did."

She paused while the bartender brought two more ryes, her chin resting on her fist.

"Do you see, Jake? There's been something heroic and gay about Mona all this time. The bet itself—the gesture of sending that muff—everything. We kept finding motives for other people to have killed him—Lulamay, the whole Sanders family, Mrs. Ogletree—but not Mona. So it seemed that the motive must be something as heroic as the bet itself. Now to have it come down to this, a sordid, ugly, ordinary motive for a commonplace crime—!" Suddenly, without warning, tears began to stream down her face. "I can't bear it. I can't bear to have it turn out this way." She fumbled in her purse for a handkerchief, didn't find one, and said feebly, "Hell!"

Jake stared at her, drew a handkerchief from his pocket, and handed it to her. She mopped her face, blew her nose noisily, and said, "Now it's all over and we know just why it happened," and immediately began to weep again.

Jake suddenly realized that the enormous bulk of the bartender was shadowing their table.

"Are you picking on the little lady?" the bartender demanded indignantly. He gentled his voice, looked at Helene, and said, "There, there, there."

"Go away," Jake said vaguely and inadequately.

Helene buried her face in her handkerchief and howled. The bartender made a sympathetic, clucking noise with his teeth, and said soothingly, "Never mind now, never mind. What's the matter, is he picking on you?"

"Yes he is," Helene said from the handkerchief. "I'm crying because he won't buy me another drink."

"The big palooka," the bartender said reproachfully. He murmured, "There,

there," again, gathered up the glasses, and added, "If he won't buy you a drink, I will." Seeing that the tears had stopped, he scowled once more at Jake and went away.

"A fine reputation I'll have when you get through with me," Jake said irately. "This place is half a block from the *Herald-American* and it's full of my friends."

"I'm just making sure they'll never forget you." She removed the last traces of tears from her face, took out her compact, and began powdering it carefully and artistically.

The bartender returned to set the refilled glasses on the table. He shoved one in front of Jake and said, "You don't deserve this, Jake Justus."

"It isn't Jake Justus any more," Jake said absent-mindedly, "I'm married now." He thought for a moment and added, "I mean, this is my wife. This is Mrs. Justus."

"You're drunk," the bartender said suspiciously.

"That may be," Jake told him, "but she's my wife just the same." He downed his rye, motioned to Helene to do the same, looked at his watch, stood up, and began fastening his overcoat. "We were married day before day before yesterday."

"Well, well," the bartender murmured. "Congratulations. Have another on the house."

"Thanks," Jake said, shaking his head. "We'd love to, but we've got to go see my lawyer." He waved Helene to the door and nodded good-by to the bartender, who worried over the whole thing for days.

Out in the street, Helene waved at a taxi.

"It's only a couple of blocks," Jake began.

"We're not going to Malone's office yet," she said. "State and Madison," she called to the driver. The car lurched forward in the snow.

"What's the idea?"

"You'll find out. Have you a tooth to spare?"

"One or two, in a good cause. Why?"

"A tooth for a tooth is worth two in the head," she said happily. "I want to get a look at that dentist's office Fleurette was in so conveniently when Gumbril was murdered."

"Oh no you don't," Jake said indignantly. "I'll have every tooth in my head knocked out for you, if needs be, but I'm damned and double damned if I'll have any of them pulled."

"Sissy," she flung at him. "Anyway, the dentist probably went home hours ago."

"Helene, be reasonable."

"You might as well have it pulled," she said soothingly. "It's better than having the toothache, and you never know—!"

Jake was silent. He had begun to have an uncomfortable feeling that all the teeth in his head were beginning to ache.

Holiday crowds still swarmed about the corner of State and Madison, despite the snow and the lateness of the hour. The cab stopped on the northwest corner. For a moment Helene stood staring up at the office building that overlooked the spot where Joshua Gumbril and his sister Fleurette had been slain. Suddenly she caught Jake's arm and pointed toward the building.

"There it is."

Jake looked up at the line of gold lettering that announced the doctor's name, and shuddered. "Helene, I don't feel well."

"You'll feel better when it's over. Maybe you can take gas." She dragged him into the building and shoved him toward the elevator.

As they went down the corridor, a girl emerged from the doctor's office, switching off the lights behind her, and locked the door. Helene hurried to speak to her.

"Oh, I hope the doctor hasn't gone. My husband has a tooth that has to come out at once—immediately."

"Look here," Jake began weakly.

The girl looked at them in surprise. "This isn't a dentist's office. I'm sorry, but there isn't a dentist anywhere in the building. Maybe if you'd call the—"

"Are you sure?" Helene demanded.

"Yes, I am. You might find—"

Helene said, "But I was positive that this was a dentist's office. Why, I had a friend who had some work done here just two days ago."

The girl shook her head. "It couldn't have been here. The doctor's been away for the past week. And anyway, he isn't a dentist. He's an obstetrician." She went on down the hall toward the elevator.

"Well," Jake said, "it seems to be your move. What do you suggest?"

She ignored him. "My hunch was right. Let's go back and tell Malone."

"What the hell would he want with an obstetrician?"

"Never mind," she said fiercely. "I was right that Fleurette didn't see Joshua Gumbril murdered from a dentist's office or any other office. I'd suspected as much, but now I'm sure of it."

"I'm sure of something else," Jake said happily. "I've had a very, very narrow escape."

They found Malone hunched over his desk, talking into the telephone. He looked up as they came to the door and motioned to them to come in.

As they entered the room he said, "Thanks. See you later," to the telephone, put it down on his desk, and said, "That was Von Flanagan."

"What has he found out?" Jake asked, as if he really needed to be told.

"He says he traced the ownership of the gun with three telephone calls. It was one of a pair sold to Mona McClane four years ago."

"It was, eh?" Jake said calmly, reaching for a cigarette. "Did it fire the shots that killed Joshua Gumbril and Fleurette Sanders?"

"It did," the little lawyer said quietly. He stood up and began getting into his overcoat very slowly and deliberately. For the first time Jake realized how terribly tired he seemed. "Yes, it did," Malone repeated. He added, almost as an afterthought, "He'll meet us at Mona McClane's in a little while."

Suddenly, his overcoat half on, he picked up the telephone, clenched his cigar, and called Mona McClane's number.

"I'm coming up to see you," he said into the phone. "I'm on my way now. I wonder if you can assemble the people who were present when you made that bet with Jake. I'd like to have them hear how it came out." He listened a moment, murmured, "Yes, all of them. That's fine," and hung up.

"Do we need to make a Roman holiday of it?" Helene demanded.

Malone said nothing. He stood by the desk, apparently deep in thought, for an instant. Suddenly he unlocked a desk drawer, took out the box containing Mona McClane's muff, and tucked it under his arm.

Helene told him of their discovery about the dentist's office.

The lawyer nodded. "I hate to break your heart, but I'd already found that out. Fleurette probably learned of Gumbril's death the same way we did, from the newspapers. Not having to waste time identifying him, like ourselves, she was able to hike right along to his room and beat us to the box. Being his sister she was probably familiar with his hiding place, and went straight to it."

"Then did she—" Jake began.

Malone motioned him to silence. He ushered Jake and Helene into the hall, followed them, and unlocked the door. They rode down the elevator and crossed the lobby without a word. As they got into the car Malone said, "Helene, just how fast can you drive to Mona McClane's?"

Jake groaned. Helene said, "Do you really want to know?" Her voice held the pleased surprise of a small boy asked to demonstrate his ice-cream capacity.

She started the car as Malone said in a husky, painfully tired voice, "I'd like to have time to make a few explanations before Von Flanagan gets there, that's all." He added a few blocks farther, "Don't think I like this, because I don't. But you got me into it and I've got to go through with it now. And if either of you say one word on the way, I won't answer for the consequences."

## Chapter Thirty-Five

At first it seemed remarkable to Jake that the big, comfortable room in the old McClane mansion should look just as it had when he had seen it last. Then he remembered that had been only the night before.

The same room, the same, oversized luxurious furniture, the same people. Save for that terribly large gap left by the absence of Fleurette Sanders. She had been sitting on that couch, that one right over there. Strange, Jake thought, that such a little person as Fleurette could leave such an enormous space behind in a room. It was like the tremendous, yawning canyon that always seemed to be left by the extraction of a quite small tooth, a canyon of which one was perpetually conscious. Everyone in the room was trying to pay no attention to the space left by Fleurette Sanders, and everyone was unbearably aware of it.

All of them avoided the couch where she had been.

The others were there. Jake looked around the room. There was Willis Sanders, pale and visibly shaken, with George Brand right beside him and an unobtrusively solicitous Partridge hovering in the background. Willis Sanders was beardless, Jake observed, while his companion's neatly trimmed mustache and imperial were back where they seemed to belong. He wondered how Partridge had managed it. Some kind of glue, of course. There was Daphne Sanders, sitting quite by herself, like an alien in the room, trying to look as though she hadn't accused the dead Fleurette Sanders of murder only the night before.

There was Mrs. Ogletree, pleasantly excited and doing her fluttering best to appear shocked and horror-stricken. Jake was reminded of people on trains and buses reading the accounts of disasters in the morning paper, saying, "How awful!" in exhilarated and almost elated voices. There was something almost vulturelike about her. Jake remembered Max Hook's revelation, and wondered how many tender morsels of gossip had been turned into lucrative blackmail by the arrangement with Mrs. Ogletree.

Wells Ogletree, beside his wife, looked as though he were trying, with his aristocratic nostrils, to decide on the exact location of a mouse that had perished, not too recently, in the wall.

Ellen Ogletree and Leonard Marchmont sat together on a sofa. Ellen looked very bored and extremely discontented, Marchmont acted like a man who has just been called to the telephone from a sound sleep. Both of them seemed to feel that the whole procedure was not only definitely distasteful, but also extremely dull.

Yes, all of them were there, Jake thought, all as tense as harp strings, yet pretending that nothing in the least unusual was going on. None of them looked at him, none of them seemed to remember that he had bet he could pin a murder on Mona McClane, and now was here to collect.

The only person who looked entirely calm was Mona McClane. She wore the same dark, clinging dress she had worn the night before, with the glittering pendant on its long, slender chain. Her small, pointed face was pale but, Jake thought, no more pale than it had always been. She showed no sign of agitation, only an intense interest in whatever might be going to happen next.

Opposite her 'sat John J. Malone, his dark-blue suit wrinkled and a little dusty, his black hair mussed and damp. There was a small smudge on the side of his nose.

Jake felt for the comforting pressure of Helene's slender hand, and told himself fiercely that owning the Casino was going to be worth all this.

Malone cleared his throat and said, "Captain Von Flanagan of the Homicide Bureau will arrive any minute now. I came here first because I wanted to explain a few things before he arrived."

The room was very still. Someone struck a match. It sounded as loud as an explosion.

"A few days ago," Malone began again, "you heard a bet made between Mona McClane and Jake Justus here. Perhaps most of you put it down as a rather absurd joke. Perhaps some of you took it seriously. I don't know. At any rate—" he paused for a long breath, "the following afternoon one Joshua Gumbril was shot at the corner of State and Madison Streets under circumstances corresponding to the terms of the bet.

"It was not my bet," he said, "and I had no intention of becoming involved in subsequent events. However, circumstances were such that I did become so involved, and that is why I am acting as spokesman for Mr. Justus now."

No one spoke. No one stirred.

"Usually," Malone went on, "the discovery of a motive for the murder of a man or woman is a great step in the direction of finding and proving the identity of the murderer." He appeared to become less tired as he continued. "Curiously, the reverse was true in this case. A crime was committed. It was not the discovery of a motive, but the discovery of the absence of a motive that pointed to the identity of the criminal."

Jake wrestled with that statement. He wondered if the exhaustion of the past twenty-four hours had been just a little too much for Malone.

The little lawyer continued, "Because the motive for a crime points so clearly in the direction of the criminal, the first act of the criminal after committing his crime is the destruction of the apparent motive." He paused and repeated, as though to himself, "The apparent motive—!"

With a great effort Jake brought his eyes to Mona McClane's face. It had become very white; her eyes were as large as a fox's in the dark, but she retained enough of her poise to smile at him.

"By a curious coincidence," Malone said, "when that bet was made, there were a number of people present who had excellent reasons for desiring the death of the late Joshua Gumbril."

Jake was sure that he heard a faint, tremulous sigh from somewhere in the room.

"I trust you know what you're talking about," Wells Ogletree said coldly.

"I do," Malone told him, "and so do two others who are here. One of them murdered Joshua Gumbril and Fleurette Sanders. The other is Willis Sanders, who knows who committed those crimes—though he had no part in them himself."

Willis Sanders' face turned gray. Suddenly he buried his face in his hands with a kind of sob. Everyone in the room tried to look away from him, save Mrs. Ogletree. She seemed to be trying to look everywhere at once and miss nothing that went on.

Malone went on again almost dreamily, "A motive is always the key to a murder. But this time it was not the discovery of a motive that made everything clear. It was the absence of one. The motive for the murder of Joshua Gumbril should have been in a green metal box in his room. It was not, and because it was not, there was no doubt left as to *what* it was."

Wells Ogletree's voice cut sharply into the silence. "Did you come here to tell us something definite, Mr. Malone, or to ramble on about motives and a lot of pointless rot none of us understand?"

Malone looked at him coldly, yet almost pityingly. "I'll be more specific if you like, Mr. Ogletree. The person who murdered Joshua Gumbril because he was a blackmailer, and then murdered Fleurette Sanders because she too—"

A cry from Helene interrupted him. She sprang to her feet and started for the hall. As Jake went after her, he heard the library window thrown open, and ran into the library just in time to see a car starting in the driveway. He realized then that its driver had gone quietly out of the room while Wells Ogletree was speaking. The drawer of the library table was wide open; it took only one quick glance to tell him the gun it had held was gone. As he raced back into the hall and down the steps he could hear Malone swearing close behind him.

At the same moment that the car he had seen turned out of the driveway another passed it, coming in. It stopped before the house just as Helene, in her own car, started the motor. Jake slid into the seat beside Helene as Von Flanagan called, "Who drove away?" and Malone shouted back, "The person you want!"

Then Malone was in the seat beside him, Helene was pressing her foot on the accelerator, and they were spinning around the corner into the street. Far ahead he could see a tiny red taillight flickering in the dark, threatening to disappear. The police car with Von Flanagan was right behind them.

The car ahead, Mona McClane's, was built for speed. So was Helene's.

They turned into the Drive and headed north, driving with a fine disregard of red lights, stop signs, and icy pavements. Traffic hastily turned aside to let them go by. Now and again the big, heavy car would slide sideways, right itself by some miracle, and continue in the right direction. Once the car ahead, rounding the curve into Lincoln Park, missed a southbound Chicago Motor Coach by inches, skidded insanely for half a block, and kept on going.

Behind them the police car's siren wailed mournfully.

Inside Lincoln Park, the traffic thinned, yet once or twice the car ahead was almost lost to them, only to reappear as the stream of cars spread out.

Jake found himself wondering what time it was. It occurred to him too that he had had no dinner. No dinner, and no sleep for what seemed to be days and days. None of those things mattered now, in this insane chase up the outer drive with the siren on Von Flanagan's car screaming somewhere behind them, and the car ahead slowly and steadily losing its lead. None of those things mattered, but he remembered them just the same.

He glanced at Helene; her profile was dead white against the darkness, as though it had been cut out of cardboard.

Suddenly he wished with all his heart that the car ahead would magically acquire miraculous speed, be lost forever to its pursuers. He thought there must be a time in every hunt when the hunters wished desperately, passionately, that the fox might get away.

But even as he wished it, the pursued car streaked past the Edgewater Beach Hotel, struck an unexpected patch of ice a few blocks farther north, spun madly around for one terrible moment, missing several passing cars by a shuddering hair's breadth, and skidded off to the lake side of the Drive as though it had been shot from a cannon. There was a splintering crash as it struck a tree, and then silence.

He felt Helene's big car shiver like a living thing as its brakes were applied, closed his eyes for one sickening second as it slid sideways, opened them in time to see Helene skillfully maneuver it to the right and bring it to a stop just off the pavement.

The screaming siren was right behind them now.

Jake was out of Helene's car almost at the instant of its stop, two seconds behind Malone. He saw a small figure in a tan polo coat emerge from the wreckage ahead of them, stagger a moment, and run toward the lake.

After a few steps the figure turned suddenly. There was the sound of a shot, the sharp crack of breaking glass as a bullet struck the windshield of Helene's car. The figure ran on blindly a few feet farther, wheeled to fire again.

Jake could think of nothing but to dive at Helene and get her out of the line of fire. With only a fraction of his mind he realized that Von Flanagan and the red-faced policeman, Kluchetsky, had caught up and were ahead of them.

There were two more shots from the fleeing figure.

He dimly heard Von Flanagan shout something at Kluchetsky. The big policeman slackened his speed, drew his gun, and fired three or four times, even in that moment taking careful, deliberate aim.

Jake caught Helene in his arms. As in a dream, he saw the small figure of Ellen Ogletree as it stopped suddenly, wavered for only a moment, and then fell.

## *Chapter Thirty-Six*

The little patch of sand and snow between the Drive and the lake was suddenly full of people. Not more than a minute after the police car had screamed to a stop, another car coming from the same direction paused at the curb. George

Brand emerged from it, Leonard Marchmont, and then Mona McClane. They came over to join the group around Malone and Von Flanagan.

The tall, lanky Englishman was a little ahead of the others. He walked up to the huddled little body in the snow and stood looking at it.

"She's dead, isn't she?" His well-bred English voice seemed curiously incongruous in that setting.

Kluchetsky looked up from where he was kneeling in the snow. "Yeah."

"Oh." That was all Marchmont had to say. He stood a little away from the rest after that, half in the shadows, his face impassive.

Von Flanagan gave a few quick orders to the men with him; the body of Ellen Ogletree was covered to protect it from the snow that was beginning to fall again. Then he turned to Malone.

"What did she have to do with it?"

"She murdered Joshua Gumbril," Malone said wearily, "and Fleurette Sanders. When she realized I knew it, she tried to get away. That's all."

Mona McClane started to speak, glanced at the wreckage, at the covered body, at Kluchetsky examining his gun and putting it away to use again, and said nothing. Malone reached out and tucked her arm through his.

"That's your car she was driving, isn't it?" he asked.

She nodded.

"Your keys were in it?" the police officer asked.

She nodded again. "I always leave the keys in the car when it's in front of the house."

"Would she have known that?"

"I imagine so."

Von Flanagan finished dusting snow from the gun that had fallen from Ellen Ogletree's hand. He held it out to Mona McClane.

"That yours?"

She examined it closely. "No. I never saw it before."

Jake looked and turned his face away. He had seen that gun before. He himself had put it in the library table drawer from which Ellen Ogletree had snatched it in her mad attempt to escape.

"Do you have a gun?" Von Flanagan asked.

"Yes. Two, in fact. One is kept in the library table, and one in my dressing table. They're a pair."

Von Flanagan described the gun Malone had given him. "Are they anything like that?"

Mona McClane nodded. "That sounds exactly like mine."

Waving the police officer aside, Malone said, "Do you have a large platinum fox muff?" He added a few descriptive details.

"Yes, I have. I had it made for me in Paris."

"Where is it now?"

She smiled wanly. "In a blue cardboard box in my closet, labeled 'fox muff.' "

"That's where you're wrong," Malone told her. "It's in the back of Helene's car, in a bright red box labeled 'Merry Christmas.' "

Mona McClane and Von Flanagan said, "What are you talking about?" almost simultaneously.

Malone told them about the muff, the gun that had been inside it, and the way he had received them both.

The snow was falling more heavily now. On the sidewalk two policemen were keeping back the growing crowd of curious onlookers.

"I don't understand," Mona McClane said.

"What's the last time this girl visited you, before Gumbril was shot?" Von Flanagan asked.

"The night before. She spent the night at my house."

"Could she have gotten that muff and the gun out of your house without your knowing it?"

"I suppose she could."

"Well, I guess that explains that," Von Flanagan said. He turned to Malone. "How do you know so ding-danged much about it?" He added without a pause, "How come she did it, anyway?"

Malone ignored the first question and said, "He was blackmailing her. A few years ago Ellen Ogletree was kidnaped, her father paid fifty thousand ransom money. That money went to Ellen herself less Gumbril's cut. She wanted it because she had an expensive boy friend and her old man always gave money to her a nickel at a time."

Jake looked through the gloom and snow for Leonard Marchmont. He had disappeared.

Von Flanagan said, "What—?" stopped, and said, "Go on."

"Fleurette Sanders was Gumbril's sister," Malone said. "She put the girl in touch with Gumbril in the first place. After the kidnaping, Gumbril began systematically blackmailing the girl until she was all out of money. Then to keep Gumbril quiet, she got herself engaged to a wealthy young man—what was his name?"

"Jay Fulton," George Brand said.

"That took care of Gumbril for a while. She promised him that as soon as she was married to Fulton, she'd go on paying him. Then she decided to murder Gumbril, and broke her engagement to Fulton. That same night she stayed at Mona McClane's house, helped herself to the gun and the muff, next day she made an appointment with Gumbril that would necessitate his going up State Street to keep it, trailed him to the corner of Madison, and shot him. Then she went to his hotel room, searched it, removed and destroyed whatever evidence Gumbril had kept for the purpose of blackmailing her."

"But the Sanders woman," Von Flanagan said, brushing the snow from his face."

"She was Gumbril's sister, remember," Malone told him. "She knew all about the kidnaping and the subsequent blackmail. As soon as she heard Gumbril was dead she went to his room too and made a search of her own. When she saw the evidence that Ellen Ogletree had planned her own kidnaping was missing, she knew who murdered her brother. Evidently she decided to tell me what she knew. Today Mrs. Ogletree, Mrs. Sanders, Ellen Ogletree, and Mona McClane lunched together. Mrs. Sanders left the table to make a telephone call. Ellen excused herself and listened in. When she heard Fleurette Sanders make an appointment at my office, she guessed why. Fleurette had already threatened her."

"She had checked the muff and the gun in a department-store checkroom. Probably when she shot Gumbril she went right into the store there on the corner, got a gift box at the first counter she came to, put the muff into it, had the whole works wrapped, and checked it. Today she got it out again, trailed Mrs. Sanders—figuring she'd pass the same corner on the way to my office from Field's—and just repeated her performance. But this time she got a messenger boy and sent the muff with the gun inside it to my office."

Von Flanagan shook his head and murmured, "The things people will do!" In a louder tone he asked, "Why did she send it to you?"

"She wanted me to defend her," Malone said quickly. "She knew the game was up. You'll find notes on all this in my stenographer's notebook in my office, just as she told it to me."

Helene started to speak. Jake kicked her quickly on the ankle.

"You told me you didn't know where the gun came from," Von Flanagan said angrily and accusingly. "What's more, you told me you didn't have any client—"

"I didn't, when I talked to you," Malone said smoothly. "The gun came to my office, tucked inside the muff, this afternoon, delivered by a messenger boy. I had a crazy hunch it might be the one used in the killings, and so," he assumed an air of righteousness, "the first thing I thought of was to deliver it to you." He added with an air of injury, "You don't think I'd hold out on you, do you?"

"Oh no," Von Flanagan assured him hastily. He stood for a moment staring into space, as though he were trying hard to remember something of great importance. Suddenly a light broke over his face. "But what happened to the clothes on Mrs. Sanders' body?"

"Oh, that!" Malone cast a look around him, indicated by gestures to Von Flanagan that some things could only be discussed apart from the presence of women, and drew the police officer away from the group. For a minute or two he carried on a dramatically gestured discussion with the officer, during which the latter nodded twice, shook his head in blank incredulity once, and lifted his eyebrows four times. As they returned to the group Jake heard Von Flanagan say, "Yes. I understand. Yes, I'll fix it up somehow for the papers. But honestly, Malone, I never would have believed it of him."

That was the last Jake ever heard about Fleurette Sanders' clothes. Malone never would confess what he had confided to Von Flanagan.

The little lawyer took a quick glance at the tiny mound under the police blanket and looked away again.

"If she'd known what a good lawyer she had," he said gloomily, "she'd never have tried to make a break for it." Suddenly his voice rose in anger. "Your damned Kluchetsky. I ought to sue him. In fact, I think I will."

Von Flanagan roused himself from thought long enough to ask, "Why?"

"The son-of-a-bitch," Malone growled. "He did me out of a client!"

## Chapter Thirty-Seven

George Brand poured a double rye into a glass of seltzer, gazed at it dreamily, and said, "How did you know all that?"

"I didn't," Malone said promptly. "I was making it up as I went along. But damn it, I had to tell Von Flanagan something."

It was past midnight. There were five of them in the booth in Gus's place on 72d Street: Jake, Helene, Malone, George Brand, and Mona McClane. They had selected Gus's partly because it was easy driving distance from the airport from which Jake and Helene were to take the dawn plane (though Malone swore that Milwaukee would be easy driving distance with Helene at the wheel) and partly because Helene declared that she liked Gus and refused to go anywhere else.

"You mean," Mona McClane said, "that Ellen didn't tell you anything?"

"Not a thing," Malone said cheerfully.

"But that stenographer's notebook," Jake said, "with notes in it. How did you manage that?"

Malone said, "While you two were out, I got hold of Maggie and had her come down to the office in a hurry and take it all down as I told it to her." He poured his drink down his throat, shuddered slightly, and said admiringly, "I think of everything."

"You mean none of that was true?" Jake demanded.

"All of it was true. But I couldn't prove it. The notebook was the clincher. As long as Von Flanagan had the case closed, he didn't give a hoot anyway."

The little lawyer took out a cigar, looked at it, lit it, and said, "If I'd used my head I'd have known it this afternoon."

"You'd have known what this afternoon?" Helene demanded.

"That it wasn't Mona McClane. At least I should have tumbled the minute I looked at her."

*"Why?"*

"Because of her furs," Malone said. He cast a quick glance around the table and bawled an order to Gus. "She never would have had time to go home and change her furs in the time between Fleurette's murder and when we met her."

"I may be dumb," Jake began, "but—"

"You are," Malone said acidly, "if you don't see right away that no woman as well dressed as Mona McClane would carry a big platinum fox muff with the pale beige fur she had on this afternoon."

Gus delivered five more ryes.

Malone took a folded paper from his inside coat pocket and handed it to Mona McClane. "You might want this," he said. It was the marriage certificate.

"Thanks," she said. She glanced at it, her eyes suddenly softened, and she said gently, "It was one of those mad impulses you can't resist when you're very young and impressionable and sheltered. You wouldn't believe it, but he was an extremely attractive young man, with no money and no prospects. I didn't dare tell anybody, and all of a sudden I found myself being pushed into," she made a wry face, "a fashionable marriage. I didn't dare do anything about an annulment, and he had disappeared. When you're seventeen and something like that happens to you, you don't know what to do. I just went ahead with the fashionable marriage, scared to death. It was years before I saw him again."

She drew a long, quivering, sighing breath and went on, "I only saw him once. He'd become wealthy then, he'd also become a criminal. I learned then that he'd gone away when he read in the papers of my engagement because he thought it was the only thing to do."

"Did he ever try to blackmail you?" Malone asked very gently.

"Never. It was one of those things one forgets. Because there was nothing to be done about it. After that meeting I didn't even think of him again until," she smiled with just one half of her mouth, "I read of his murder in the newspapers." She looked long and thoughtfully at the certificate, folded it and put it in her purse, and said, "Where did you find that?"

Malone told her of its discovery in the metal dispatch box.

"Until I found that," he said, "I believed that you'd killed him."

Jake stretched his long legs under the narrow table and said, "What the hell is all this about motives and no motives, anyway?"

Malone said, "As long as I couldn't find her motive for the crime I believed Mona had killed him. As soon as I found it, I knew she hadn't." He paused and said, "Look. Suppose Mona knew of the existence of that certificate in that box. Suppose Gumbril had been using it to blackmail her, and, consequently, she killed him. That's how it appeared, wasn't it?"

"Well?" Jake said crossly.

"Would she, then, have calmly gone away and left that certificate there for anybody in the world to find?"

After a moment Jake said sheepishly, "No, she wouldn't. But maybe she wouldn't have known where to look for it."

"Neither did you," the lawyer said, "but you found it. And you didn't have the advantage of knowing what to look for. Even if she hadn't discovered the box was unlocked, she'd have guessed that the certificate was in it and carried the whole thing away. That's why, when I found what was in the box, I knew I'd been wrong all along. That's why I was so dumfounded when I discovered it, because, by all my reasoning, it shouldn't have been there." He finished his rye, wiped his lips on his handkerchief, and said, rather pompously, "Any more questions from the audience?"

"Thousands," Jake said, "but I'm damned if I'll ask."

Mona McClane said, "How did you know it was Ellen?"

"For the reverse of the reason I knew it wasn't you," Malone said. He paused and yelled, "Gus!"

"Don't mind him," Helene said. "He makes his living by confusing people."

Malone ignored her. "Of the people in that room tonight, five had definite reasons for wanting to murder Joshua Gumbril and, later, his sister. Mona McClane, Willis Sanders, Daphne Sanders, Ellen Ogletree, and Mrs. Ogletree. The same line of thought I applied to you applied to them. Before Gumbril was killed, there must have been papers in that box relating to the killing of the first Mrs. Sanders and to the Ellen Ogletree kidnaping. Possibly, something relating to Mrs. Ogletree's personal-information service." He explained to Mona McClane what he had learned from Max Hook. "When I opened the box, only that marriage certificate was there. The Ogletree papers were missing because they were the reason Gumbril was killed. The Sanders papers were missing because Ellen took them to use in blackmailing Willis Sanders into giving her boy friend a job. Anything about Mrs. Ogletree was missing because she was Ellen's mother."

George Brand emerged from a long, trancelike communion with his glass. "But those papers about the murder of the first Mrs. Sanders—" He paused, gulped, and said, "They're incriminating to Willis."

"Incriminating is a mild word for it," Malone said.

George Brand turned pale. "If they should be found—! My God, Malone! Where are they?"

"In my pocket," the little lawyer said complacently. He drew out two typewritten documents on cheap paper. "There's the receipt Little Georgie was so anxious to get, stating he'd received one grand for his part in the arranged kidnaping of Ellen Ogletree. I'll give it to him and let him burn it—after his performance this afternoon he deserves that pleasure as a reward." He looked at the other paper, held it over the ash tray, and set a match to it. "That was signed by the man who shot and killed the first Mrs. Sanders because he was paid to do so by Fleurette."

They watched it burn in silence.

Suddenly Jake said, "How the hell did you get those papers?"

Malone said proudly, "I knew Ellen Ogletree was the sort of girl who would carry important papers in her handbag. While I was talking to Von Flanagan there on the beach I moved the handbag from his pocket to mine, slipped the papers out of it, and put the handbag back." He paused and added, "I had a client once who was a pickpocket."

"He must have been a damned good one," Jake said in admiring reverence.

"How much of what you told Von Flanagan was true?" George Brand asked.

Malone sighed and said, "I wish to God I knew." He rubbed the burned paper from his fingers and picked up his cigar. "I knew Ellen had a motive for murdering Gumbril. She was kidnaped. He received fifty-grand ransom money and his bankbooks told me he didn't keep any of it. As we learned tonight, Max Hook's boy only got a grand. Someone got the rest. It might have been Ellen's father or it might even have been Ellen's mother. Or it might have been Ellen. Helene told me once that Ellen's father never gave her any spending money. Yet Daphne told me that Ellen was winning Leonard Marchmont's affections with valuable presents."

Helene nodded. "It adds up. Then Gumbril blackmailed her?"

Malone nodded. "Fifty grand seems like a lot of dough, but on the one hand the boy friend was expensive, and on the other Gumbril was shaking her down regularly. The first thing Ellen knew, her bank account was down to rock bottom again. Speaking of rock bottom—" He looked in his glass and bawled, "Gus! How do you expect to get rich if you don't tend to business?"

Helene said thoughtfully, "I thought there must have been some good reason for getting engaged to a guy like Jay Fulton."

"Maybe she really meant to marry him," Malone said. "She was desperate. Then she heard Mona McClane make that bet with Jake. She saw a chance to murder Gumbril and lay the blame on Mona McClane. Maybe even then she knew about that certificate in the green metal box. But even if she didn't, she probably figured the bet would do the trick. She couldn't wait to break her engagement to Fulton, she did it right away. Then she spent the night at Mona McClane's, took the muff and the gun the next morning, probably called Gumbril and made some appointment with him that would cause him to walk to State Street, trailed him to a crowded corner, and shot him."

He drew two lines on the table with a match. "Here's Ellen and here's Fleurette. Ellen's first act after the murder was to break into Gumbril's room—she'd probably been there before when she paid him off—found the box and the key to it, and removed the paper dealing with the kidnaping. When she found the paper dealing with the Sanders shooting, she saw a chance to induce Sanders to give her boy friend a job, and took that paper along too. The other she left to be Mona McClane's motive for murdering Gumbril. She even called up the county clerk of Walworth County and had him check up his records to make sure the certificate was genuine."

He moved the match to the second line on the table. "Here's Fleurette, now. She read in the papers that her brother had been killed. Her first act was to hurry to his room to get hold of that incriminating paper. It was gone. The Ellen Ogletree paper was gone too—and Fleurette must have known of its existence. That gave her a hint as to what had happened. Then when Fleurette learned that Willis Sanders had given Ellen's boy friend a job, Fleurette knew for certain that Ellen had killed Gumbril."

"But why did she make up that yarn about the dentist office?" Jake asked.

"She was trying to frighten Ellen into giving back that Sanders paper," Malone said. "That's why she telephoned me today, too. She knew Ellen would overhear her make that call. You can't tell me a smart woman like Fleurette would be overheard if she didn't intend it. She figured that if Ellen thought she was coming to see me and spill what she knew, Ellen would trade that paper for her keeping her mouth shut. Instead," he said after a long breath, "Ellen killed her."

He took up the match and drew a third line, a little away from the other two. "Willis Sanders knew that Ellen had killed Gumbril, as soon as she came to him with what she'd found in Gumbril's box. But he was in no position to talk. Then Daphne went berserk. He was scared clear through. When Daphne left home, his first move was to ask Ellen to help find her and talk her into returning. Daphne went home when she cooled off, but Sanders was still scared, and so he came to me. When he learned of Fleurette's death he knew who had killed her, but he didn't dare speak, not even to me."

He sighed heavily and said, "What a lot of bother would be saved if clients would only be honest with their lawyers. Well, that's how it all happened. Of course, it's speculative. But hell, everything in the world is speculative."

Jake said nothing. He'd heard all the explanations he'd wanted to hear. His dream of owning the Casino seemed to have faded, but somehow it didn't matter much now. Frankly, he was a little bored with murder.

He squeezed Helene's hand under the table and whispered in her ear, "Listen, sweetheart. When people are married—"

She squeezed his hand in return. "What are you looking so gloomy about? We've nothing to do now but honeymoon."

"I've just been remembering," he whispered back, "that there's no damn privacy on those transport planes."

George Brand looked at his watch. "Time for one more before we leave."

Malone muttered something about damned good riddance.

Mona McClane leaned across the table and smiled at Jake. "Too bad about the bet."

He smiled back at her. "Imagine my surprise," he said, "when I found I was tracking down the wrong murderer."

Mona McClane stirred her drink for a moment before she spoke. When she did, her voice was almost gay.

"Imagine *my* surprise," she said, "when I found you were solving the wrong murder!"

**THE END**

AND, YES, DEAR READER, THE NEXT TITLE IN THIS SERIES IS CALLED
*THE RIGHT MURDER.*

THE EDITORS

# About the Rue Morgue Press

"Rue Morgue Press is the old-mystery lover's best friend,
reprinting high quality books from the 1930s and '40s."
—*Ellery Queen's Mystery Magazine*

Since 1997, the Rue Morgue Press has reprinted scores of traditional
mysteries, the kind of books that were the hallmark of the Golden Age of
detective fiction. Authors reprinted or to be reprinted by the Rue Morgue
include Catherine Aird, Delano Ames, H. C. Bailey, Morris Bishop, Nicholas Blake, Dorothy Bowers, Pamela Branch, Joanna Cannan, John Dickson
Carr, Glyn Carr, Torrey Chanslor, Clyde B. Clason, Joan Coggin, Manning
Coles, Lucy Cores, Frances Crane, Norbert Davis, Elizabeth Dean, Carter
Dickson, Eilis Dillon, Michael Gilbert, Constance & Gwenyth Little, Marlys
Millhiser, Gladys Mitchell, Patricia Moyes, James Norman, Stuart Palmer,
Craig Rice, Kelley Roos, Charlotte Murray Russell, Maureen Sarsfield, Margaret Scherf, Juanita Sheridan and Colin Watson..

To suggest titles or to receive a catalog of Rue Morgue Press books write
87 Lone Tree Lane, Lyons, CO 80540, telephone 800-699-6214, or check
out our website, www.ruemorguepress.com, which lists complete descriptions of all of our titles, along with lengthy biographies of our writers.